STORM WARRIORS

TRYSTAN STARED DUMBLY at the spot where Emyr had been. The knight's riderless horse whinnied and tossed its head, and might have bolted had not Moraint Heilyn taken hold of its rein.

Ghosts! The word echoed in the harper's mind, as he knew it must be echoing in Herla's.

'We are enchanted!' said Moraint, more wrathfully than fearfully. 'The elves have cursed us. They have not kept their word!'

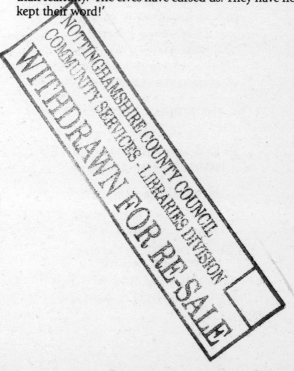

More Warhammer from the Black Library

· THE TALES OF ORFEO ·

ZARAGOZ by Brian Craig
PLAGUE DAEMON by Brian Craig

· THE VAMPIRE GENEVIEVE NOVELS ·

DRACHENFELS by Jack Yeovil
BEASTS IN VELVET by Jack Yeovil
GENEVIEVE UNDEAD by Jack Yeovil
SILVER NAILS by Jack Yeovil

· GOTREK & FELIX ·

TROLLSLAYER by William King
SKAVENSLAYER by William King
DAEMONSLAYER by William King
DRAGONSLAYER by William King
BEASTSLAYER by William King
VAMPIRESLAYER by William King

· THE KONRAD TRILOGY ·

KONRAD by David Ferring
SHADOWBREED by David Ferring
WARBLADE by David Ferring

· WARHAMMER NOVELS ·

CLAWS OF CHAOS by Gav Thorpe
ZAVANT by Gordon Rennie
HAMMERS OF ULRIC by Dan Abnett,
Nik Vincent & James Wallis
GILEAD'S BLOOD by Dan Abnett & Nik Vincent
THE WINE OF DREAMS by Brian Craig

A WARHAMMER NOVEL

The Third Tale of Orfeo

STORM WARRIORS

Brian Craig

10 9 8 7 6 5 4 3 2 1

Cover illustration by Clint Langley

A CIP record for this book
is available from the British Library

ISBN 1 84154 259 8

Set in ITC Giovanni

Printed and bound in Great Britain by
Cox & Wyman Ltd, Cardiff Rd, Reading, Berkshire RG1 8EX, UK

See the Black Library on the internet at
www.blacklibrary.com

Find out more about Games Workshop
and the world of Warhammer at
www.games-workshop.com

STORM WARRIORS

Being the Third Tale of Orfeo

PROLOGUE

ORFEO LEANED BACK in his chair. His eyelids were heavy – as well they might be, given that he had been telling his tale for several hours. The chair was by no means the most comfortable he had ever sat upon; the men of Araby preferred low couches and cushions, and had it not been for the fact that Alkadi Nasreen, Caliph of Mahabbah and the Twin Seas, was Estalian by breeding and birth, there might have been no chairs in Arjijil at all. Orfeo felt so tired he had begun to think that the Arabians had the right of it, and that chairs were a ridiculous folly devised for torment rather than comfort. In order to spare his aching back he leaned forward, resting his elbows and forearms on the table.

The two candles set before him on the table had burned low in their brass holders; the remaining tallow had flowed into grotesque shapes, and the points of the spikes upon which the candles had been impaled were very close to the wicks. The more substantial candle, which was set in a recess in the wall, was not quite so near to extinction, but it too seemed tired and languid. No light showed as yet through the cracks in the shutter but he judged that dawn could not be far off.

Orfeo was uncomfortably aware of the fact that Alkadi Nasreen was still studying him carefully. Although the caliph had agreed to let him go, with horses and money to help him on his way, there was still a sense of something unsettled between them. Nasreen was intrigued by his enigmatic visitor, curious about his reasons for being aboard the vessel which his pirates had attacked and taken. Orfeo could not help but feel that he was not yet entirely safe from the threat of that curiosity – and would not be – until he was beyond the bounds of the pirate king's tiny realm.

It is, thought Orfeo dully, an uncomfortable destiny which compels a man like me to harbour so many secrets... but I suppose a talent for honesty is the last thing which would work to the advantage of a storyteller.

'If you have no more need of my wisdom and my voice,' he said aloud, in an amiably ironic fashion, 'I ask your permission to go to my bed. I will sleep more easily, now that I know exactly what my situation is.'

Nasreen shrugged his shoulders slightly as he leaned back in his own chair. 'You are a free man,' he said, not without a certain ironic inflection of his own. 'You need not ask my permission. Your horses and your saddles will be ready when you wake. I will give you the money myself, when you come to say good–'

The word 'goodbye' was never completed, being rudely interrupted by a loud crash.

Orfeo was sitting with his back to the door of the room, and could not see what was happening, but the amazement and alarm which suddenly possessed the caliph's features were warning enough that he should not turn lazily around. As he came to his feet he snatched the chair up with his right hand, so that when he had whipped around, its four legs were extended before him as a defence.

That instinctive move saved his life. The door which had been so rudely hurled open rebounded on its hinges, but the two persons who had moved through it were already well clear of its swing. The first of the two was poised to strike with a long-bladed dagger, and if Orfeo had stood up unguardedly nothing could have stopped the point finding a target in his flesh.

As things were, the hurtling fury of the attack proved to the attacker's disadvantage – for when he found the four legs of the chair jutting and jabbing at him he had abruptly to change his course. Seeing that his assailant was off balance, Orfeo immediately thrust out with his makeshift weapon, and the man with the knife had to fall backwards, interfering as he did so with the similarly precipitate progress of his companion.

Neither of the attackers was huge in stature – one was only a few inches shorter than Orfeo – but the bare forearms revealed by his loose sleeves were thin almost to the point of emaciation.

The lightness of the invaders, however, seemed not to signal any lack of strength or skill, for they overcame their initial disadvantage very quickly. When they separated to stand side-by-side, thin daggers at the ready, Orfeo could see that they were hardened and practiced fighting-men who would not be easy to defeat even in the best of circumstances.

These were certainly not the best of circumstances. Orfeo had no weapon at all, save for what he could improvise; the caliph wore no sword, and any blade concealed about his person must perforce be smaller than those which their assailants had.

The attackers were dressed in a remarkable fashion. Their loose-fitting nether garments were dark grey, while their heads and shoulders were covered in cowled shawls of jet black. Their faces were darkly veiled, so that the only parts of their flesh which were visible were their hands and wrists. Their feet were raggedly bandaged in such a way as to suppress the sound of their footsteps.

While they paused momentarily before relaunching their assault, Alkadi Nasreen called: 'Beware poison!' The anguish in his voice was as revealing to Orfeo as the words which he spoke, for the caliph was an uncommonly bold man, and it was clear that even he found cause now to be direly frightened.

Orfeo shifted the chair from his right hand to his left. This was necessary because he had been hurt in the right shoulder when he was first taken by Nasreen's pirates, and though the wound had healed his left arm was more equal to the task of bearing the chair's weight through the coming conflict. Also, the move set his right hand free to reach behind him – though he did not take his eyes off his opponents while he did so – and seize one of the heavy candleholders from the tabletop.

Hot wax stung his hand as he flicked the molten ruin of the candle away to expose the spike atop the brass stalk, but he did not wince. The spike was blunt, and the candlestick had not been weighted for fencing, but it was a weapon of sorts just as the chair was a shield of sorts. With his rapier in his hand Orfeo would not have been desperately fearful of enemies like these, for his long reach would have given him a great advantage, but the candlestick was much shorter than his favourite blade, and if the long daggers had indeed been dipped in poison he must do more than keep them from his heart and throat.

From the deep recesses of his memory an elven voice spoke to him, saying: *'Poor clumsy oaf! Too slow, too slow! How do you pretend to be a master of the dance when you are so slow in the dance of war that you are more dangerous to yourself than to another?'*

He knew only too well how inadequate his talent was – but these were men, not wardancing elves, and if they had the need to dress their weapons with poison, perhaps they had not much faith in their ordinary skills.

Behind him the table was turned on its side by Alkadi Nasreen, who was constructing a defence for himself, but the caliph toppled the table gently, so that its edge would not fall on Orfeo's ankles.

Orfeo did not turn to see whether Nasreen had produced a knife, or whether he too was reduced to candlestick and chair for his armoury – and it was as well that he did not, for when the attacker who had been first through the door hurled himself forward again he came so swiftly that it required all of Orfeo's skill and strength to get the chair solidly between them, prodding with one of the legs at his opponent's head.

Alkadi Nasreen was howling now, but not with wrath – he was yelling for aid.

Orfeo realized, with a nauseous thrill of anxiety, that the caliph of Arjijil should not have to yell for aid in the heart of his own citadel – there should have been guards enough even at this hour to prevent invaders ever getting near to him.

Was it possible, he wondered, that the caliph had been betrayed by his own adopted people? Did the pirates want a man of Araby to lead them in his stead?

He had to move the chair very cleverly then, to stop both attackers as they came forward together in careful unison. Had the two separated, it would have been easier to keep them back, but they knew that. Orfeo realized that by over-turning the table to make a wall Alkadi Nasreen had in fact erected two lines of defence for himself. Because Orfeo was outside the barrier the attackers must kill him first, before turning their attention to the man who was presumably their true target.

From two different angles they thrust at him with their daggers, one coming high from the right and one low from the left. Though he brought the chair down neatly enough to cope with the latter thrust he had to raise the candlestick to meet the former, and it was as much by luck as by judgement that he managed to catch the blade and turn it aside. Then he lashed out with his right foot – and was very grateful that he wore good Bretonnian boots instead of soft Arabian slippers, for the kick went home in a very satisfactory fashion and he heard his opponent grunt in shock and pain.

It was a small advantage, but he knew that it was the only one that he was likely to find, and so he attacked. He came forward, jabbing hard with the chair at the man who had ducked in order to come at him low. Again it was as much by luck as by judgement, but he managed to catch the man a solid blow upon the temple with one of the legs of the chair. Had he been able to lift it high and bring it down again he might have knocked the man unconscious, but he could not – he could only continue to shove and prod, and though he drove his opponent back, the man had the opportunity to collect himself and make ready for another thrust.

In the meantime, his second assailant was already manoeuvring to strike back at him – and would certainly have done so, were it not that the wine bottle which Orfeo and Nasreen had emptied during the night was hurled suddenly and fiercely into his face.

Had the bottle broken instantly, the shards of glass might have done more damage, but in fact it did not shatter until it hit the floor; the blow was nevertheless sufficient to make the knifeman miss his thrust completely, and gave Orfeo the opportunity to stab with the candlestick. This thrust too might have been a good one but for the fact that Orfeo had a chair to burden his other arm, and an opponent to keep at bay with it; as things were, it could be no more than half-successful. It struck home upon the man's cheek, but having neither sharp point nor powerful poison at its tip it could only inflict an inconsiderable hurt.

Both attackers had been momentarily driven back, but both were still in full possession of their faculties, and as they came at him again Orfeo knew that he would need even better luck to hold them back for another minute, let alone to put one or other of them out of the fight.

But Alkadi Nasreen was still shouting for aid, and while Orfeo tried to balance himself to meet another two-pronged attack, the caliph used the second candlestick as though it were a javelin. It was not weighted to fly point-first, and did not, but Alkadi Nasreen was a powerful man, and the candlestick made a more satisfactory missile than the bottle. The assailant to Orfeo's right saw it coming, and tried to fend it off with his arm, but in doing so he had to turn so that his own weapon was briefly behind him, and Orfeo judged the opportunity too good to miss. The move required of him was a very difficult one, but he was after all a dancer, if not a wardancer, and he had complete trust in his well muscled legs.

Orfeo lashed out with his left foot at the man who was now more dangerous, aiming to make him jump backwards. Then he let the hand which held the candlestick fall, and brought the chair around in a long fast arc, wielding it almost as though it were a battle-axe.

As an attacking move it worked perfectly – the leading leg of the chair hit the veiled man hard on the side of his head, and he went down stunned. The defensive part of the manoeuvre, however, was not so perfect. The kick was good and accurate, and the man at whom it was aimed should indeed have moved back to avoid it – but he did not. Instead, he was content to fold himself, lessening the blow's force as it went home to his belly. It hurt him, to be sure, and unbalanced him completely – but he was still in a position to slash at Orfeo's calf with his dagger before he was tumbled over.

The cut was by no means as effective as it was intended to be – the hard kick jarred the man too badly for that. In any ordinary fight, it would have been irrelevant – no more than the merest scratch. But in this fight, Orfeo knew, even the merest scratch could not be reckoned irrelevant.

Knowing that he might have only a few seconds left to act, Orfeo was very quick to balance himself again, as only a dancer could. Then he brought the chair back in an arc as vicious as the first, aiming to bring the whole weight of the object into violent collision with the head of the man who had hurt him. He could not tell whether it was the effect of his kick, or whether the man no longer cared whether he was hit or not, but the blow went home with a very satisfying thud, and the veiled man was thrown back against the stone wall of the room, hitting it as a dead weight.

Knowing that the other was only stunned, Orfeo was quick to turn again – but now Alkadi Nasreen had leapt out from behind his barricade, and while his fuddled opponent was trying to raise his long blade into a threatening position the caliph plunged a much smaller dagger into his throat, letting go as soon as the blade was home so that he could keep his distance from the stricken man's last reflexive thrust.

While the hooded man was still falling the door was thrust back again and armed men jostled one another in the doorway in their hurry to join the fight. They did not seem to realize that it was all over – perhaps they thought that Orfeo was the villain and not the hero of the play – and for a moment Orfeo thought that he would go down in a confused whirl of blades as the swordsmen piled into the dimly-lit room cutting furiously in all directions; but Alkadi Nasreen was bawling again, crying out angry instructions, and the newcomers lowered their blades.

Orfeo went down anyway, as his scratched leg suddenly lost all feeling and all ability to support him – and though he kept his wits about him for three or four seconds more, while he tried to support himself with the chair which he had used so cleverly as a weapon, it was all to no avail. The light of his consciousness was snuffed out like a guttering candle, and fell into an ominous abyss of oblivion.

HIS DREAMS WERE of storms and of music.

His dream-self was not bound to the earth at all, but his powers of flight were too feeble by far to oppose the driving and whirling of the wind which tossed him wherever its whim dictated, through tempests of freezing rain or rolling clouds of desiccating dust. He could not tell whether he was high above the rocky shores of the misty Isles of Albion, or lost in the tropic haze of the *harmattan*

which blew from the hot heart of the great desert of Araby,
and while he was so rudely hurled about, the wind wailed
at him like some eerie stringed instrument, with far more
melody in its voice than it had any right to have.

It was as though his weightless substance was possessed
by a kind of weird music, as though his furious movements were a kind of wild dance. He had the curious
feeling that if only he knew the rhythms and steps of the
dance, if only he could learn its paces and its turns, then
the power of flight might return to him, and that the wind
might be his friend and not his enemy – but he could not
do it, because no man could control the music of the
storm. Such storms, he somehow knew, could be magically
conjured up, and could be mirrored in the sound of an
instrument built for the task, but they could not in the end
be commanded – for they were, after all, storms... and no
matter that their substance was the substance of the world,
their souls were the souls of Chaos...

HOW MUCH TIME passed before the storm of Orfeo's dreams
tossed him casually back to wakefulness he could not tell.
When he opened his eyes, he found himself in near darkness, in a room which had no windows and was lit by a
single low-burning candle.

In a way, that was as it should be – for had he not fallen
into his unnatural sleep in exactly such a dim-lit room?
But in another way, it was deeply disturbing, for this was a
room in which he had never been before, gloomier than
any of the chambers in which he had been incarcerated
while he was a prisoner in Arjijil.

It disturbed him that he could not tell whether it was day
or night. It disturbed him, too, that he could not tell
whether he was still in Arjijil, or on the other side of the
world. He might have believed himself on the far side of
death, in Morr's realm, had it not been for the fever which
was burning in his body and the nausea in his belly.
Whatever death was like, he thought, it could not be like
this. Only the living could feel as bad as he did.

He lay quietly for some time, unable to move and unable to think coherently. He was awake, but his dreams had not entirely surrendered him to the empire of reason. He tried hard to wonder where he was, and being a man of strong mind he succeeded, after a fashion, in wondering; but he could only echo the question and its attendant anxiety. All that he knew for sure was that he was alone, and suffering.

In time, the suffering eased. The turmoil which was ravaging his body and his mind relented by slow degrees. When he burned, he burned less hotly; when he shivered, the cold was not so intense. The occasions when he wished that the fire in his guts would spill out through his mouth grew rarer. Hours might have passed, or only minutes cruelly extended by his heightened perceptions; he could not tell. But the candlelight did not die; there was light enough to show him what a bare and comfortless prison he was in.

Eventually, he was well enough to ask himself why; but he could not find an answer.

It was not until someone raised his head to give him water that he realized he was no longer alone. He found it strangely difficult to focus his eyes on the face of the man, and by no means easy to recognize his benefactor once he could see the face clearly. 'My lord of Mahabbah and the Twin Seas,' he whispered, when he had enough strength, 'I do believe that yours is the most dangerous realm to which my travels have ever taken me.'

'I cannot believe it,' Alkadi Nasreen replied. 'I have heard enough of your tales of the Old World to be certain that Arjijil is a haven of peace in a sorely troubled universe... or was, until capricious fate delivered you to my doorstep.'

The caliph was squatting on a rug beside Orfeo's pallet, after the customary fashion of the Arabians. There were no chairs here, nor tables.

'Will I live?' he asked.

'Aye,' replied Nasreen. 'Though the poison was powerful, you will live. You are a strong man, and the wound was very slight. I wish I could say the same for all my servants, but four lie dead – one of them a girl and one of them the strongest of my bodyguards. I had thought my inner sanctum impregnable, but the *hashishin* are very clever in their work.'

'Who are the *hashishin*?'

'A company of assassins – hirable for those who have the stomach for dealing with their kind, but with purposes of their own also. Arjijil has grown tolerably rich by piracy, but they say that the mountain stronghold of the *hashishin* is a kind of paradise on earth, which has its counterpart on the other side of death, set aside for those who serve the company most loyally. They take their name from a drug which is widely used in Araby, but which they take most immoderately and in an unusually pure form – they are the masters of many other curious drugs in addition to the poisons with which they anoint their weapons. They are difficult to fight because they bring to battle a kind of exaltation which adds greatly to their fury, if not to their skill. Many a brave warrior has fallen to their weapons, and many a haughty ruler. You may carry your scar with pride.'

'I have too many scars to be proud of any,' Orfeo muttered. 'This is a curious hospital to which you have brought me.'

'It is a secret place,' said Nasreen. 'The most secret of all my secret places, in fact. None but I can come to you here – but then, none but I know that you are still alive. Those men who came too late to defend me must have spread the word throughout the city by now. The *hashishin* have tried to kill our beloved caliph! They were defeated by the brave Bretonnian player, who died like a hero in saving the caliph's life! You will appreciate better than most men what a fine story can be made of it – you might become the very stuff of legend in Arjijil.'

Orfeo was thinking clearly enough by now. The effort of conversation had clarified his mind, and though his body still ached, the pain seemed remote and untroublesome. He was sure that he would not die of his poisoned wound – but he was not sure why Alkadi Nasreen was mocking him like this.

'Why have you not told them that I am alive?' he asked faintly.

'That would spoil the story, I think,' said the caliph, mildly. 'You of all people must understand that a tale of self-sacrifice works so much better if the sacrifice is fatal. If my people knew that you were alive they would doubtless applaud your heroism politely, but while they believe you to be dead they can exaggerate it to the limits of belief. Profound and powerful feelings are awakened by tales of heroes who die, are they not? I would be glad of correction, if my opinion is wrong.'

Orfeo looked around at the featureless walls of the hidden room. It was not obvious to him where the doorway was, or how its opening might be triggered.

'Am I a prisoner again?' he asked.

Alkadi Nasreen frowned. 'You are very insistent in your belief that I am not your friend,' he said. 'I am a man of honour, and I have set you free. I brought you here because you were hurt – and because I am not a fool. The report of your death is not the only lie in that tale which my men are innocently putting about, and we both know it. I think you understand well enough what generosity I have showed in allowing this tale to go abroad, and I must insist that the time has now come when you should stop lying to me.'

'What do you mean?' asked Orfeo.

'You know what I mean,' the caliph replied tautly. 'Those men did not come to kill me – they came to kill *you*. When my servants saw dead *hashishin* in my private room, they leapt to the conclusion that I was in mortal danger, and that you had saved me – but I saw what they did not. I saw the attack begin, and I know that both knives were aimed at you.'

'They had to kill me in order to pass me,' Orfeo said.

'I know the *hashishin* far better than you do,' Alkadi Nasreen told him, 'despite that you seem to have attracted their attention in a way I hope never to do. If I had been their target, they would not have concentrated their attack in the way that they did. You did not save me, Master Player – *I saved you!*'

Orfeo remembered the bottle and the candlestick, thrown with such telling force and accuracy, and knew that it was true. He knew too that if Alkadi Nasreen had let it be known that he was still alive, the news would very soon have reached those who wanted him dead. Unlike the caliph, he did not know the ways of the *hashishin* at all, but it was easy enough to guess that they would not like to fail in their missions.

'Who hired them?' asked Alkadi Nasreen, speaking more softly now. 'Who – and why?' The caliph spoke as a friend, and Orfeo knew now that he was fully entitled to do so. He felt ashamed of the doubts which he had harboured about the caliph's sincerity and good intentions.

'I do not know,' he said – but repented immediately of the transparent half-truth, and said: 'I go to meet another, who has enemies about which I know little or nothing. They have evidently discovered that I was interrupted on my journey, and sought to take advantage of the fact to make sure that the meeting will not take place.'

There was a pause before Nasreen spoke again. Eventually, he said: 'You lied to me, friend Orfeo. You said to me that you had no mission in Araby but your own, which was to spread the wisdom of lore and legend throughout the world.'

'My mission is my own,' said Orfeo, 'and that is what it ultimately is. Oh, I lied, after a fashion… but what you wanted to know was whether I was a spy for the Estalians, carrying secret messages to the great sultan. That I am not, and there is nothing in what I am which poses the slightest threat to you or to Arjijil. At least, I thought so, until–'

'Until the assassins came, and killed my servants in order that they might try to kill you. Blood has been shed in Arjijil because of you, Orfeo, and were I not your friend I would be angry. But if I am your friend, you must tell me the truth.'

Orfeo could see no way to refuse, but when he did not immediately speak Alkadi Nasreen touched him gently on the shoulder, and said: 'You are tired now, and ill. I will bring you food, and more water. When you are strong enough, you may tell me what you will.'

This gesture of kindness confirmed Orfeo in his determination that he would be as honest as he could when the time came for him to make his explanation.

'YOU KNOW', SAID Orfeo, 'that I lived for a while among the elves of the Loren Forest. I had been abandoned there as an infant of three or four years; they discovered me, and could not bear to let me die. They could have taken me to a village of men and given me to someone willing to look after an orphan, but they did not.

'I had always thought the reason for that was because they knew how unkindly men are wont to treat those who are recipients of their so-called charity – but while I was in Estalia, not long after my sojourn in Zaragoz, I met an elf of Loren who told me otherwise, and said that my foster-father had not dared to give me into the charge of my fellow men, lest I meet a violent death. This elf claimed that he knew who my true parents were, and that it was a secret of some weight and value, for which he was inclined to ask a price.

'I did not know this elf, and I am not so gullible a man that I accepted what he said unquestioningly. Indeed, I had the suspicion almost from the first moment I met him that he was of a different kind from the wood elves I had known. I even wondered whether he might belong to a company against which my foster-parents took great care to warn me: the *druchii* or dark elves, who have forsaken the worship of Liadriel for that god of luxury which seduced your own brother. Despite that I did not trust him, though, I could not ignore him. While there was a chance that he spoke the truth, I was forced to deal with him.

'I asked him what price he required for the information which he claimed to hold. He told me that he had urgent reasons of his own for journeying beyond Araby, and the fabled land of the dead, to the heart of the Southlands, and he needed to assemble a group of clever companions if his expedition was to be successful. It was, he said, a matter which required great discretion, for he had enemies even in Estalia; it would therefore be necessary for the members of his group to travel separately and secretly to an appointed place of gathering – a place which lies hundreds of miles to the east of Arjijil. He asked if I would consent to join him, and promised me material rewards as well as the information which I sought if his adventure were to prove successful.

'I did not have to pretend to be reluctant, but he knew well enough how strong a lure he had laid down. I questioned him as thoroughly as he would permit, and he satisfied me that he did indeed know my foster-father, and more about my own particular circumstances than common gossip could have told him. He threw out dark hints about matters to be settled, and blood-debts to be paid, but he would not say anything specific about who I might be or why I should bear an extraordinary grudge against those who had left me to die in the wilderness.

'On the subject of his own schemes I could get no more out of him save for a promise that he would give me further details of the planned expedition when the entire company was gathered. He assured me that his party included one man who could see us safely across the sand-sea and another who had considerable knowledge of the Southlands, and that he had every reason to suppose that his plans would be successful if only he could outrace his Old World enemies.

'In the end, I agreed to his terms. I do not like him, and I do not trust him, but I am a wandering man by nature and I have told you honestly enough how I love to visit strange places in order to exchange the tales I know for those which I have never heard before. You must have guessed while you have listened to me how passionate I am about my tales, but you cannot begin to understand what a craving I have to hear wilder and better ones. I can invent marvellously – but there is something about the tale discovered, the tale which combines the force and profundity of legend with the conviction of honesty – which can never be duplicated by mere invention. I told myself that even if this elf was an evil man – even if his intention was to use me as a bodyguard while he braved great perils – still he might take me to places where fabulous tales might be learned… still he might make me part of a tale as fabulous as any I knew.

'In addition, as any other would who found himself in my situation, I have a gnawing curiosity to know what my real name might be, and who my true parents were.

'I do not expect a practical man like you to think well of me for agreeing to the mad terms which this elf offered me, but I could not resist temptation. I was on my way to my rendezvous with this mysterious person when my ship was attacked by your pirates – and I have been very anxious to depart from here in order that I might still attend the meeting. Mine may be a foolish mission, but it is my own – and I could not possibly know that my temporary imprisonment in Arjijil would bring such deadly creatures here as you and I were forced to face yesterday morning – if it was in fact yesterday, and not the day before.'

When he finished what he had to say, Orfeo poured himself a cup of cool water, and drank it thirstily. He could sit up now, and take food, but the fever in his blood was not entirely dead and the flesh around the scratch made by the dagger was ulcerated and very ugly.

'If this is the truth,' said Alkadi Nasreen, 'it is somewhat less credible than the two long tales which you have already told me.' But he said it in a way which suggested that he did believe it.

'They too were true,' Orfeo reminded him.

'Aye,' said the caliph softly, 'and I remember what you told me of the doom of Zaragoz, when the daemons which my brother sought to control were turned against him. I remember how you were seduced by a worshipper of this dark god of luxury, and were held in thrall by her – and I remember how you reached out from your place of safety, when you had reached it, and touched that greater and more gorgeous world of which my brother spoke to you. You have travelled far since you were in Zaragoz, my friend – but I wonder whether you have brought something with you, which has not let you alone and never will.'

'I have wondered the same thing myself,' said Orfeo, quietly. 'In fact, I wonder whether anyone who is touched by Chaos is ever let alone thereafter. There is something in men which responds to Chaos, my lord of Mahabbah, which eventually serves to bring them to the forthright worship of dangerous gods but works in the meantime in subtler ways to tempt and corrupt them.'

'Not only men, if your suspicions about this strange elf are correct,' observed the caliph. 'I have heard it said that elves are proud and boastful, but never that they are weak of spirit. When elves make treaty with daemons, they must become fearsome indeed.'

'I have heard that they are,' agreed Orfeo. 'Indeed, one of the oddest tales I know tells of elves who turned to the worship of that god your brother learned to love… but you will forgive me if my mind returns to more pressing matters. I think you understand now how anxious I am to leave Arjijil, and I know that you will keep the promise which you kept to help me go. How may my leaving be contrived – and when?'

Nasreen shifted his position slightly, and reached up with his right hand to stroke his black beard thoughtfully.

'It must be done secretly,' he said, 'for the sake of your safety. No doubt the rumour of your death will reach the *hashishin* soon enough, but they may not be as ready to believe it as everyone else. We must have a funeral, of course, but while necessity dictates that the casket be closed they may still be hard to convince.

'I fear that I must counsel caution, and beg you to wait a while. Your leg is still poisoned, in any case. In three days… perhaps four… their watchers will have begun to believe. Your friend Maro must not be allowed to know that you are alive, because they are sure to keep a close eye on him… I know that you wanted to take him with you, but I ask you now to leave him in my care, safe in the knowledge that I have sworn that I will never hurt or sell him. If that be done, then I am sure that I could find a way to smuggle you out of the citadel by dead of night, with no one the wiser. I implore you to agree, for I am sure that any other course of action would dramatically lessen your chances of reaching your intended meeting-place alive.'

Orfeo considered what had been said, and could find no flaw in it. He knew full well that without the friendship and help of Alkadi Nasreen he was certainly a doomed man. He had to trust the other's goodwill, and that meant that he had to trust his judgement too.

'Very well,' he said. 'I will consent to wait until my leg is better, and I will place myself entirely in your hands. No doubt you are the one man in Arjijil who could take me out of it without anyone knowing. I thank you, my friend, for what you have promised and for what you have already done. I am sorry that I ever doubted you.'

'Of course,' said the caliph smoothly, 'such generosity must have its price.'

Orfeo could not help but scowl, though he was very quick to suppress his annoyance. 'Price?' he repeated, trying not to sound resentful.

'Oh yes,' said Alkadi Nasreen. 'There is always a price. This one is to be paid in two parts. First of all, I want a promise from you – a promise that if you should live to go forth upon this mad adventure into the heart of the continent, and if you should also live to return, then you will visit Arjijil again, to tell me the story which you have so provocatively begun.'

Orfeo smiled, albeit rather wanly. He could see that he had deserved this well enough, but he knew only too well that it would be an easier promise to give than to fulfil. 'And secondly?' he asked.

'Secondly,' said Alkadi Nasreen, 'I want to hear the story which you have just mentioned to me – the story of the elves who had dealings with daemons of that same dark god which destroyed my brother.'

'I cannot vouch for its truth,' said Orfeo. 'It is a wilder tale by far than the tale of Harmis Detz. I do not find it impossible to believe, but I cannot pretend that it is aught but hearsay. Still, if you are determined to hear it, we have the time.'

'Good,' said the Caliph of Mahabbah and the Twin Seas. 'This time, I can promise you that we will not be disturbed. But first, I have some funerals to arrange – including yours. Eat, my friend, and sleep if you can. Be ready for my return, and have your story ready for your tongue.'

'I will,' said Orfeo. 'And...'

Alkadi Nasreen had already risen to his feet, but he paused to say: 'And what?'

'Lay my empty casket gently in the earth,' said Orfeo, 'But be sure that you bury it so deeply that none will be tempted to dig it up again.'

'You will rest safely in your grave,' his friend the caliph told him. 'You may be absolutely sure of that.' And though he smiled, to show that it was a joke, Orfeo could not help but feel a little thrill of fear.

But after all, he told himself, it will make a tale. Whatever else comes of it, it will make a tale.

WHEN THE CALIPH was settled upon his cushion, Orfeo took a draught from his wine-cup. His leg was more painful now than it had been before, and the last lingering traces of delirium were agitating his thoughts, but these afflictions did not seem inappropriate, given that his tale had much to do with stormy dreams and delirious bravery.

'First,' he said, 'I must explain how this tale was told to me. I heard it from a man I met in l'Anguille, the port city in northern Bretonnia. He was en route to Marienburg in the Wasteland, I to Couronne.

'Like me this man was a player, but he styled himself a bard and said that he came from Morien, one of the group of islands that lies off the western coast of the legendary land of Albion. The instrument which he played, which was strange to me, he called a harp. Most players, of course, carry lutes – which have the virtue of being easily portable and easily repaired.

'A harp, by contrast, is more than half as tall as a man, and has three times as many strings as a lute. Its frame is so heavy that it needs a strong man to lift it, and it must be set on a pedestal to be played. If it is to be carried from one town to another it requires a beast of burden – and it makes a very full load for a donkey, if not for a horse.

'This man said that bards do not often travel from place to place. They are men of some importance in the courts of Morien and act as advisers to the petty kings as well as taking a leading part in all ceremonies and festivals. The harps which they play are usually set in places of honour, from which they are rarely moved. His own harp, he added, was a smaller instrument than many, but was nevertheless a much more satisfying thing for a musician to play than a mere lute.

'I pointed out that for the purpose of leading a civilized dance it was imperative that a player should have a portable instrument, and one which was capable of carrying a plain and unencumbered melody. Complexity, I suggested, should not be automatically reckoned among the musical virtues.'

'Bravo,' murmured Alkadi Nasreen.

'My informant,' Orfeo continued, 'went on to explain that it is not the function of the harpers of Morien to play for the dance. The bardic order is closely associated with the priesthood of the druids, for in that island a particular sect of the Old Religion retains its orthodoxy, and the Mother-Goddess – who is known throughout most of the Old World as Rhya, wife of Taal, the God of Nature and Wild Places, and also mother of Manann, the God of the

Seas – is held sacred. Those gods who are worshipped in Bretonnia and the Empire – including both Taal and Manann – have fewer worshippers in Morien.

'The priests of the Old Religion are shy men who love the wilderness, shunning courts and council chambers, and bards have become the lay ambassadors of druidism in Morien and the neighbouring isles. They have their own share of the wisdom of the faith to protect, preserve and use, and they have modest powers of magic associated with this wisdom. The harp, therefore, is required in some measure to be an instrument of magic as well as of music, and the harmonies of magic – unlike the melodies of the dance – benefit greatly from complexity of sound.

'I asked for a demonstration of the alleged magical power of the harp, but I was not entirely surprised when my request was refused. His excuse was that magic is not to be used for mere amusement; it has its particular place in the ordered scheme of things, and rules which bind it to that place. I could only take his word, while remaining privately sceptical. But the bard offered to provide a further explanation of the nature of his calling and the quality of bardic magic in the form of a tale. He warned me – and his other listeners – that it was a dark tale, full of mystery, but that it would, amongst other things, serve to demonstrate what manner of man the bards of his native land are. You understand me well enough to know how eager I was to hear him out.

'This is the story which he told me.'

CHAPTER ONE

THIS IS THE tale of Herla, King of Plennydd in the isle of Morien, and of his bard Trystan; but in order that you should understand it, you must first know something about the history and folkways of Morien.

It is believed in Morien that all the isles were once united in one realm under the rule of the great and good Agam Rund, who had taught his knights a code of honour which all were proud to embrace and to obey. In Morien, that code is carefully preserved, binding the island's kings as tightly as its commoners.

According to the men of Morien, the days of Agam Rund were a time of great druids as well as great kings, and Agam had for his chief adviser a bardic wizard of very considerable power, named Bavian. Bavian had prophesied that while the Code of Agam Rund was observed in the Isles of Albion, there would be peace, prosperity and happiness; but by the time of King Herla those days were long gone. Some said that the prophecy had been spoiled even before Agam's rule came to an end, because Bavian had turned his power to illicit magic, hoping to discover the secret of immortality. The bards of Morien, however, are taught that Bavian did achieve an immortality of sorts, and that he remains a friend to the realms of Albion, ready and able to help in times of distress, provided only that the Code be kept by those he comes to help.

The men of each of Morien's three kingdoms consider that their noblemen keep Agam's Code more faithfully than their neighbours, though each consider their own kingdom least fortunate in terms of its geographical situation. The men of Gwron, in the east, complain that they have ever to contend with the ravages of the dark elf raiders. The men of Alawn, in the south-west, think this burden trivial compared with the problem of insistent winds which carry the lowland soil up into the mountains at the heart of the island. The men of Plennydd complain that they have the worst of both worlds, having the wind to face in the west and the isle of Aeryn to the north, from which come fierce boat-borne brigands.

These differences of opinion give rise to some dissent, but for the most part Morien is a placid isle. The castles of its kings are all built on high ground, and while there are three kingdoms on the island none of the kings dare take an army to lay siege to another lest the uninvolved king be tempted to send his own forces against the castle left unguarded. In any case, Morien has only one good road, connecting Caer Plennydd with Caer Alawn, and that winds through many gorges and narrow passes as it threads its way through the mountains.

Though Morien is by no means rich by comparison with the better parts of Bretonnia or Estalia it is not barbaric; gold and iron are mined in its mountains and the best of its valleys are so rich in coal that its forests can be kept entirely for hunting, because there is no need for the labour of charcoal-burners. Despite the natural poverty of the soil the lowlands grow good wheat, because the farmers take care to manure their fields by ploughing in seaweed which grows in great profusion on the western coast. The farmers in the lowlands also keep pigs descended from the wild boar of the forests, while the hillmen keep sheep whose fleeces are exceptionally thick, and which therefore produce excellent wool. These resources are the treasure of the three nations – but they all require to be moved and marketed, and in a land without navigable rivers, roads are very precious things, whose closure inevitably creates hardship. For this reason, the friendship of Plennydd and Alawn is a very precious thing – a treasure in its own right – and the kings of each nation are ever eager to marry their daughters to the princes of the other. Herla was some months short of his twenty-first birthday when he became King of Plennydd, but he was already betrothed to Morgana, the younger daughter of the King of Alawn.

At the time when Herla's father first sickened, the noble families of Plennydd provided sixty-one knights of an age to bear arms. Only one of the sixty-one – Moraint the son of Hywel, of the house of Heilyn – was younger than Prince Herla, and there was a good deal of whispering about Herla's unfortunate lack of years in the corridors of the court and in the ringholds from which the noble families supervised their lands. These whispers argued that although the prince had demonstrated his swordsmanship in the tournament, and his courage in the hunting field, his judgement and cleverness were less certain. Some doubted that he had the cunning to outwit the wily kings of Alawn and Gwron in the games of diplomacy which monarchs must play.

These anxieties were increased because Plennydd had lost its old bard less than a month before the king took to his bed. The new bard, Trystan – though he was a Plennydd man and had been a boyhood friend of Prince Herla – was looked upon with some suspicion because he had not been nobly born. The bardic order had augurs and seers who were normally trusted to know what they were about, but there were many in Plennydd who could not help but be uneasy about Trystan's elevation to such an office at such a tender age. That he had a prodigious talent for musical magic no one doubted, but there were those who muttered that raw talent was not wisdom.

A few, in seeking to be scrupulously fair, expressed the hopeful opinion that a young king and a young bard might grow old and wise together, and become a partnership so rich in skill as to be indomitable when Gwron and Alawn passed into younger hands; but not many men can set aside thoughts of tomorrow in favour of hopes for more distant times, and so anxieties came to triumph over optimism in the hearts of Plennydd's noble subjects, even before Herla was crowned. Had it been otherwise, the course of this story might have been different, but destiny is destiny and cannot be questioned or denied.

ALTHOUGH THE DOUBTFUL whispers about his fitness were not supposed to reach the prince's ears, it was inevitable that they should. They troubled him, in part because he shared the same anxieties. His one ambition was to be a good king – a stout upholder of the Code of Agam and a benefactor of his people – but he was prey to gnawing doubts about his suitability for such a role. Affairs of state had always bored him, and he faced the prospect of his arranged marriage with trepidation. His greatest pleasures were combat and the hunt, when he could forget matters of status and responsibility, and narrow his mind to the glorious urgency of the moment; and he harboured the secret conviction that he would make a far better free forester than a king.

At the very moment when he became the king, Herla was at the hunt, unable to hear the news. It was winter, and all Plennydd knew that the snows would soon come to put an end to hunting for a while; the prince had been avid to go out despite the fact that his father was ailing. He had promised to return by evening, so as to be by his father's bedside, but the excitement of the chase had made the promise unkeepable, and when the sun set he was alone on the wooded slopes of a mountain, having lost all sight of his companions.

For two hours Herla had followed a valiant stag up slope and down, hurdling bushes and leaping streams, utterly lost in the vivid excitement of the chase. There was not a horse in the realm which could have carried him through such an adventure but the one he rode, and there was not another man in the realm who could have stuck to the task with such fierce single-mindedness – and in the end, when he had run the stag to exhaustion, he was possessed by a marvellous glow of pride. When the desperate beast turned at last to threaten him with its broad antlers he shot it cleanly in the neck with an arrow, and cried out in triumph, believing it to be the finest shot he had ever released.

It was not until the stag shuddered and fell, and all became still, that Herla noticed how dusky the world had become, and how cold the wind was which blew from the north. He dismounted in order to go to the fallen stag.

There was no way he could bring the entire carcass back to Caer Plennydd, but he was determined to take its antlers in order to commemorate his achievement.

As he knelt down beside the animal, though, he was seized by a sudden chill of anxiety. He looked up uneasily at the top of the mountain, which was shrouded by a dense cloud so dark as to be almost black.

Such clouds, so Morien's legends said, were of the kind which carried the riders of the Storm Hunt out of the frozen north when they were minded to sport for the souls of men. Herla had never seen the Storm Hunt, even in the distance, though he had often looked out for them on stormy nights when he had been a little boy, and had had a bedroom under the eaves of Caer Plennydd's highest tower. Now he looked at the cloud, saw only a cloud, and laughed at the quaint innocence of childhood.

He made haste to cut the antlers, knowing that he must return home while twilight still lingered, because he had no lantern with him. But as he severed the first of them with his dagger, he heard the sound of another horse approaching, and looked up in surprise to see who it might be.

It was a pale-featured man wearing light armour and a plain helm, mounted on a mist-grey mare so tall she might have been closer kin to Plennydd's warhorses than the swift coursers used in hunting. The rider wore no colours to identify him, and Herla could not judge whether he might be a knight – foreign, if so – or a mercenary soldier such as kings were wont to hire for their secret missions.

'Hail to thee, noble Herla,' the rider called out. Herla was not surprised that the man could guess who he was, for he wore his own colours clearly enough, but he thought the archaic mode of address somewhat strange.

'And to thee, friend,' Herla replied. 'You are far from home, are you not?'

'Further than thou knowest,' answered the rider hollowly. 'And yet, no further than thee from the only home which men of our kind have.'

'What do you mean?' asked Herla, pausing before taking the second of his trophies.

The rider answered with a bitter laugh. He had reined in his mare a dozen yards away, but made no move to dismount. 'I have a favour to ask of you, King Herla,' he said, after a pause. 'Will you give me the antlers of that deer which you shot just now?'

'Why should I?' answered Herla. 'I killed him, did I not?'

'Aye,' said the other. 'But had you been where you ought to be, he would have been mine to kill, and his headdress mine by right. Had you been a dutiful man, King of Plennydd, you would not have beaten me to my allotted prize – but I bear no grudge, I do assure you, for I am a huntsman too, and I understand how the thrill of the chase can carry a man beyond his natural limit. I only ask you to give me the antlers, which are no use to you.'

Herla was angry when he heard this, not because he had been called King of Plennydd, though he believed that his father still lived, but because he had been called undutiful.

'If you are a huntsman too,' he said hotly, 'you will know that I have the right to claim these antlers – and if you were a dutiful man, you would not try to prevent me doing it.'

'I have not tried to prevent you,' answered the rider. 'I have only asked you for a favour. The antlers are worth far more to me than to you, though your turn to wear them will doubtless come in time. I only ask you to be generous.'

Herla was by no means an ungenerous man, but he had chased the stag hard and long, and was still aglow with the memory of his triumph. Had others seen the kill, it might have been different – for their tales would have been testament enough to his skill – but he was alone, and felt the need of physical evidence to bolster the account which he would give of it. In addition, prickings of guilt regarding his broken promise to be home by nightfall told him that he would seem a sorrier failure if he went home empty-handed. The antlers, he believed, would help to justify his decision to follow the stag when all the others had given up the chase.

'I am sorry,' said Herla stiffly, 'but the prize is mine by right, according to that Code which all in Morien observe. I am the man who killed the stag, and the trophy is valuable to me on that account – I cannot see that they have any value at all to anyone else, and I do not understand what you mean when you say that I will one day wear them. I can assure you that I will never do any such thing.'

The rider on the grey horse frowned, and said: 'So be it, then. You have done me no wrong by your refusal, and I have no right to be angry. But I say this to you, King Herla – I serve a master who does not like those who are overly careful with the letter of the law, and who will sometimes take the trouble to put a man's devotion to his code to the test of temptation. I was once as you are, and bear you no grudge – but if in time to come we meet again, I will ask you to remember the words you have spoken today.'

Then the mist-grey mare turned, and walked away and as she walked it seemed that the cloud which covered the crown of the mountain crept down to welcome her, and draw her in – and the rider vanished with her, into the gloom.

Herla cut the second antler, and went quickly to his own horse. Only when he mounted up did the significance of the rider's mode of address strike him. King Herla! he repeated to himself, wondering why it had not seemed strange before. Am I in truth King Herla? All of a sudden, the importance of that question seemed great enough to outweigh all others, including the enigmatic nature of the horseman.

He spurred his own horse to a trot, and then to a gallop, but his attempt to race against the fall of night was hopeless, and he soon had to slow down again because he could not see his path clearly enough. The horse knew its way back to the royal stables even in the dark, and carried him there in due course, but it lacked only an hour before midnight when he finally clattered through the streets of Caer Plennydd to the gate of the citadel itself. By that time, his father had been dead for five hours. There was none sorrier than he for his long absence, but sorrow did not help to quell the new whispers which had taken wing – nor, indeed, did it help to banish Herla's own doubts about his fitness to follow in his father's footsteps.

CHAPTER TWO

ONE EVENING IN the spring of the following year found King Herla looking down from his throne upon the last of those who had been brought before him for judgement. He was trying hard to maintain his expression of stern authority, but weariness was taking its toll, and he felt sure that the distress which he felt must also show upon his face. This was no mere peasant accused of theft, nor even a franklin charged with false accounting to the tax-collectors; this was a knight – a Codebreaker.

To judge this case was the heaviest duty which it had so far fallen to Herla to perform since he had ascended his father's throne. It could not be reckoned a test of his cleverness, because the man had offered no contest to the accusations laid against him, nor even any plea for clemency; all matters of truth and culpability were clear and settled, and all that remained for Herla to do was to pass the sentence prescribed by tradition. It was not a matter in which he could fail, or lessen the esteem in which he was held by his court. Nevertheless, he felt a deep regret that this

37

necessity had arisen. It was a shadow cast upon the record of his brief reign; a hint of dishonour. The dishonour was not his own – but he felt that as King of Plennydd he must answer for Plennydd. Hallam, son of Meilir of the House of Larne, was a knight of Plennydd, who had carried with him wherever he went some tiny part of Plennydd's honour; in disgracing that trust Hallam had hurt the realm itself.

Herla could see that Hallam understood well enough what he had done. The dishonoured knight stood before him, stripped of all colours, with head bowed. His entire posture spoke of defeat and despair. Herla could not find his way through the intricate mazes of ancestral marriage which determined the relatedness of the House of Larne to the royal family, but exactitude mattered little. All the knights of the realm could be reckoned cousins to the royal line; their blood was Herla's blood. In this case, it did not show: Herla was a dark man with jet black hair, while the luckless Hallam was a copy of his straw-haired, grey-eyed father.

Herla could not imagine what had possessed Hallam to do what he had done. Hallam was no reckless boy – and was certainly no fool. To judge by his appearance now, the man was probably unable to account in retrospect for his actions; he had become a stranger to himself, astonished by his own betrayals.

'Hallam, son of Meilir of the House of Larne,' said Herla, striving mightily to keep his voice level. 'The charge is laid against you that you did enjoy an adulterous liaison with the wife of your kinsman Berwyn, son of Beredir of the House of Aglavin, in violation of the sixth point of the Code of Agam, which you swore to uphold. Will you now declare publicly that all this is true?'

Hallam lifted his head very briefly, though he could not bring himself to look directly at Herla, much less to glance sideways at his father. 'Aye,' he said hoarsely, with an evident effort to speak loud enough to be heard. 'It is true.'

'The penalty for this crime, in the law and custom of Plennydd,' Herla continued, 'is that you must leave the realm, and never set foot within its borders until twelve full years have elapsed from the day of the next festival. You may not return to your own lands, nor to the lands of any of your kin, until Beltine Day in the thirteenth year of the reign of Herla, son of Bryn. Will you swear to accept the terms of this sentence, upon pain of death?'

'I will,' said Hallam, this time without lifting his head.

'Go, then,' said Herla, a little more softly than the occasion warranted. 'Go, and make haste to leave the bounds of the realm before Beltine.'

Hallam turned abruptly on his heel, as though he desired nothing in all the world but to be gone from this council chamber. A full seven days remained before Beltine, but Herla knew that Hallam would not linger long on his father's land. Nor would he long remain in Morien.

And, in all probability, Hallam would be in no hurry to return when Beltine came again twelve years hence. Few exiles chose to return to the realm which had cast them out, and those who did often chose to double the sentence passed upon them, in order to demonstrate their penitence beyond the shadow of a doubt.

Poor Hallam, thought Herla. If ever we see one another again, I shall have sat upon this throne for more than four and twenty years. I will be well-schooled in the arts of kingcraft by then, if I am here at all… but what will become of you, in Albion, or the Empire – or wherever your destiny takes you? You are too proud to be a servant, and those arts of combat in which you are practiced will not qualify you to be a foot-soldier. Will Meilir send you money, even though he will refuse to speak your name?

The king permitted himself a slight and sorrowful shake of the head, though he put up his hand to wipe his brow in order to conceal the motion. The eyes of his court were upon him, and he was determined to meet the collective gaze with the imperious stare which was required of him. He had been told, but had never fully understood, that callousness was born with kingliness; and that no matter how frequently he might be disposed to show mercy and generosity, he must never make mercy the rule – for the king was the law and the Code, and must be stern.

It would have been better if the business of the day could have been concluded then, but it could not. When this proclamation had been written down there was another to be issued also. An hour later, Herla was still sitting on his wooden throne, fretfully picking at the sleeve of his robe while he waited for the scribe to finish writing. The scribe was a patient man who took great care to form each letter perfectly; he was forever pausing to look critically at his handiwork and quietly bemoan the poor quality of his ink. Only a small number of the nobles of the court had chosen to remain, and Herla wished that the few who were still there had left, though it would have been a serious impoliteness had any of the nine noble houses left itself unrepresented.

'If we do not hurry,' observed the king, trying with all his might not to seem harsh, 'the criers will be baying at the moon and the stars.'

'A crowd is waiting,' observed the bard Trystan, who was waiting by the window. 'When Alawn's herald rode away this afternoon the news was carried by flying rumours into every corner of the castle and all of its surrounds. Your subjects are desperately impatient to be told what they already know – that the marriage is arranged, the settlements all agreed, and the date set for Lugnasad.'

The scribe did not deign to acknowledge Herla's mild criticism – but Emyr, of the House of Siun, who was the lad's uncle, offered the opinion that the crowd could not possibly know the date of the marriage, which had only been determined two hours before.

'On the contrary,' replied the bard. 'They will apply the same logic which we brought to the determination, and will arrive at the same result. Only a major feast-day will suffice for a royal wedding, and Beltine – being only a few days away – is far too soon. By the time Samain comes the season will be cold and dreary, and King Coll will not want to commit himself to a long trip northwards when the

weather is likely to be foul. Next Imbolc would be even
worse and next Beltine too far away. Lugnasad it must be,
and therefore will be. Nothing remains to be revealed –
and yet the people of the town are anxious to hear the
news cried before nightfall.'

'All the more reason,' murmured the scribe, 'that the
news should be accurately cried. Kingdoms have been lost,
it is said, because of proclamations distorted in the crying
by one misread letter.'

'Aye,' said Trystan, equally softly. 'No doubt they were
near neighbours to those luckless kingdoms which were
lost because of a single bad nail in a horse's hoof.' He
glanced as he said it at Herla, who smiled in honest
amusement.

Herla knew that he should not be impatient, but he
found the robes of ceremony less comfortable to wear than
armour even on the best of days; they were softer, but in
their way no less heavy. Chainmail was a barrier between a
man and the world, which made him self-
sufficient, but the robes which a king wore when he sat
upon his throne were connections which bound him to
the world with sinews of ceremony and law, which forced
him to hear the complaints and pleas of his subjects and
proclaim the labyrinthine rituals which guided and regu-
lated the life of the realm. Herla could not help but regret
his captivity within the walls of duty, and he was pro-
foundly glad when the scribe looked up at last, after a final
flourish of his quill, saying: 'It is done, your majesty, and
clear enough for any man who has the art to read.'

Herla signalled to his secretary, who hurried forward to
take up the paper, so that the king might set his seal upon
it before it was borne away by the crier to the palace gate.
Herla waited for the red wax to be softened, then carefully
impressed the face of his ring upon it, to make a mark as
bold and clear as any of the careful letters.

He was about to step down from the throne, intending
to hurry to the disrobing chamber, when a man-at-arms
came abruptly into the room, anxious lest he be too late.

Herla sighed, and resumed his seat.

'What is it, Gwilym?' he asked.

'Sir Godwin of Conwy, your majesty, asks most urgently for an audience. He has dire news, he says, of a threat to the kingdom.'

Herla frowned. Godwin was the holder of a lowland tract in the west, which lay to the northern side of the border with Alawn. The House of Conwy was not reckoned a noble one – a fact which caused some resentment among its members – and was unrepresented in the council chamber. Godwin rarely came to Caer Plennydd and was not normally a man to bring demands or requests.

'Bring him in,' he said – a command which proved unnecessary, for Godwin had not waited for an invitation, and was already shoving poor Gwilym aside.

'I beg pardon, sire,' said the white-haired knight, who wore his colours but no armour and had clearly ridden hard all day, 'but I have done my utmost to reach you by nightfall, and cannot stand on ceremony now.'

'Have your lands been attacked?' asked Herla, unable to think of anything else which could cause such panic. 'Have the pirates of Aeryn come ashore?'

'There has not yet been an attack, sire,' answered Godwin. 'Nor is it men of Aeryn who have come ashore, but elves – about sixty of them, I think. They have not yet raised a hand against any of my people, but they have bows which they have used in hunting stag and boar, and nine in ten of them have the look of fighters.'

'Elves!' The exclamation came simultaneously from Herla and Trystan, but Trystan took instant control of his surprise, and it was only Herla who added, wonderingly: 'Elves, in Morien?'

'Elves, sire,' said Godwin, very positively. 'I think they are come from the sea, perhaps survivors of a shipwrecked trading vessel who made their way to our shore in a small boat. They certainly have no ship now, and must therefore be stranded. What they mean to do I cannot tell, but if they go a-raiding my ringhold has not men or steel enough to stand them off.'

'Elves are not raiders by nature,' said Herla uncertainly, feeling that this matter brought a most unwelcome end to an already-overburdened day. 'They have no love for humankind, but they have a reputation as honest traders. Bold warriors they may be, but they are not quarrelsome or vicious. If they have indeed been shipwrecked, they might need and welcome our assistance – though they are probably too proud to come begging for it.'

'You may be right,' said Godwin, with a trace of resentment in his tone, 'but whether or not you are, I wish that these folk had landed ten miles to the south, where they would be in Alawn instead of on the land which I hold in your name. Whatever the case, it was my duty to report their presence to you as soon as I possibly could.'

'Aye,' said Herla patiently 'you did right, Sir Godwin – and you have my thanks for your expedition.'

'Coll had best be told,' Emyr Siun put in. 'Even though they are in Plennydd, they are close enough to his border to make him interested.'

There was a murmur of agreement from the others present, which Herla took as an echo of doubt in his own capacity to make the decision. He was quick to endorse the opinion, to dispel any illusion that he might have done otherwise.

'Gwilym,' he said, 'send a man to ride after Coll's herald, and ask him to tell his master that a company of shipwrecked elves has landed on our western shore. Tell him that I will order a full investigation to be made, and will send news as soon as I have any.'

The man-at-arms saluted, and ran to do as he was bid. The herald's party would not have ridden far before stopping for the night along the road which led to Caer Alawn; there would be no difficulty in catching up with him.

'Is it your desire that I should approach these folk, and question them?' asked Godwin, when the door had closed behind Gwilym.

'No,' said Herla thoughtfully. 'If half of what I have heard of elves is true they are a haughty people, and it might be politic to send a special emissary from the court. Trystan – is this a task more fitting to your talents that to any other's, do you think?'

There was a murmurous whisper among the attending knights which suggested that they could not all agree with this suggestion, but king and bard were equally careful to ignore it.

'I cannot tell,' answered Trystan cautiously. 'But it seems to me that the order might also have an interest in this matter, and I would be glad to go on their behalf and Plennydd's.'

'So be it, then,' said the king. 'We may discuss in private, I think, exactly what you should say. Has any other aught to add?'

Again there were murmurs, resentful of the exclusion – though the thought uppermost in Herla's mind was simply to bring the session to a belated end. It seemed for a moment that Emyr Siun might say something more, but the old knight thought better of it, and no one else showed any inclination to step forward.

Herla stood up and bowed, concealing as he did so a deep sigh of relief and then he hurried from the chamber, beckoning to Trystan to follow him.

CHAPTER THREE

LATER, WHEN THEY had dined on roast mutton, cabbage and bread, washed down with ale, Herla and Trystan continued the discussion which Herla had peremptorily postponed.

'What has the wisdom of the order to say about stranded elves?' asked the king. 'If they are indeed the survivors of a wreck, what will they do now that they have come ashore?'

'I never heard of any such thing happening before,' Trystan told him. 'If there is aught recorded which bears upon the case it will be in the order's enclave in Caer Gwron – but I would prefer to rely on the evidence of my own eyes and ears. When I have visited these people I will be in a better position to judge their intentions. If there are only sixty of them, I doubt that they can pose any threat to the realm – and if nine in ten are fighting-men they cannot have more than a handful of women with them, so there is little likelihood of their desiring to make a permanent settlement here. They might try to make their way to Aeryn or Great Albion if they can, for that is where the ports are to which the elves sometimes come when they are in the mood for trading with the isles.'

'This could hardly have come at a worse time,' said Herla moodily. 'My wedding is but seven days and a festival away. You must return before Beltine – you will be needed then, though I had not thought of it when I decided that you were the man for the mission.'

'I will return in time,' Trystan assured him. 'And the timing of your wedding may prove more fortuitous than inconvenient, for if these folk seem friendly it might be a good idea to cement the friendship. Perhaps I might have your permission to invite the chief of the elves to your wedding-feast? That would give our own knights – and the nobles of Alawn and Gwron – an opportunity to examine him. The sea elves are the masters of the Western Ocean, and it will do no harm to have friends among them. Nor would it harm your own reputation to be known as the man who found such friends for Plennydd.'

'If they are friends,' said Herla grimly. 'Godwin clearly thinks that they are not. You must be careful in judging them, in case they are not what they seem. You and I are educated men, but there are many among my subjects who see the world in simpler terms, and think that anything which is strange is to be feared. There will be those among my knights who will say that the elves should be expelled forthwith, or destroyed, in order that we may be certain of our safety.'

'That would be against the Code, which commands us to help those in distress,' Trystan observed. 'Such a conflict would certainly spoil your wedding, and might store up trouble for the kingdom.'

'I know it,' said Herla. 'But there are many who say that the Code applies only to friends and neighbours, not to those who come from beyond the bounds of Agam's empire – and certainly not to elves.'

'You do not construe the Code in that way,' replied Trystan quietly. 'I know you too well to think so for a moment.'

Herla looked at his companion in a speculative manner. How well, he wondered, did Trystan really know him? Though they had been boyhood friends they had been apart for seven long years – the ordinary length of a bard's apprenticeship – before being reunited in their present roles. When they were very young they had played the game of 'when I am king and you are my bard,' and now that reality had suddenly come to pass they had fallen into it as though it were a mere extension of those games, but Herla was not so sure that King Herla was the same person as the youthful prince he then had been, and he had every reason to suppose that Trystan the bard had changed his character in no small way during his absence.

So far, it had been possible to be king by playing at it, and Herla had only had to use his bard as lightly as he might had their plotting been no more than a game. But a change was looming which would affect them both, for Herla would have a queen, and must live as the world and his wife expected him to. Now, there had also emerged a matter which required sound advice and proper action. These were the first real tests of Herla's kingship, Trystan's bardship, and the friendship which united the two of them.

'It is said,' observed Herla, 'that it is sometimes more difficult for kings to live by the Code than it is for lesser men.'

'Oh no,' replied Trystan. 'It is ever lesser men who find themselves too faint of heart to live by the Code. The tragedy is that there are sometimes lesser men to be found among kings, as well as in the ranks of gentlefolk and commoners.'

'But not among the ranks of the harpers, I am to presume?'

'Never among the ranks of the harpers, we are to hope,' said Trystan. 'For I fear that if the order were to fade and crumble, the Code would certainly fade and crumble with it. We, not the knights, are its true custodians.' He spoke very soberly, in a manner which Herla had not heard him use before.

Yes, thought Herla, he is changed. The order has put its strength into him, and its conviction. I am supposed to have found my own strength and my own conviction to mirror his – but have I? How can I tell, until I am tested – and when I am tested, might it not be too late to make the discovery?

Aloud, he said: 'You are the right ambassador to send to these elves. If they are shipwrecked they may be in dire need of common things, and you must take them gifts of needles and saws, cloth and thread, salt and spice, and hooks and nets for fishing – but nothing too heavy, for you must not be slow in reaching them. Deal with them as you think they deserve – you have a free hand to issue whatever invitations you see fit. But you know how vital it is that you should return for Beltine's feast, to play the music of the spring.'

'I would not miss it for the world,' his bard assured him. 'This is my first Beltine as Plennydd's bard as well as yours as Plennydd's king, and it means as much to me as it does to you that the music should be well played, so that it may work its kindly magic for the good of the realm.'

EARLY NEXT MORNING, while the sun was still nestling among the peaks of the heartland, Trystan set forth on his journey. His horse was a lightly-framed courser, and he was perforce dressed lightly, but he had put on as much finery as he could in order that he should not seem insignificantly drab to those he went to meet.

Over his woollen jerkin he wore an embroidered tunic which was quartered to contain the symbols of his rank. In the upper left corner were the blue-and-silver colours of royal Plennydd, arrayed in rightward-slanting bars. To their right was the badge of the bardic order of Morien: three concentric circles, the first being coloured green for the fertile earth, the second blue for the vault of heaven, the third gold for the fount of life; with the three circles were the runes displaying the motto of the order: The Truth Against the World. Below Plennydd's colours were

Herla's own figures, which showed three drops of red blood on the nation's ground; below the bardic badge was Trystan's own, displaying an owl in flight against the blue and russet colours of the House of Peredur, to which he was affiliated.

His mount was not dressed, but in the pack which his second horse carried Trystan had packed an ornamental cloth in Plennydd's colours, so that he might put on a proper show for the elves. He went unarmed, as befitted a messenger of peace, but he took with him two men with light bannered lances. These also carried bows and full quivers, and wore swords of an unceremonial kind; but they had no armour beneath their livery, because their mounts and spare horses were also of the speedy kind.

The distance between Caer Plennydd and the nation's western shore was not vast but the country was not easy to cross, and the journey could not be done in a single day even with the change of horses. It could be done in two, though, by well-mounted men who knew the best paths over the hills and through the woodlands. The two men-at-arms had both been born on Conwy land, and knew the territory well; thanks to their skill as guides, it was not long after noon on the second day when Trystan came in sight of the encampment which the elves had made.

He saw the settlement first from the ridge of a distant hill, and promptly dismounted in order to dress his horse. Then he paused for a little while to take stock of the situation.

The elves had come inland a little way from the bleak and dismal shore, into an area of woodland between two rocky promontories, where a stream ran down to the sea. Already they had begun the work of making the place habitable, having cut down and trimmed more than a hundred thin-boled trees in order to build a cabin huge enough to provide a temporary shelter for them all. Although a dozen elves still swarmed busily about the roof, it was very nearly completed. The other elves were

working at a great multiplicity of tasks; they had already
built three large ovens and a massive kiln, and made an
earth-mound for producing charcoal. The carcasses of two
boars and three stags had been hung, skinned and
butchered. Trystan could see that although his gifts would
be welcome, the elves had contrived to make very considerable progress without them.

If they have done this in a matter of days, he thought,
what might they not build in a year? A whole village of
cottages with a protective palisade as big as any ringhold in Morien, perhaps. He could not help but note
that although the elves' camp was low-lying – as it had
to be in order to be sheltered and to be close to the
resources of the woodland – it would not be easy to
attack.

The elves must have seen Trystan's party while they
stood on the hill, but once they were among the trees
the bard and his two fighting-men were lost to their
sight for a while. Nevertheless, they were met in the forest, while they were still some distance from the camp,
by two wary elvish bowmen. Trystan told them his name
and his business, and they replied in fluent Old
Worlder, telling him that he was welcome to accompany
them to an audience with their captain, whom they
named Thoron.

When the archers brought their guests into the area
which the elves had begun to clear, Trystan found that the
company had become uneasily quiet. Half a hundred pairs
of eyes were upon him as he rode up to the huge hut, and
he wished that he did not look quite so gaudy. He had
heard that elves were usually fancy in their own dress, but
these were all clad in plain colours.

Trystan judged that Godwin was probably right in his
estimate of the elves' strength. There were no children
among them, and only a few who showed signs of ageing
– though Trystan knew that elves were long-lived by nature
and rarely exhibited the common human signs of decrepi-
tude. Though all wore similar clothing, with little to

distinguish male from female, he judged that only a few were women. He counted forty-one, but he knew that some must be inside the hut, while others were probably out foraging in the forest and along the shore.

It was not until he brought his mount to a stop before the wooden house that there emerged from within it a person whose bearing suggested authority. It was rumoured that the elves who plied the seas were considered uncouth by others of their kind, little better than humans, but it was obvious that these elves did not share that opinion; Trystan had been in the company of high druids and bardic masters, and had seen all three of Morien's kings, but he had never met a human who looked at him with quite such lofty condescension as this elf, who was presumably no more than the captain of a trading-ship. And yet, as the elf contrived a bloodless smile, Trystan could see that the other was making an effort to be welcoming, and had no intention of seeming openly contemptuous.

'Hail to thee, good herald!' said the elf leader. 'Welcome to our house, despite that it is not yet wholly built. I am Thoron, late of the elfship *Moonshadow*, unhappily cast away upon this shore.'

Trystan was not surprised that the elf spoke perfect – if deliberately archaic – Old Worlder. The elves were traders, after all, and often visited the ports of the Old World. Some had even settled in the more important ones, such as l'Anguille on the northern coast of Bretonnia, though they reputedly lived apart from humans in their own quarter of the city. The largest of these trading communities was in Marienburg in the Wasteland, the greatest of all the Old World ports, and several hundred of these sea-faring elves were said to live there, administering their own affairs according to their own customs and laws.

'I bring you greetings from King Herla of Plennydd,' Trystan stated formally. 'He is glad to welcome you to his land, which is governed by the Law of Agam Rûnd. I must ask you if you know that Code, and if you are prepared to abide by it while you are within these bounds?'

Thoron smiled again politely. 'We have heard of the famous Code of Agam Rund,' he answered, 'and we have heard that it is a good law. As unwitting guests in Morien we accept that we are bound to obey it – but I cannot say that I know it, in every detail. If you can tell us now what rules there are which we are supposed to obey, I will give you a promise on behalf of all my people that we will keep them to the best of our ability.'

Trystan was prepared for this. 'There is a written law which is kept in a secret place,' he said. 'But there is a spoken law also, which is taught to all the men of these isles when they are young, so that they may know what is expected of a knight of Albion. All those of gentle birth must swear an oath to abide by these rules, and the oaths of loyalty which commoners swear include them too. The commandments of the Law of Agam are these:

'One, you will do no harm to any man who has not harmed you.

'Two, you will deal honestly in commerce with all men, and lie to none.

'Three, you will lend succour to the injured and aid to the needy.

'Four, you will not injure or violate the privacy of another man's house and property.

'Five, you will defend the weak who cannot defend themselves, against any and all unlawful oppressors.

'Six, you will respect all the ties and obligations of lawful marriage.

'Seven, you will bravely bear arms for our kingdom against its enemies, under the command of its king and his appointed generals.

'Eight, you will stand firm against the temptations of daemons and all foul magic.

'Nine, you will honour the dead and will not injure or violate their places of burial, or the sacred places of the forest, or the holy circles made of stone.

'Ten, you will be courteous and mild even with those you do not love, and will resist all wrath which is not righteous.

'It is not required of guests and birds of passage in any of the isles of Albion that they should swear to uphold Agam's Code, but it is required that they should know what the law is, and should not do anything which is forbidden by it. In return, those who are sworn to uphold Agam's Code are bound to give hospitality to their guests.'

Thoron was still smiling, but the others watching seemed serious and studious as they contemplated what Trystan had said. Trystan let out his breath, glad to have got the cumbersome address out of the way.

'All here have heard this,' said Thoron, after a brief pause, 'And I enjoin all here to take due note of it. We mean no harm to any of your people, man of Plennydd, and while we are fated to be guests in the realm we will do our utmost to be untroublesome. It is our hope and intention to build a ship – a task which may take one year or three, as fortune will permit – and then to sail away again. We hope that our presence upon this land will be tolerated, and ask that our use of it will not be counted as theft. We acknowledge that we will be indebted for this tolerance, and will pay a just price for it when we can. Will that satisfy your king, sir herald?'

There was just a tiny hint of ironic insult in the last question, but not enough to imply that what had been said was insincere. This was an elf, after all, who must presumably think that all this careful formality was mere pomposity, ill-befitting *human* beings.

'My name is Trystan,' replied the harper, 'and you need not call me sir, for I am not a nobleman. I am bard to the Court of Plennydd, friend and counsellor to King Herla. I have brought gifts for your people – not jewels or trinkets but things which might prove useful to shipwrecked mariners. I see, though, that you are very clever and industrious folk, who have already accomplished more than any man might have expected in securing the necessities of life.'

Thoron nodded to acknowledge the compliment. 'Come down from your horse, sir herald,' he said. 'Bring your companions into our house. We thank you for your gifts, which will lend us much-needed assistance, in accordance with the third commandment of your excellent Code.'

Trystan got down, and passed the courser's bridle to an elf who came to take it. He signalled to his companions that they might also dismount and lay their lances down. He paused to show the elves who came to take the horses away which of the packs were intended as gifts, and these were brought into the wooden building for unpacking.

Inside, the hut was as huge and empty as a barn; it was plain that the elves had been hasty to make some kind of structure which could shelter them all from the wind and the rain, and a base from which more carefully-planned projects could be launched. Its windows were neatly squared but not yet shuttered. It had a crudely-made stone fireplace but the chimney was as yet under construction. The first few floorboards had been laid down, and there were half-a-dozen carpenters working on others as well as on a long table and chairs, but the bulk of the internal woodworking still remained to be done. Daylight shone through the roof in a dozen places, and such gaps as had been sealed had only been patched with leaf-pulp and clay, pending more effective water-proofing.

There were, as Trystan had expected, no animals; the elves had not a single horse or goat or hunting-dog. But there were a few piles of personal possessions stored here, with the boat which must have brought them to the shore and four long oars. Whatever storm had overcome their ship had not left them utterly without resources.

'We have a little coin,' said Thoron, as he watched the careful scanning of Trystan's eye. 'Your people need not fear to trade with us – and when our coin is gone, we will find further goods to trade. These hooks and nets will enable us to become fishermen, in which art we are very skilled; and if your king will let us hunt freely our bowmen will soon produce a superfluity of meat. You need not fear that we will take mothering hinds or young deer, but we would be glad to capture a dozen sows and piglets if we can, to prepare for the coming winter. We have all summer ahead of us yet, but we must plan for the future.'

'You may take forty deer a season for meat,' answered Trystan, 'and make captive half as many sows – but you may have to range far in search of them, for this is not rich land. I must warn you that the border of our neighbour realm, Alawn, is but ten miles to the south; if you wish to forage across that border you must seek other permissions than those I can give you. The fish in the sea are yours to take as you please, and the seabirds too if your archers are clever enough. The gulls' eggs are good, if you have climbers skilled enough to reach them.'

'And the wood?' said Thoron. 'We must cut wood to build houses and barns, and that ship which will ultimately take us away.'

'I will confer with the king,' answered Trystan carefully, 'and he with his landholders. They must decide where trees can be cut, and how many, for we must be sure that poor Godwin of Conwy does not bear the entire burden of your gleaning – but I am certain that we can find you wood enough for all your purposes.'

'You are generous,' said Thoron, with no hint now of irony or condescension. 'We are grateful – and you may be sure that when we leave, the landholder who has given us such hospitality will have everything that we have built here for the use of his own people, to compensate him for all that we have taken.'

Trystan finished looking about him, and turned his gaze directly to Thoron's face. It was an uncommonly handsome face, by human standards – but by human standards, the elves were a comely race. The elf captain's eyes were large and brown, and seemingly frank, but his mouth was narrower than the mouths of others of his company, and the points of his ears more backwardly-directed. His skin was smooth and polished; the only sign of age and weathering it showed was a slightly uneven darkening in colour – and yet, Thoron did not seem to be a young man, and was certainly far older than Trystan.

The elf knew that he was being closely studied, and spread his arms slightly as though to invite the harper to make a full inspection. Trystan noted that the elf's clothes, though plain of cut and colour, were at least as well-made as his own woollen jerkin, and that his brine-worn leather boots were the product of first-rate craftsmanship. Though Thoron wore neither colours nor ornaments of office Trystan did not doubt that he was high-born within his clan. His only unique adornment was an amulet of some kind, which was hidden from view – though Trystan could see the chain which bore it above his collar, and the circular outline which it pressed into the cloth of his shirt.

'How did you come to be stranded here?' asked Trystan. 'The ships of the elves are famed for their unsinkability, and are said to have powerful magic which protects them from the power of storms.'

'Our great clan-ships are worthy of such a reputation,' agreed Thoron. 'But each such ship is the parent of a flotilla of lesser vessels. I was the captain of a smaller ship, which was unlucky enough to be separated from its fleet nearly sixty days ago. We were bound for Marienburg when we were driven far across the sea by a tropical storm, which left us dismasted and badly holed above and below the water-line. We made what repairs we could, but were helpless in the warm current which flows north-west across the Great Western Ocean; by the time we had recovered a measure of control over our course and speed we were anxious enough to surrender to the good wind which blew us here. Alas, the leaks grew worse and we had in the end to take to our one remaining longboat.'

'And have you no magician with you, who might have summoned help from your kin by magical means?' asked Trystan, trying not to sound suspicious or disbelieving.

Thoron pursed his lips before replying. 'There is one among us, named Kerewan,' he admitted, 'who has some training in the arts of navigation and shipcare, and a thorough knowledge of the stoneworking magic of our folk – but we are of the *Uranai*, and are expected to conduct ourselves like full-grown elves, not children. We do not fear the darkness, and do not cry in the night for comfort. We must prove ourselves the masters of our ill-luck. We have lost our ship and must make another; it is for us to find our way back to the clan, and not for the clan to search for us – that is *our* code, sir messenger.'

This speech reassured Trystan, and told him that what he had always heard about the elves was true: that they were a proud and self-sufficient people, who minded their own business as far as they were able. He nodded, to signify that he understood – and then he issued the invitation which he had suggested to Herla, saying that the king would be pleased to welcome Thoron and a few of his followers to Caer Plennydd, to be guests at his wedding-feast – when further discussion might be held regarding the terms of their residence within the realm.

Thoron seemed very surprised by this invitation, and when first he began to reply his face was clouded with doubt. Trystan guessed that he was about to say that he could not spare the time for such an expedition; but then his expression changed, and he answered that the invitation was very welcome, and that he would be glad to come to Caer Plennydd. 'But when,' he asked, 'is Lugnasad? We do not know your festivals at all.'

'Five days hence is Beltine,' Trystan told him. 'Lugnasad is the hundredth day thereafter. If you come on foot, the journey will take you four or five days, for the way is very difficult. But you need only go east, and anyone you meet will point you the way to Caer Plennydd – you will see it soon enough when you begin to climb into the higher hills.'

'We will keep account of the days,' Thoron promised him, 'and we will come at the appointed time.'

CHAPTER FOUR

THAT NIGHT TRYSTAN and his two companions slept in the house which the elves were building, having shared their meat for an evening meal. Although Thoron continued to be friendly the remainder of the company were inclined to keep their distance – only two or three others spoke to Trystan, and then with a careful politeness which made him feel awkward. In the main, though, they seemed to have concerns of their own which absorbed their full attention. They continued to work long after twilight had faded, apparently well able to see by the light of the two moons and the stars despite the obscuring effect of inter-mittent clouds.

Not all the elves returned to the hut even in the dead of night, so Trystan was never able to make his count of their numbers conclusive, but he judged that there must be at least fifty-five of them. He was curious to meet Kerewan, who had been named as the magician of the company, and asked Thoron if he might; but the elf lord explained that Kerewan was about his own arcane business and would not return for two days and more. Thoron promised, though, that he would include Kerewan in the party which he was to bring to Herla's wedding-feast on Lugnasad Eve, saying that Kerewan would no doubt be as interested to meet the magicians of Herla's kingdom as they would be to meet him.

Perhaps because he had dined on meat alone, without bread or ale or greenstuff, Trystan slept badly. He was well-used to lying on hard ground – and the ground within the hut was no harder than most – but he could not seem to find a comfortable posture in which to lie, and was forced to turn hither and yon, while his dreams were so near to the interface of sleep and wakefulness that they were close kin to delirium.

Trystan had been prey to violent nightmares as a child, but the achievement of maturity and the disciplined years of bardic training had combined to give him greater peace of mind for some years. Now, it was as if those years had melted away, and reason's empire within his soul had dissolved into the confusion of childhood fears and misunderstandings. He dreamed that he was pursued by dark horsemen, hunted and harried like some fugitive stag while the wind plucked at his hair with its airy fingers and mocked him with a reedy voice which whistled and whispered in the treetops.

It seemed that he fled for hours on end. Whenever he found a moment's peace he would barely have time to sink to his knees or to turn and listen when the chase would begin again. Evil shadows would descend like a great flock of predatory birds avid to rend him with their claws... but in the end, he did escape, and found some haven where the hunters could not follow him – some ancient druid circle drawn in stones upon a wooded hill.

If that had been the end of the nightmare, it would not have troubled him too much, but when he woke up in expectation that the dawn was nearly come, he found the night still at its darkest, and he was carried away again, as though into some some magic underworld. Here was more movement, more restlessness, more urgency – but this was the urgency of the dance, not of the hunt, moved by fever and not by fear. There were shadow-daemons here as there had been in the earlier part of his dream, but these were not the cold shadows of ghostly huntsmen but the hot and musky shadows of incubi and succubi – spirits of languor and lust, whose greed for his soul was of a different but kindred kind. As these shadow-beings crowded him – for their pursuit of him was more intimate by far than the pursuit of the huntsmen – he felt the sensuous warmth of their soft clothing, like moleskin leather, and it seemed that the cloth caressed his flesh as freely and as hungrily as the hands which groped at his private parts.

The faces of these spectral beings were hard to see, but it seemed to Trystan that they were painted or tattooed in many colours. Their eyes were like the eyes of flies much-magnified, compounded from thousands of rounded cells, red or gold in colour. Each one seemed to possess a pair of horns, though these horns varied very considerably in style and magnitude, some being shaped like the antlers of yearling stags, others like the curling horns of burly rams, and others like spiralled sea-shells. They all had hair in great abundance, which was always soft and very fine, and which seemed to have a flowing life of its own, as anxious in the caress as their blunt-clawed fingers and their silken sleeves.

Trystan was more helpless in the grip of these tender creatures than he had been when he fled the huntsmen; he was made captive by them, and borne away into the bowels of the earth – and while he went he was thrilled and tantalized by their competing touches, which twisted his soul into a state of unbearable excitement. But in the end they left him unsated and unrelieved, abandoning him before a throne of awesome dimensions, upon which there sat a deity which was the very personification of the primal forces of lust and desire for luxury.

This god was both male and female, and though he wore armour of a kind, as if he had once been a warrior and might condescend to be so again, his mail was as bright as crystal and as brittle. In his right hand he carried a strange sceptre of jade; his face was very delicate, and passionate, and wide-eyed with deceptive innocence. His twin horns were beautifully curved, and decked with countless tiny jewels.

He spoke to Trystan, and said: 'Though you imagine that you owe your soul to the mother which suckled you, you have that in your soul which yearns for me. When you play the music of the harp, it is not the Mother of all Things which echoes in the harmonies of your soul but the thrill of life and luxury. Do not deny me, my little lover, for I am a direly jealous god, and when a soul has such a stamp upon it as yours, I do not like to see it pledged to others. You have made some very silly vows, my beloved, but you have time enough to unlearn that which you have done to prison and cripple your appetites. Only give yourself to love, as your nature inclines, and the rest will be so very easy. Only follow your yearning heart, my pretty one, and it will lead you to the rewards which you truly deserve. Only remember that love is the highest of all life's offerings, and makes all else worthless if it cannot be enjoyed. Only remember that everything can be betrayed, save the rule of truest passion. Be mine, dear one, be mine, and you will find what you have lost, and discover that which you have never had.'

Not until this speech was completed was Trystan allowed to wake, though he struggled to do so from the very first syllable – and even when he woke, cold darkness was still all about him, and had to be endured for a doleful half-hour before the dawn came.

It did not occur to Trystan to connect his dream with the elves, because it touched more personal resonances in his mind and memory. He had always had doubts about his true fitness to be a bard, and though he loved the harp with an uncommon ardour, he was not sure that what he found in the music he had learned was the authentic pulse of that Great Mother of All of whom the druids spoke. He was much troubled by the extravagance of his nightmare, and by the way in which it had entangled seductiveness and menace.

The aftermath of the dream made him thoughtful while he and the men-at-arms made preparations for their return to Caer Plennydd, and he was not able to give his fullest attention to the formalities of his departure – nevertheless, he contrived not to offend Thoron in the slightest, and when they made their farewells Trystan was satisfied that he had done his duty.

THE DAY WAS the brightest and warmest of the year so far – a fact much appreciated by Trystan and his two companions, for a homeward journey always gives birth to more impatience than an outward one, and heavy rain would have made theirs very troublesome. With the warmth of the sun on his head Trystan was quick to forget his nightmare. When they first had occasion to pause, Trystan undressed his horse, but he kept his own dishevelled colours on. There were few in this region who would recognize his face, and it would be as well to display his badges of rank to all who saw him.

Some time after midday Trystan took care to stop at a farmhouse where he bought a meal for himself and the men-at-arms, and discussed the elves at some length with the farmer – a franklin named Dewi Lwys – and his two sons. He told Lwys that the elves seemed like placid folk, who would not be troublesome, and with whom profitable trading might be conducted. He sang the praises of their craftsmanship, and suggested that in time the elves might have valuable goods to trade for livestock and vegetable produce, and that those who were their nearest neighbours might reap rewards from their proximity.

Trystan knew full well that all this speculation would be swiftly and widely repeated, and that the rumour of what he had said would spread out behind him like ripples in a pond. He was pleased to think that he was sowing the seeds of a peace which, if the gods were willing, might long outlast the sojourn of the elves in Plennydd. Like all new bards, Trystan hoped that he might play his part in keeping the security of the realm for the whole of his tenure.

He was still basking in contentment as the sun began to sink behind him and the vivid afternoon turned to golden evening. He thought that he had never seen the heather on the hills so purple, nor the singing birds of the woodland so bright in their plumage, nor the humming bees so busy about their work.

This is a fine land which has been given into Herla's care, he thought. It is wilder than Gwron and Alawn, and its soil is less yielding, but it has a stubborn pride which they have not. It is good to be a man of Plennydd, and doubly good to be a warden of Plennydd's well-being.

He carried this thought into a stand of ash trees, and was astonished to find them already burst into leaf – for the ash was the latest of all the trees in Plennydd to take its summer raiment, and was said never to do so until the tenth day after Beltine. Having observed this oddity he was not surprised to find that the stand was gathered about a small grove, whose configuration marked it to the educated eye as a sacred place; nevertheless, he thought it peculiar that the place should be unfamiliar to him, given that he was supposed to be retracing a route which he had taken only two days before.

He reined in and turned around to tell the men-at-arms that they should not cross the sacred place, but the men-at-arms were nowhere to be seen. He realized with a small start of alarm that he had lost himself in his reverie, and wondered why his companions had not called out to him when he had wandered away from the path they thought best. He made as if to turn his horse, but he was interrupted by a deep, soft voice, which said: 'Do not go, Trystan Harper, for I would have words with thee.'

When there was a voice there was no man in the clearing, but as soon as the words were spoken he was there;

and, no matter how paradoxical it was, it seemed that he had always been there.

Always!

Trystan's heart was hammering in his breast; he was a bard, entitled to receive true visions and certain supernatural visitations, but this was the first time he had seen any manifestation of Nature's messengers outside the context of a druid ceremony, when he was no more than a single insignificant figure in a crowd of wiser men.

The man who had spoken was tall and broad and heavily bearded. His aged skin had the texture of a tree denuded of bark, and his eyes were as green as the leaves which had sprouted in untimely fashion upon the ash-boughs. Despite his apparent age his profuse hair was not white but brown, tangled and matted like forest undergrowth, and though he was dressed as a forester in green and brown, with no robe and only the plainest of staffs, he was every inch a druid.

'This is a clever spell, which so skilfully defies the season and the moment,' observed Trystan, trying hard to act his part. He had been reminding himself only minutes before how stubbornly prideful the men of Plennydd were, and he knew that a bard should not be intimidated by a measure of natural magic – but he could not help being awed and afraid.

'The season and the moment are not so difficult to defy as you might suppose,' answered the other. 'To those who have the wit to see it, blood of my blood, time itself is but an illusion. Time is a foundation-stone of order, but order is a more precarious thing than you would like to believe.'

Trystan was troubled by this observation, which was unlike anything he had ever heard a druid say before, and which had a hint of sacrilege about it. He was troubled, too, by the appellation 'blood of my blood,' which implied that this astonishing person was kin to him.

'That is not what I have been taught,' he said. 'I had thought that the words of the ancient wisdom were: *To every thing there is a season, for Mother and Man alike, and the passing of the seasons can neither be helped nor denied.* But if the ash may burst forth before Beltine, perhaps I am wrong.'

The bearded man sighed so heavily that the sound was almost a groan. 'You know not how you taunt me, my child,' he said. 'We are both right, after our different fashions. There is more than one world, and more than one wisdom, and dire danger wherever the several worlds collide. You belong to time, and must labour under the burden of destiny, which says that the season which is come is come, cannot be unmade and must run its course. I was of that kind once, but I remade myself in another way, and now can enter time only when time itself is set a-quiver by dark menace.'

This speech allowed Trystan to guess who the bearded man was – and made it all the more worrying that such a man should name him kindred.

'What do you want with me?' asked the harper. 'Are you truly numbered among my forefathers?'

'You are blood of my blood,' said the other, again. 'And for me there is a reward in being near to you. But I cannot return to time and the land for such reasons as that; I have come to issue doleful prophecies concerning the season which has come to Plennydd. I must say to you this: that it is in the nature of prophecies that they be uttered in a way that what they promise must come to pass; *but it is also in the nature of true prophecy that it cannot deny choice and it cannot deny hope.* Whatever you may forget of what I say to you, remember that!'

It seemed to Trystan that his heart was in his mouth, and he could feel the blood in his head buzzing like the bees; he knew that he would have the utmost difficulty in forgetting a single word of what was said to him here and now, no matter how peculiar it might be.

'Who are you?' he asked, though he already knew the answer.

'Time has changed me,' replied the other. 'Once I was Bavian, son of Llew... now I am Bavian the Accursed and

Bavian the Maligned, and Bavian the Undying. I am the time-denier and the time-defier, but I must tread my allotted course until it brings me to my doom.'

'My teachers told me I might meet you one day,' muttered Trystan, remembering that he had not quite believed it. 'I had not expected the day to come so soon.'

'It might have been better had you been a man and not a boy,' answered Bavian, with another sigh, 'but it might not. Even the ash tree may sometimes be green before Beltine, and sometimes wisdom and power may come early to those who have not quite deserved them.'

Trystan set his jaw at this speech, resentful of the pessimistic tone in which this speech was delivered. He wanted to show that he was no fool, and that he could think as quickly as any man, and so he raced ahead of himself to guess what it was that Bavian wanted with him. 'Is it the elves?' he asked. 'Have you come to warn me that the elves are not what they seem, and that they will bring trouble to the realm?'

Bavian shook his head, and lowered his green gaze for a moment. 'The elves are not your real enemy,' he said, very carefully. 'The real enemies of the realm are within the realm, as the real enemies of Agam's Code are among its keepers. If the storm is to come, do not blame the ragged gulls which flee to shore before it; if night must fall, do not blame the owls which can only hunt in darkness. A blight is in the realm, Trystan Harper; it comes to Plennydd as it comes to the world entire. It must be fought with blood and iron, but it must also be fought with heart and reason, for souls in peril cannot in the end be redeemed by violence. Herla's knights will be tested, and Herla must try his sword against the swords of those he never thought to face, but the true battle is above and beyond the travails of combat.

'That is my prophecy, blood of my blood, of which all must come to pass. But I am free as you are free, and I may give warnings as well as pronouncements of doom. The warnings that I give to you are these, Trystan Harper: *Beware*

the music of the blood-born storm, and beware the music of ten-
derness! And when all else fails, remember the watchword which
I gave to all my kind: The Truth Against the World.'

When the voice had finished uttering the motto of the
bardic order it did not merely pause, but ceased to be –
and when the voice was gone, so was the man. When
Trystan looked around at the crowding ash-boughs he saw
that they were not yet in leaf. The sacred grove was still
there, but it was very different in appearance – all dull and
dusty with the lazy air of approaching dusk and the golden
sunlight creeping through the unclad crowns of the surrounding trees.

Trystan soon emerged from the trees into an open space.

'That is not the way, sire,' called one of the men-at-arms,
as casually as if he had only that moment turned his
mount in that direction. 'Bear right, my lord, bear right.'

Trystan's horse, unbidden by his hand upon the bridle,
bore right, and took him speedily on towards his destination, while the harper bit his lip in the turmoil of his
anxiety and vexation.

CHAPTER FIVE

THE SWORD-BLADE stabbed at him like the head of a striking snake, forcing Herla to throw his weight backwards and bring his own blade up. It was a move which few men could have made without falling, but the king's sense of weight and position was uncommonly good, and he not only contrived to parry the strike but to throw his lunging opponent off balance. While Moraint Heilyn floundered the king came about with astonishing grace, and tapped him gently upon the right breast.

The tap had perforce to be gentle, for Moraint and the king had long since ceased to fence with wooden practice-swords; instead they used metal ones which were accurately weighted, though not properly sharpened. Poorer swordsmen might easily have killed one another with weapons of that kind, but these two were the best in all Plennydd, and they rarely inflicted a serious bruise on one another's tender flesh.

'You are too good for me today, sire,' confessed Moraint, wiping sweat from his brow.

'I do not think so,' replied Herla politely. 'Less misfortunate, that is all. Had you not stumbled…'

'Stumbling is not misfortune,' answered Moraint, determined to take no credit where none was due. 'It is clumsiness. You do not stumble, for you are as light and sure of foot as any man I ever saw. I cannot match you, and never will, no matter how strongly my arm bears my sword or how clever I am in learning my passes.'

Addressed to any other king, such words might have been the mere flattery of a loyal courtier, but Herla's reputation as an outstanding swordsman was well deserved. The light fencing-sword, however, was rarely used in the three kingdoms of Morien as a weapon of war; uplifted as they usually were by their huge horses, the knights of Morien preferred heavy broadswords which could be slung from their saddles in capacious scabbards. Such heavy swords were usually single-bladed and blunt-ended, designed for crude hacking and slashing. If a knight were forced to continue a combat after being unhorsed, he almost always found that he must hoist his sword two-handed, or become very rapidly fatigued.

When they learned the arts of fencing the knights habitually used weapons far lighter than the ones which they routinely carried into battle, and for this reason fencing had become more sport than art of war in the isles.

Herla had access to an armoury more ample than any other in the realm, and when he had grown to manhood he had taken care to cultivate the skill of using a weapon with a thinner blade than was common, with two edges and a point, so that with stern practice he could bear it one-handed far longer than was usual, and cut with it most skilfully. Among the other knights of the realm only Moraint was good enough to spar with Herla using such a weapon. Some of the older knights frowned upon the idea of carrying a light and pointed sword into battle, saying that it was too easily broken and that its extra edge and point gave it no real advantage when it was wielded from the back of a warhorse, but Herla – like the

stubborn man of Plennydd that he was – had persisted
in his own ambitions.

'Another bout?' asked Herla – but Moraint was shaking
his head even before the messenger arrived to say that
Trystan had returned from the elves' camp.

Herla did not delay in putting his weapon aside and
going to the audience chamber where the bard awaited
him.

'What news?' the king demanded, with unseemly breath-
lessness. 'Are the elves friendly?'

'They seem so,' answered Trystan, in a rather halting tone
which suggested immediately to Herla that the bard had
good reason to doubt the semblance.

'Why do you doubt it?' asked Herla, trying hard to quiet
his anxiety. 'What did they say to disturb you?'

'Nothing,' confessed the bard. 'They declared their intention to be peaceful while they provided themselves with
food and shelter, and said that they wished to build a ship
as quickly as they could, in order to sail away. I invited the
captain to attend your wedding, and I have put the word
about that they are to be treated as friends, but...'

Herla became instantly grave. He seized a cup of water
from the hand of a servant who had followed him from
the armoury, then sent the man away immediately.

'Tell me what you said to them,' he instructed the bard,
'and how they replied, as fully and as accurately as you
can.'

Trystan gave a detailed account of his observations of the
elves, and everything which had passed between Thoron
and himself. When the bard had finished, Herla said: 'This
all seems satisfactory. What was it that alarmed you?'

'While I was coming home,' said Trystan levelly, 'I met
Bavian.'

Herla's first impulse was to laugh, though he knew that
it could not possibly be a jest. He knew that the bardic
order claimed descent from the man, and had a very
solemn attitude to his name, but he also knew that Bavian
had been dead for centuries; it was in his estimation no

more likely that Trystan should meet him than that he, Herla, should meet Agam Rund or the leader of the Storm Hunt.

'What do you mean?' he asked – and then was forced to listen to a very painstaking description of an event which tested his credulity to the limit. He believed the bard to be sincere, but he was not so certain that what the bard believed was the truth of the matter. He recalled that when he and Trystan had been boys together, Trystan had often suffered from delirious nightmares. He knew little about the training of bards, but he had heard that they were taught to trust their visions, and sometimes deprived of food and sleep in order to educate them in that means of supposed communion with the Mother of All.

'This troubles me,' he said truthfully, 'but I do not know what to make of it at all. You say that Bavian told you that the elves are not our enemy. Why then do you make this vision a reason for doubting them?'

'He said that the elves are not our real enemy,' replied Trystan carefully. 'But I took that to imply that they have something to do with the blight which he prophesied. Our real enemies, he said, are within the realm – but it may be the coming of the elves which will prompt those enemies to action. What he said was said to some purpose, and was not mere gibberish intended to confuse or amuse us.'

'But he also said that what is fated to happen must happen,' Herla reminded the bard.

'He did,' admitted Trystan uncomfortably. 'I do not pretend to understand what he meant us to do. I only report to you everything which happened, as I am bound to do.'

Bound to do! thought Herla. He deals with me as he is bound to do, though he is my closest friend. What has happened to the trust we once shared?

'You are my adviser,' said the king softly. 'You – not Bavian or any other. Do you tell me that we should take up arms against these elven invaders? In spite of what you saw at their camp, do you say that we should kill them all, or drive them from our shores?'

There was a pause while Trystan looked very troubled and uneasy.

Ah! thought Herla. He likes the business of judgement no more than I do, who am bound by law and custom to sit upon my throne and decide the fates of men. Yet judgement must be made, in this and all matters – and must be well-made, lest it lend credence to those who say that we are too young and too unwise to care for Plennydd as we should.

Trystan finally shook his head. 'No,' he said. 'If this blight is fated to come upon us, we cannot prevent it by going to war, and may fatally weaken our own strength. We must deal peacefully with the elves, but cleverly – and we must look out for the real enemy with which they are supposedly allied. We must be polite and scrupulous in all our dealings with Thoron's people, but we must be secretly on guard, taking nothing at face value. There is nothing else we can do.'

Herla lifted his hand, feeling the slight ache in the muscles of his arm which was the echo of a sword's weight.

'I prefer an honest fight,' he said, 'where I can see my adversary clearly. But that is not the way of kings. Sometimes, my friend, I wonder whether I have the makings of a king, or whether I should have been a younger son, free to be my brother's champion.'

'Bavian promised that you would have an opportunity to try your sword,' Trystan reminded him dully.

'Against the swords of those I never thought to face,' Herla quoted. 'Who might they be, do you think? The elves?'

'I think that you can imagine the elves as adversaries well enough,' said Trystan dubiously. 'Those you never thought to face must be stranger still, or...'

Herla could see the implication of that dark hint well enough. 'Or far too familiar,' he said, in a voice hardly above a whisper. 'Those I never thought to face might be my friends... my kin...'

'If there are truly enemies within the realm,' murmured Trystan, 'I cannot begin to guess who they are. Though some may doubt whether you truly have the making of a great king, there is surely not a man in the realm who would like to see you fail. The men of Plennydd are honest and loyal, and will stand by you if you are tested. For myself, I know that you have the makings of a great king, and I do not like to hear you doubt yourself. Perhaps, if there is a time of trouble to come, you will prove it even to yourself.'

Herla would have liked to believe it, but he was not quite as certain of Trystan's conviction as he had earlier been of Moraint's. The bard spoke as a friend must speak, and Herla was glad enough of that – but whether he really believed what friendship compelled him to assert was another matter.

'You did right to invite the elf captain to Caer Plennydd,' said Herla, having weighed the matter as well as he could. 'I will be glad to have the opportunity to meet and study him. You are right, too, to say that we must be on our guard. I do not pretend to understand this visitation which you have had, but where I can make sense of the advice which was offered I think it was good. The Code must be our guide in dealing with the elves, as it is in our dealings with our fellow men, and if there are enemies within the kingdom, we must watch out for them. But we must be careful in what we say outside this room, for there are many who already have too great a fear and mistrust of the elves, which might lead to disaster if it were carelessly fed. We must handle the old men of the court very carefully – and King Coll of Alawn more carefully still. I fear, Trystan, that what you have heard might be the kind of prophecy which makes itself true, if its substance becomes known and twisted, for there is nothing which can blight a land so comprehensively as evil rumour. Will you keep secret from everyone else what you have told me today about Bavian?'

'I will do whatever my king wishes,' Trystan assured him, again unduly awkward in his punctiliousness. Herla knew that it might only be embarrassment which made him so, but feared that it might signify some deeper lack of trust.

If I have enemies within my realm, he thought, I dare say that the worst of them are ignorance and doubt – not merely in my own mind, but in the mind of every man who must think not only of the summer to come but also the winter which must follow.

HERLA TOOK CARE to inform his court publicly that Trystan had formed a favourable impression of the elves, and that they were not to be molested. He sent a herald to Alawn to inform King Coll of what he had done, and advised him to do the same. Then he sent a messenger to Thoron to give him licence to hunt across the western demesnes for the number of deer which Trystan had promised, and for pigs to keep.

Godwin of Conwy had no representative at court to complain about the terms of this licence but there was, as Herla had expected, some protest from those whose landholdings bordered on Godwin's estate, who were also likely to be affected by the edict. Herla dismissed the objections, believing that they were born of mere habit rather than the fear of any tangible loss. In any case, the deer of Plennydd were held by custom to belong to the king no matter whose land they ran on, and the men of Plennydd did not put a great value on wild pigs.

Beltine came hurriedly upon the nation thereafter, and for three days Caer Plennydd thronged with people. On the eve of the festival there was a market and fair, at which there was much discussion of the far huger market and the grander fair that there would be on Lugnasad Eve, when the king's wedding-feast would be held, and of what would happen on Lugnasad Day when the marriage itself would take place.

Because the weather had been good for four days, optimism ran high for a glorious summer and an excellent harvest. The prospect of the king's wedding was an attractive one to the common folk, who would have their fair share of the generosity of the occasion, and all of this added up to make a good and happy Beltine for all its celebrants.

The weight of these hopes and expectations was added to the burden which Trystan carried on Beltine Day when he went to the great harp to play the music of spring for the first time as Bard of Plennydd, but he did not mind that. He thought it far better to make his first performance on a happy day than an anxious one, despite his own private fears regarding what Bavian had said to him.

He still puzzled over the meaning of the warning which the ancient magician had so passionately intoned, but he did not think that it applied in any way to what he must do on Beltine Day, for custom did not demand that there be any tenderness in the music he played, nor any quality which he could honestly compare to 'the music of the blood-born storm.'

The entire court was gathered in the hall for the bard's playing, and the doors had been thrown open so that the common incomers might hear the music too. This was magic, of a kind, and all the men of Plennydd had the right to hear it made and judge the artistry which went into its making.

For all his careful training in the Enclave of Gwron and the mountain fastnesses of the Old Faith, Trystan was not sure how good a player he was, or how truly important the quality of his playing might be. In ancient times, it was said, the rituals by which the men of Albion had sought to ensure the fertility of the Mother of All had been cruel ones, involving the spilling of innocent blood – and it was still common in some regions for a measure of animal blood to be added to the mulch ploughed in to enrich the soil of the fields.

It was said, however, that the wisest among the druids had discovered and gradually developed a magic which served the cause far better, and had allowed human sacrifice to be outlawed under Agam's Code without loss to the realm. The bardic order had been appointed the custodians and instruments of that special magic, which was made by the music played at every feast-day.

In the eyes of the common folk, what was to happen in the hall was simple enough: Trystan, Bard of Plennydd, would play the music of spring, whose rhythms would spread out to stir the clouds of the air, and the water of the streams, and the good earth itself, calling them magically to life and beneficence – and the better the bard played, the better the summer and the subsequent harvest would be. But the bards themselves knew that it was no mere matter of string-plucking skill, for the quality of the summers did not increase smoothly as a bard grew practiced, nor did it steadily decline as an ageing bard's fingers were stiffened by the years.

In the eyes of the bards themselves, the task was not so much to cause the summer to be good, but rather to help the summer to be born; a bard's playing was not to create the rhythms of air, water and earth but rather to discover them. The Mother of All was not, after all, a trollop to be paid or a coquette to be seduced; she went her own way after her own fashion, owing no particular favour to any of her myriad children, but capable of loving and cherishing them, of showing a little more kindness or indifference as they contrived to delight or disappoint her.

The true situation, thought Trystan as he put his fingers to the strings of Plennydd's great harp, has much in common with what Bavian said of prophecy. What will be will be, and no man has authority to command the wind or the ocean or the sun – and yet, nothing is finally settled in advance but that which still leaves room for choice and chance. If the summer is to be good, I will not have made it so, and if the summer is to be bad, I shall not be to blame – but in either case, if I play to the limit of my talent, and find the rhythms of the world unerringly, things will be better than they would have been had I done nothing at all. And so it is with all the affairs of men, which is why we need a Code to guide us, despite that we have a Destiny to meet.

And so he played, making the fullest use of that talent which his masters had called prodigious, and trying with all his might not to undermine his power by lack of skill or precision. His fingers stirred the strings to life, then guided them into the infinite range of their harmonies, with never a false note to spoil the spell.

The music of spring was bright and quick, the notes liquid and eager; the music of spring was bold and full of promise, calculated to warm the hearts of all who heard it. It was the music of the gentle rain and the benign sun; it was the music of prancing stallions and mares in season; it was the music of birth and proliferation; it was the music of colour and flowering. It had the sounds in it of crooning birds, of droning flies, of squealing young animals; it had the cadences of butterfly wings, of lambs at play, of the wind in the tall grass and the leafy treetops.

All this Trystan knew, and all this Trystan played.

As he played though, he became conscious of other rhythms which had always been in the music, and which he had learned with his fingering, but which he had never quite identified until he played them on the great harp, for their proper purpose.

He realized for the first time that much more of human life was in the music than he had supposed while practising its parts – that the rhythm of the heartbeat was always there, and the pumping of the lungs, and the jollity of the dance, and the pace of the sprint, and the thrust of lovemaking. It was all in there, in the music of spring: all quickening phases of emotion. There was hot temper as well as joy, there were sharp pangs of pain as well as surging hope; but there was no anguish, and there was an abundance of hope.

He lost himself in his play, as he had never done before, but he felt that he played well, and that the magic which he made was both potent and good.

When he had finished, the courtiers set up a mighty cheer, which echoed outside. Trystan was determined not to believe that he fully deserved the acclaim, for the people of Plennydd knew as well as he did that he was playing the music purposefully for the first time, and their generous inclination would be to flatter him a little, but when he took his seat of honour by the throne, Herla whispered to him that he had excelled himself, and brought honour to his reign, and Trystan could not help but be very pleased.

Later, when evening had fallen and the Beltine fires had been lit, Trystan and Herla stood in the king's private apartments watching the festivities wind down.

'It has been a fine day,' said Herla. 'This is what we dreamed of, is it not, when we were boys? It is all we desired, and more.'

'Aye,' said Trystan, readily enough – though there was inside him a curious lack of feeling; a numb emptiness left by the end of the music and the end of the magic. But it had been a good day, which had gone as well as any man had any right to expect. Bavian's prophecies seemed far less ominous now than they had when first they had been spoken.

'I wish,' said Herla slowly, 'that one of us had saved the other's life, when we were children playing.'

Trystan laughed, and said: 'Perhaps we did, a hundred times and more. Every choice that one of us made, which took us one way when the other might have chosen another, might have steered us away from some fatal accident.'

'No,' said Herla earnestly. 'I mean that I wish one of us had once been in evident and mortal danger, from which the other had snatched him to safety. I wish that I might have nearly drowned in the lake yonder, and that you had risked all to pull me out, or that you might have been savaged by a mad dog, and that I had shielded you while I beat it away with a stick.'

'Why?' asked Trystan, putting away his amusement. 'Why do you wish such a strange thing? We could not have been faster friends had some such thing happened… we could not be faster friends now.' But even as he said it, he saw that the heart of the matter was that they did doubt one another, just as others doubted them. They could not help it.

'Perhaps not,' answered Herla, in a perfectly level tone. 'But I sometimes fear that we do not owe one another enough. We are not bound by life itself.'

'We are bound as closely as men ever are,' Trystan assured him – as he felt honour-bound to do, despite that he could not quite mean it. 'We need no melodramatic tale to recall in order to make sure of it. I know what manner of man you are, and I trust you far more than I could trust any person who happened to see me drowning in a pool and fished me out – who might easily be a dolt or cunning villain in spite of what he did.'

Herla did smile then, with frank generosity. 'I am glad that you say so,' he said. 'I hope it is true. It did not matter, when we were boys, that I was royally born and you were not even a noble – we were of an age, and that was all that seemed to matter. It should not matter now that we have spent so much time apart, and that I am a king while you are a bard. We must trust one another as firmly as any two men can.'

Trystan was surprised to hear Herla talk so forcibly in this vein, and did not like himself for thinking – not without a certain bitterness – that it was all very well for a little prince to think that it made no difference that his playmate was a commoner, while the commoner could hardly ever be unaware of it for an instant.

What he said aloud was: 'We must – and we do.'

He tried to say it as if there could be no doubt about it, and was pleased that the king accepted it thus. But he was puzzled by what Herla said next, which was: 'Do you still have those dreams which you used to have, and which used to trouble you so much?'

Since the night he had spent with the elves Trystan had indeed had other nightmares, but they had been much vaguer ones, easy to forget when wakefulness came.

'I am a harper now,' he answered, 'and it is part of what I am to dream, and to learn from my dreaming. But I still have occasional nightmares of a very personal kind, which trouble me a little.'

'I have had nightmares myself,' confessed Herla quietly. 'Although I never had them when we were children, I have them now. But this is not the time to think of such things. This is Beltine, and a time for hopeful expectation. It will not matter, will it, that I am soon to be married? We will still be the best of friends, and no less close?'

'We will,' promised Trystan. For just a second, it was on the tip of his tongue to add: *and we would be, even if you were to marry a woman you truly loved*; but there are some things which cannot be said, especially to a friend, and he chided himself for having thought it.

There was another silence, which it fell yet again to Herla to break. 'I wish the elves had not come,' he said. 'Whether they mean us harm or not, I wish they had not landed on our shores. But they are here, and I suppose that we must make the best of it.'

'The world is as it is,' said Trystan, 'and we must make the best of what we find in it. That is what it is to live, whether we are bright-eyed harpers, dark-browed kings or black-faced miners.'

CHAPTER SIX

UNFORTUNATELY, THE SUMMER was not as fine as the highest hopes of Beltine had anticipated; the forty days after Beltine were too dry and the forty thereafter too wet and grey – but it was nevertheless a good and fruitful summer, better than most of those in the living memory of the old men who kept count of such things.

When the solstice came, some fifty-seven days after Beltine, Trystan was required to leave Caer Plennydd in order to go to the stone circle high in the mountains where the three kingdoms of Morien touched. There he played his allotted part in the sacred ceremonies of the druids, of which he was not allowed to speak. He was gone from the castle five days. He returned, in due course, a little leaner, and very tired – but he was forced by custom to present himself immediately to Herla, and he found the king by no means eager to let him go to his bed.

'There is more news of the elves,' said Herla, 'and there are some who dare to say aloud that I made the wrong decision in treating them so kindly.'

'What news?' asked Trystan. 'Have they hurt someone?'

'They are building some kind of stone citadel,' said the king. 'Godwin has sent word – and Coll has also taken care to mention it, which presumably means that he has set a watch upon his border to make sure that nothing untoward can happen there. While Thoron's folk had only wooden huts Godwin was tolerant, but now he is very anxious lest the castle be intended as a permanent base. Furthermore, he says that they are raising it by means of powerful magic, for they have not had time to cut the blocks of stone which they are using by any ordinary process. They are raising this edifice on the headland above their camp, quarrying the stone from the headland's heart – and you know well enough that none but the druids have ever been able to work stone as hard as that, even crudely.'

'Thoron told me that one of his party is exceptionally skilled in some kind of stoneworking magic,' Trystan recalled. 'And it is said that the elves have built miraculous fortresses in several other places in the Old World. Is Godwin so certain that this is a castle, and not merely a better house?'

'Oh yes,' said Herla drily. 'Godwin is certain, of course – but it may only be his trepidation which makes him so. Nevertheless, a stone wall is a stone wall. I could reassure Godwin, I suppose, by saying that when the elves go he will have the castle for himself – but how can I be sure that they do intend to leave?'

'Did Coll's spies – or yours – mention the ship that they are supposed to be building?' Trystan asked.

'Godwin concedes that a large keel has been laid and that a goodly proportion of the company seems to be busily employed as shipwrights. He admits, in fact, that when the ship is completed it will have room for twice as many men as Thoron has – but still, he argues, the building of a stone citadel implies that some will stay here when the others go.'

'Do nothing hasty,' advised Trystan, after a moment's thought. 'The elf captain will soon come to Caer Plennydd for all to see. Then we will all have the opportunity to judge whether he conducts himself as a civilized guest in a civilized country.'

Herla nodded, and said: 'That was my own plan.' Then he sought immediately to change the tenor of the conversation by saying, in a teasing fashion: 'Did you enjoy yourself at the ringhold of the gods? How fares the Mother of us All, now that the sun has turned in its course again?'

'The Mother fares well, as always' said Trystan brusquely. 'How fare the preparations for your wedding?'

'Well, I think,' answered the king. 'The contests have all been announced, and there is no shortage of entries for any of them. If the prizes were not enough to ensure a keen interest, there have been some considerable wagers laid these last few days. My knights are wary of betting on their own competitions, but they have no scruple about backing their liege-men. Caer Plennydd will certainly provide the winner of the crossbow contest, but it is a very different matter to judge the longbow, when so many foresters and huntsmen from the remoter demesnes will be entered, and several of the landholders believe that they have a dark horse in reserve. As for the running-races and the wrestling, there is not a nobleman in the realm who does not have a fancy of some sort among his servants.'

'No one would bet on the fencing, in any case,' Trystan observed. 'You cannot enter, and that will leave the field entirely clear for Moraint. And you should forbid wagering on the lance-contest, because there are always arguments about the judging; we do not want any resentful men who have been defeated with weakened lances attempting to redeem their pride by challenging their conquerors to return matches with proper weapons.'

Herla laughed. 'I can assure you that there will be no blood shed at this festival,' he said. 'Any quarrels which arise must wait for another day. I would like to make a good display of our warhorses, though. I doubt that the elves have ever seen their like, and if Thoron has any thought at all of bringing conflict to the realm the sight of such chargers as we can put in the field should certainly give him pause.'

'Let us make a good display, by all means,' said Trystan, 'but let us make it for your sake, not for the sake of cunning politics. Let our bravest knights show off their skill in your honour, and let us put all thoughts of enmity out of our minds until such time as we may be forced to entertain them. It is your wedding, sire, that we are talking about!'

'Why yes,' said Herla ironically, 'I had forgotten that! I knew there was a reason why I could not enter the lists myself, but could not quite bring it to mind.'

And with that, Trystan was allowed to go at last, to bathe himself and then to sleep – and if he dreamed at all, he had forgotten it by the time he woke again.

THE ARRIVAL OF the elves in Caer Plennydd, two days before Lugnasad, was an occasion of much excitement. It was not that the event seemed to anyone to be more significant than the wedding itself – there were only a few oldsters in the castle who had seen Bryn married, and there were at least as many merchants and one-time mariners who had seen elves in the ports of Aeryn, Albion, Bretonnia, or even Marienburg – but only that the presence of the elves added an extra dimension to their eager anticipations.

Thoron's party came on foot and plainly clad – and thus presented a picture far more prosaic than the noblemen of the distant ringholds, who took care to dress in all their most colourful finery and mount their most imposing horses – but the fact that they came at all was remarkable enough in itself to put the strutting popinjays in the shade.

Thoron had dressed himself all in black, but his jerkin, hose and boots were all made of different kinds of leather, every one of a quality rarely seen in Plennydd. He had seven companions, of which six were clad in russet browns and dark sea-blues; only the seventh – who wore a grey cloak, decorated with patterns of bright silver thread that resembled downward-pointing arrowheads, and hemmed with pale fur – stood out as one who took proper trouble with self-adornment. But this seventh was the only one who did not bear a heavy pack upon his back, or carry a bow and a sword; instead he had a wizard's staff carved from white heartwood and dressed with glittering crystals.

All eight of the elves were tall by the standards of the men of Plennydd – who were, admittedly, not noted for their stature – but they were also slim, and there was many a barrel-chested hewer or horse-tamer among the crowds who opined that they looked too delicate for proper fighting. There were many among the crowd, too, who suggested that the elves' reputation for comeliness was not entirely borne out by this company. Though handsome enough in fundamental form, there were few in the group whose faces were entirely unblemished – and though there were very many watching who were uglier by far, they took the view that humans were not so vain in making claims about their perfection, and hence deserved to be judged less critically.

Though there were many in the streets of the town who called greetings to the elves as they ascended to the walls of Caer Plennydd, the elves never replied. There was nothing particularly disdainful in the way that they looked about them, studying the ramshackle hovels which clustered about the castle with as much apparent interest as they devoted to the smooth slate roofs and latticed windows of the better houses, but they walked as a group holding close ranks, apart and aloof from their surroundings.

Trystan was called to the battlements of the castle by Moraint Heilyn in order to watch the visitors approach, but he could not answer many of the questions which the young knight threw at him.

'The one in black is Thoron,' he was able to confirm, 'and the one attired as a wizard must be the one he named Kerewan – but if I saw any of the others when I acted as emissary I was not told their names, and I doubt that I could recognize them now. They are not as alike as legend says, but still they are not human, and it is difficult when looking at them to pay attention to their distinguishing marks.'

'Do you see their swords?' asked Moraint.

'Did you expect them to come unarmed?' asked Trystan. 'In any case, those are light weapons, such as our knights wear for ceremony, not weapons of assault.'

'No!' Moraint replied, impatient because Trystan had misunderstood him. 'It is their lightness that I intended to point out, and I doubt that they are for ceremony only. They are fencing swords, Trystan – and see how well-built an elf is for bearing a light pointed weapon! So lithe, so light of step, so long in the arm!'

'Aye,' said Trystan, with a slight frown. He was quick to apply the same logic to the bows which the elves carried, which were longer by a foot than any carried by the men of Plennydd. Those thin arms did not seem sufficiently well-muscled to string such bows comfortably, but they were long enough to permit a very impressive draw, if only the archers had the strength.

'But wait until they see our crossbows,' said Moraint proudly. 'And watch how their wide eyes will widen when first they see our horses thundering across the tourney-field.'

'They are not our enemies, Moraint,' Trystan reminded him gently. 'We have brought them here to make friends, not to intimidate them.'

'It is said that elves will not make friends with men,' said Moraint soberly. 'And I have heard tales of evil elves – said to live in a distant land called Naggaroth – whose aim is the extirpation of our kind.'

'Do not believe all that you hear in tales,' said Trystan. 'When men speak of events in distant lands they have a licence to lie, and there are few story-tellers who do not exploit that licence to the full. We must deal with these elves, here and now – and it will be best for everyone if we can all keep the tenth point of Agam's code present in our thoughts. I must go, for I must play my part in greeting these men.'

Having said this, he hurried away to put on the tunic he had worn when he went to visit the elves, which displayed his rank and nature to all who could read it. Then he went down to the hall, where the elves would be received with all due ceremony when they had been brought through the gates and the yards as honoured guests.

THORON BOWED BEFORE King Herla's throne; his expression was not easy to read, but there seemed no lack of respect in his manner.

'Your majesty,' he said, 'may I present Kerewan, who stands second to myself within our company – and who deserves a higher place by far than he is forced by our misfortune to fill, for he is a very wise man. May I also present six who stand among us as your noble knights stand among you – though they are craftsmen as well as warriors, for it is the custom of the elves to devote themselves to *kerrmieryon* in many different ways.'

'I am honoured to receive you in Caer Plennydd,' Herla replied. 'You already know Trystan, who is the Bard of the Realm. Here at my right hand is King Coll of Alawn, to whose daughter I am to be wed in two days' time, and behind him is his chief adviser, the Lord Macalla; here at my left is Prince Lin of Gwron, who will represent his father's kingdom at the ceremony. Some thirty of my knights are here gathered, with many from the neighbouring realms, and you will meet many more in the course of tomorrow and the next day. Before I order that you be shown to your allotted quarters, though, will you tell me the meaning of the word which you used just now?'

'*Kerrmieryon*,' repeated Thoron, who had plainly expected to be asked for an explanation. 'It means the pursuit of perfection in a chosen task or discipline. We of the *Uranai* – which you call the sea-faring elves – are not so fixed in our roles as you humans are, and may follow many kinds of employment in our lifetimes. In all, we are devoted to *kerrmieryon*, for we are long-lived beings and do not like to be content with a lack of mastery in anything

we do. *Kerrmieryon* defines and determines our behaviour
in much the same way that the Code which your ambassador recited to me defines and determines yours.'

Herla did not react to this explanation in any way at all,
though Trystan could see that Coll and some of the
knights of Plennydd had discovered therein a sort of criticism, as if the elf was implying that humans did not –
perhaps could not – pursue perfection in all that they did.
When the elves had gone, having been ushered away to
their lodgings in the west tower, a certain muttering broke
out among those assembled, and Coll said to Herla: 'You
will have trouble with these folk, Herla. One way or
another, you will have trouble with them.'

'Perhaps,' said Herla, in a way which implied that he had
no alternative but to wait and see. To Trystan, in a low
voice which none but Coll and Lin could overhear, he said:
'Go see them in a little while. Make sure that they have all
that they need, and explain to them what will happen
tomorrow, first at the tourney-field and then at the feast.
Take the measure, if you can, of the one they call Kerewan.
If he is truly magician enough to reshape that granite headland into a citadel, he may be more dangerous than all the
rest of them.'

Trystan bowed, and withdrew. When a decent interval
had elapsed, he went to see how the elves had settled into
their rooms. Thoron – who received him alone – was quick
to reassure him that all was well, and then sat down with
him to hear a full account of the morrow's events.

While Trystan gave his account, Thoron nodded repeat-
edly to show that he heard and understood. There was
sufficient enthusiasm in his manner to imply that he was
pleased by the prospect. When the harper had finished, the
elf captain leaned forward in a confidential manner.

'Sir bard,' he said, 'we are strangers here, and we are anxious to give no offence on an occasion of such importance.
We know that we are on trial, and we understand that there
will be many in your kingdom who are uneasy because of
our presence. Will you consent to advise me on several

matters of importance, so that we may make a good show in the test which lies before us?'

Trystan felt that there was nothing to be gained by any polite denial of the fact that the elves were on trial. 'I will give you the best advice I can,' he said.

'I am grateful,' said Thoron. 'We are no more anxious to be castaways in Plennydd than you are to have us here, and we will be as glad to take to the great ocean again as you will be to see us go. But I beg you to understand that there is for us a correct way to achieve this end – we cannot simply beg for a boat to take us to some larger port, where we might find a ship to give us passage to a port such as Marienburg where elves live. We have our pride, and a duty to follow the way of *kerrmieryon*. I understand why your king has been troubled by reports that we are building a house of stone – but I assure you that we only seek to make a better place to live while we build our ship, for we are not used to huddling together in wooden huts and cots. Though the house is strongly-built, it is no more so than the earthwalled ringholds where your landholders live, and it is certainly no castle. The magic by which Kerewan raises and shapes the stone we use for building is certainly powerful, but by that very token it tires him, and I hope you will be kind to him while he is here, for I had to make him come in order to give him a chance to recover his strength.'

There was nothing in the content of this speech to cause alarm, and Thoron's huge eyes seemed as frank as they always did – and yet, Trystan knew that he could not trust him. Whatever else Thoron might be, he was very clever. If he chose to lie, he would lie well.

'I will tell Herla what you have said,' the harper replied in a neutral tone.

'Thank you. Now, there are two matters on which I must consult you urgently. Firstly, we have brought gifts for the king, as we would bring gifts to the wedding of one of our own lords. May we present these gifts, and if so, how and when should it be done?'

Trystan confirmed that it was also the custom in Plennydd to bring gifts to a wedding-feast, and explained that they might be formally offered during the feast itself, on the following evening.

'Good,' said Thoron. 'Secondly, I am most interested by these competitions which are to take place tomorrow, for that too is something we elves love and often do. I would dearly love to demonstrate our friendship by entering into the spirit of your celebrations. Might I be permitted to enter one of my companions in each of your contests?'

This request gave Trystan much greater anxiety than the first. He could not tell whether Thoron understood that one of the purposes of the tourney was to put on a show of Plennydd's strength – and, if so, whether Thoron had a similar intention. What danger there would be in yielding to the request he did not know, but he also feared the possibility of giving offence if he did not.

He tried to think quickly, and to arrive at a compromise. 'There might be certain difficulties,' he said at length. 'Some of these competitions are open to all, but some are only for knights and some only for commoners. Despite what you have said about roles being less fixed among your own folk, I do not think it would be seemly for your elves to enter competitions of every kind – and there are some for which they are not equipped. I cannot give you permission to enter the competitions which involve lances or crossbows, for your people are quite unused to such weapons, and it would be inappropriate were you to enter the ordinary running-races or the wrestling-matches against bondsmen and house-servants. Would you be content, do you think, if I were to enter one of your followers in the longbow competition, another in the fencing competition, and a third in the middle-distance running-race which is for franklins and gentlemen? Only one of the three, I think, would be at a significant disadvantage, for the fencers will use wooden practice-swords of a kind with which an elf might not be familiar; if you prefer it, I could enter only the other two.'

'Oh no,' said Thoron quickly. 'I beg you to enter all three, if that is the most you will allow. I will nominate Jair for the running, Athdara for the bow and Seremond for the fencing – can you remember those names?'

Trystan assured the elf captain that he could – and as soon as he was able, he hurried away to give the news to Herla. Herla told him that he had done well, but it was clear that neither of them knew whether it was safe to believe it.

'Put the matter out of your mind,' Trystan said. 'This is your wedding, after all, and you must be happy.'

'It is a king's wedding,' answered Herla grimly, 'when all matters must be kept in mind, and the happiness of the groom is neither here nor there.'

CHAPTER SEVEN

THE TOURNEY-FIELD OF Caer Plennydd was a strip of level land which lay between two mountain slopes. A small stream followed a winding course along it, but left adequate space for the lists which were required for the mounted combat, as well as an open space for the fencing. Platforms had been erected for the court and the most prestigious guests, but there was plenty of space on the slopes where the common people were able to assemble.

The competitors in the long running-race had set off soon after dawn from an appointed place some miles away in the mountains, and the wrestling bouts were stopped as soon as the leaders of the field appeared; the winner came from the distant demesne of the Aglavins, but there were plenty who had supported him. Many of the townspeople had been warned by their kinfolk not to oppose him in the wagering, so he received a loud enough cheer to start the day. The wrestling too went to a borderer from the house of Gyreth, but the short running-race was won by a local man in the royal service, who was cheered mightily.

The crossbow competition was followed with the keenest interest by all, and the result proved to be close, with two of Herla's men-at-arms and one of Huw Peredur's men matching shots while the targets were carried back again and again, six paces at a time. In the end, it was one of Herla's men who won, though the cheer from the townsfolk was a little muted – understandably, given that Herla's guardsmen kept tight discipline within and without the castle walls, and were regarded by many of the common folk as enemies.

Trystan, who had been seated next to Kerewan so that he might have the opportunity to carry out his orders, asked the magician what he thought of the crossbow contest.

'It was not a true contest,' opined the elf. 'The crossbow is a powerful weapon, to be sure, but at that range the uncertainty of the mechanism outweighs the bowman's skill – it was a lucky shot which won, not a skilful one. The *Uranai* are devotees of the artistry of the bow, which is a weapon which permits *kerrmieryon*, and are reluctant to use these wind-up toys.'

Trystan studied the elf carefully, trying to guess how old he might be. Kerewan's eyes were small by elven standards, somewhat sunken and lined around in a fashion which gave the impression that he had passed too many sleepless nights. His complexion was unusually sallow and his face rather angular, both of which features made him less pretty than his companions. He had the pointed ears which so many of his kind sported, and these seemed to protrude all the more because his hair was so sparse. He was certainly not young, and might be very ancient, but Trystan did not know what signs to look for in order to know for sure.

The time had come for the middle-distance running race – which was in part a leaping-race, for the contestants had to go four times around an elliptical course, jumping the stream twice on each circuit. Because it was closed to bondsmen the race had a smaller field than either of the earlier races, but a full dozen franklins had entered along

with eight squires and the elf named Jair. Under normal
circumstances all eyes would have been on the squires,
who would one day be knights of the realm, but on this
occasion it was the elf who attracted most attention. He
was easy enough to pick out, even for those perched half
way up the mountain, because of his height.

Trystan measured Jair's lanky legs with some awe, but
privately wondered whether the thin-framed elf would
have the stamina to last the course against the wiriest of
the franklins. On the first two circuits it seemed that the elf
would be a disappointment, for he loped along ten or fifteen yards behind the pace and only gained ground when
the runners had to jump the stream, which he did with
long-legged grace.

On the third circuit, though, the leaders began to fall
away and the real race developed, with the elf lying third
to the strongest of the franklins and the eldest of the
squires. Half way around the final circuit the squire began
a sprint, and for three or four seconds it appeared that the
elf might have to let him go – but as they hurdled the
stream for the last time Jair's stag-like leap carried him to
the shoulder of his opponent, and from there he ran on
ahead very smoothly, pulling further away with every
loose-limbed stride.

The crowd cheered, not altogether reluctantly but without any conspicuous excitement – and when the cheering
died a murmurous whisper took its place.

'How much more easily could he have won had he not
bided his time?' asked Trystan of his companion. 'Thirty
paces, do you think, or fifty?'

'Oh no,' said Kerewan lazily, 'he was at full stretch, I
assure you.'

Trystan was not convinced, and was perfectly sure that
Kerewan had meant to be transparent in his deceitful modesty. The harper dared not say so aloud, but he was
privately certain that the elf bowman would have a harder
task against the cream of Plennydd's free foresters, and he
looked forward to that contest eagerly.

The targets for the longbow contest were initially placed at a close distance, because there was a vast difference in skill and strength between the best of the competitors and the worst, but at each stage they were moved back a dozen paces instead of six.

The first two rounds disposed of the weaker competitors, though few seemed displeased – those who hit the centre of the target once were well-satisfied. In the third round, only five competitors contrived to put all three of their arrows into the heart of the target; the elf Athdara, two foresters and two knights. The noblemen were the ageing Owain Dene, who had been a considerable champion in earlier days, and Berwyn Aglavin, now reckoned by all save Owain to be his superior. Trystan knew them both well, and felt for them as they watched the targets being taken back again, biting their lips because they knew that their battle, at least, would be settled now.

The first of the foresters stepped up and placed his first two arrows in the centre circle – but then his unsteady hand failed, and the third could not even make the second ring. The second was a stronger man, and a patient one; taking his time, he placed all three arrows in the centre, though one came perilously close to the rim.

The elven archer went next, and fired all three bolts into the centre with hardly any delay between shots; what was more, all three went in so close that their shafts were almost touching. Trystan felt his heart sink, and revised his optimistic opinion regarding the probable outcome of the contest.

Sir Berwyn applauded the elf's shots dutifully before taking up his own position. He too put all three shots into the centre, though they were scattered as widely as the forester's – and then he watched with open incredulity as Owain Dene, belying his years, did likewise.

The targets were moved again, and the forester stepped up. At this range, Trystan knew, the difficulty was not so much to hit the centre as to hit the target. The distance was close to the limit of a bowshot, and strength became as important as steadiness; this was where the forester, in his estimation, might pull ahead of the two knights.

The crowd moaned when the man's first shot failed to hit the centre, and groaned when the second one likewise failed – but both were in the next ring, and when the third arrow flew as true as any fired all day Trystan thought that he might have seen the winner of the competition. But then came Athdara, and when Trystan saw the way that the elf drew back his string, with his slender left arm as straight and stiff as a swordblade, the harper knew that his worst fears were justified. Thin though the arm was, it was all muscle and very powerful. While the elf took careful aim Trystan realized that the extra length of the bow and the draw might extend this weapon's bowshot ten or twenty paces beyond that of the weapons which Owain and Berwyn were using.

The elf's first shot hit the target dead centre. The second and the third followed it, and all three landed in an area the size of a man's palm – not one was near to touching the edge of the circle.

Again Sir Berwyn applauded, and Trystan could see that the knight had accepted defeat. Nevertheless, Berwyn's first shot was as good as any of the elf's, and the crowd cheered mightily. The second and the third, alas, were far less accurate, the third barely hitting the target at all. The forester, obviously believing that he would have won were it not for the presence of the elf, hung his head in disappointment.

Then up stepped Owain Dene and fired his first arrow, leaping in triumph – and perhaps in surprise – as it matched Berwyn's first. The old man took a long time in lining up his second shot, and Trystan could not have been the only spectator to judge that he had tested his own strength too severely – but again the arrow flew true, and hit the centre.

Berwyn Aglavin bowed to acknowledge that he must now be last, but then clenched his fist to urge Owain on, willing him to match the elf. But Owain's visage was grim and grey by now, and though he struggled hard to line his third shot as brilliantly as he had lined his second, he could not do it. The arrow barely snicked the target before skimming away and falling to earth beyond. Trystan wondered whether he ought to be glad or sad that the target did not need to be moved again, for he was too anxious in his mind to want to know whether Athdara could have repeated his feat yet again.

'You see,' said Kerewan softly, 'what *kerrmieryon* yields.'

'Aye,' said Trystan glumly. 'We are imperfect folk, we humans, in all that we do.' He wished that he could make his own modesty sound more deceitful. Silently, he said: Save us, Moraint, from this humiliation. Remember that the elf is not schooled with a wooden sword – but remember too that he might have tricks the like of which you have never seen!

The final round of the fencing contest was some time coming, for there were many to be eliminated from the competition, but it was clear from the very start that there were only two possible combatants who might win the final bout, and who would certainly make an exciting contest of it if they did not meet before. Normally, the opponents for each round would be decided by lot, but Trystan observed Herla issuing covert instructions to the judges, and was not surprised to see that Moraint and Seremond were kept carefully apart, each disposing of a string of adversaries with casual ease until the matter lay entirely between the two of them.

When the final bout began there was no doubt at all where the sympathies of the crowd lay. They had not shouted too loudly during the running-race, and had been compelled to be silent while the archers took aim, but now they could let themselves go, and they roared what encouragement they could at Moraint.

The knight had had little opportunity to study his opponent during the early rounds, and he began very patiently and warily, testing the other with well-practiced moves to see what kind of defence he made. Seremond, it seemed, was more patient still, for he was quite content to let

Moraint dictate the pace. Once or twice, in riposting, he tried to use his superior reach, but Moraint was well aware of the danger and was quick to elude the probing thrusts.

Twice, it seemed, Moraint almost got through the elf's guard. Trystan stole a glance at Herla, and saw that the king was utterly carried away, sharing every step and feint with his protegé, and wincing with disappointment at a particularly close-run thing.

Moraint steadied himself, as though wondering what to try next – and suddenly found himself the object of a lightning attack as the elf came forward, the wooden blade twirling and thrusting with a speed of which its lumpenness had formerly seemed incapable. Herla was on his feet, and most of his retinue with him, and for a moment it seemed that Moraint could have no answer – but then the youth slipped away from the attack because Seremond had mis-anticipated him, and again the two paused to square up to one another.

This time, it was Moraint who carried the fight forward – perhaps anxious that he should not have to face that incredible attack again. Once more he nearly hit his opponent, and for three or four seconds Seremond was in full and desperate retreat. Now it was the elf who seemed anxious not to have the experience repeated, and he drew back a little further in his address, then leaned carefully forward to take full advantage of his reach. There was a pregnant pause while each, apparently, expected the other to attack – and then both changed tactics simultaneously, coming quickly forward in a blindingly rapid exchange of blows.

Once inside the other's reach, as he quickly was, Moraint might – and perhaps should – have finished it. He knew it, and he tried, but Seremond dodged the vital thrust with what seemed an impossible contortion of his body. For just an instant Trystan was convinced that the elf would fall, but somehow he did not, and pivoting on his heel he struck the bewildered man a very sharp blow beneath the heart, which instantly knocked the breath from him.

The moves had come so thick and fast that most of the men and women in the crowd did not know immediately who had been hit, and there were cheers beginning as well as howls of anguish; but when Moraint slowly fell to his knees, all knew his fate, and that Seremond had won. The cheers and howls alike changed spontaneously into a great sigh, and Seremond dropped his sword to go to the aid of his gasping opponent, whose face had lost all its colour.

There followed a horrid interval in which it seemed that Moraint might be badly hurt – but when a minute had passed, with the elf and the judges clustering anxiously round, the knight got slowly to his feet – and though he nursed his ribs tenderly, it was obvious that his trouble was not serious.

'Three out of three,' murmured Trystan to Kerewan. 'No doubt you could have made a clean sweep of all the prizes, had I not been so unkind as to limit you.'

'Improbable,' said the wizard evenly. 'We are clever enough when wrestling, but the large hearts which make us such good runners are vulnerable to hurt, and Thoron would never have risked a man against those titans who came through to the final of *that* competition. Then again, the crossbow competition was a virtual lottery, as I argued. Your limitation probably saved us from the ignominy of at least one defeat. But your best and finest competition is yet to come, is it not? We are to see your knights in all their heavy armour, perched atop those unscaly dragons which you are generous enough to call horses, though they dwarf the animals which you used to visit us. There are those among the high elves who ride horses into battle, but I have heard that these beasts of yours are very different.'

'The men of Morien have bred warhorses for their size and weight for centuries,' confessed Trystan. 'It began long before Agam's day – and it continued thereafter with even greater pride, for it was the warhorses of Morien which made Agam's company so very fierce in battle. Even the Bretonnians, it is said, have nothing to match them nowadays, and the mightiest stallions of the breed are said to be claimed after death by the leaders of the Storm Hunt.'

'What is the Storm Hunt?' asked Kerewan.

'Daemon-kin,' Trystan answered, with a slight shiver. 'The prevailing wind, as you know, blows from the south-west – and though it sometimes blows very violently we reckon it a benevolent wind. Its lashing rain is often unpleasant, but it is what fertilizes the soil of the isles. But sometimes – almost always in winter – there blows across Morien a very different wind, which comes from the north. It is bitterly cold, and when it is stormy it brings dreadful blizzards and weirdly howling winds. Some say that it has its origins in another world, and carries monsters from that other world in its wake. It is also said that it can snatch up animals and men, and take them into a company of undying hunters whose prey is the souls of men. When the north wind blows stormily the men of Morien cleave to their hearths, bolt their doors and shutter their windows lest they be seen by the ghostly huntsmen and taken by them. It is said that those men who love warfare and the hunt too well – who are not necessarily the same men who are bravest and best in the battle – will consent to join the Storm Hunt if the choice is offered, rejoicing in the gift of being undying and content to suffer the awful cold and desolation of it.'

'If that wind blows from the roof of the world,' muttered Kerewan, more to himself than to Trystan, 'it must begin its journey in the Chaos Wastes themselves.'

'So it is believed,' admitted Trystan.

'A wild place,' continued Kerewan, as though still lost in the maze of his own speculations, 'where the unbound energies of a realm which elves call *Urrurrai* leak into this world, bringing change and metamorphosis, danger and opportunity – an irruption which the Old Slann themselves failed to control or counter.' Then, seeing that Trystan was ready with a question, he was quick to add: 'So legend has it, sir bard. The world is overfull of legends, do you not think? If only we had fewer legends and more knowledge, even elves might be better than they are.'

'Perhaps,' said Trystan carefully. 'But there is a kind of wisdom in lore and legend, I think.'

'If humans were capable of wisdom at all,' said Kerewan, speaking lightly so as to excuse the insult with wit, 'no doubt they would find it in lore and legend as well as circles of colour and stone. But "The Truth Against the World" is a good motto, and I fear that legends are more worldly than truthful.'

Trystan knew that the other referred to the three symbolic circles on his tunic and to the stone circles which the druids made to represent and embody their particular powers of divination and magic, and felt that the quotation of his order's motto was not really intended as a compliment. He did not answer, and must have looked sullen, for Kerewan spoke again. 'Come now,' said the elf, 'do not be gloomy. Your king is to be married – what does it matter if a few of your silly contests are won by elves? I do not mean to hurt you with my words, or to demean your magic. Your druids are artful men, I know.'

'But there is none among them,' said Trystan sourly, 'who could cut stone blocks from a granite headland with the power of his will. There is not a wizard in Morien or all the realms of Albion who could do that – yet it seems that it is but a little thing for an elvish wizard.'

'The *Uranai* have no special word for "wizard",' Kerewan told him mildly. 'All elves are expected to know at least a little of the arts, and to cultivate some power.' He touched a hand to one of the silver arrowhead symbols that adorned his grey cloak. 'I have the stoneworking skill, but I have the will of our entire company to use in the cutting – I believe that your bardic magic is not dissimilar, and that when you play your magical music you draw upon the hopes and dreams of your entire nation.'

This was something which Trystan had been told by his teachers, but which he had previously thought to be a metaphor; because of this, he did not know how to answer the elf.

'I would like to hear you play,' said Kerewan, to break the silence which ensued. 'When will I have the chance?'

'Tonight,' said Trystan unhappily – though he could not understand why it filled him with apprehension to say it. 'When all the gifts have been presented.'

'I will look forward to it,' said the elf – who, though he would not claim the title wizard, seemed to Trystan to be a far more powerful person than himself.

CHAPTER EIGHT

HERLA HAD ORDERED that Thoron be seated immediately in front of him on the platform from which he watched the competitions. This enabled him to watch the elf captain, to overhear his conversation, and to speak to him if he should so desire. In his turn, of course, Thoron could hear what passed between Herla, Prince Lin, Coll of Alawn and Coll's ever-present adviser, the Lord Macalla; this had the effect of making Herla's guests wary of raising the subject of the elves, which was in Herla's reckoning a further advantage.

Throughout the early part of the day Thoron watched silently, addressing neither questions nor remarks to his immediate neighbours, who were Emyr Siun and the Lady Ceithlen, wife of Huw Peredur. The elf captain seemed entirely relaxed but not disinterested; when his men won their events he applauded, but by no means immoderately – and he applauded the winners of the other events too. Occasionally he would look around him, in a lazy way, without showing particular interest in

anyone or anything – but Herla noticed that he directed
frequent glances at the place where Trystan and Kerewan
sat. Herla guessed that just as Trystan had been appointed
to find out what he could from the elf, so the magician
had been set to use his cunning on the bard.

Thoron's attitude changed, though, when the jousting
began, and the first two mounted knights took their stations at opposite ends of the field. His huge eyes drank in
the sight of the men perched atop their massive steeds,
their polished helmets glistening in the sunlight. The
armour worn by both men was concealed by ornamented
surcoats in which their own family colours were combined
with the blue and silver of Plennydd, and their shields
were decorated with gaudy patterns. Their mounts were
dressed and hooded, with armour to protect their heads
and necks.

Each man carried a twenty-foot lance, blunt at the end
and partly sawn-through to ensure that it would splinter
on impact. A true blow might still unhorse a man, and
might easily break a rib or two, but only an extraordinary
accident could result in a fatality. When a man fought a
duel in this way, or underwent a trial by combat, he would
use an iron-tipped lance of stout wood, which would spit
an opponent if it could be got past his guard, but horseback duels were rare in Plennydd, and trials by combat
employing such full regalia were even rarer. Like fencing,
the tournament was near to becoming a sport instead of a
serious art of war.

The first combatants were Huw Peredur and Meilir Larne
– both seasoned men but young enough to harbour further ambition with respect to their prowess with the lance.
Herla could not predict the result, and would have had no
preference had it not been for the fact that he could see the
expression on the Lady Ceithlen's face as she watched her
husband make ready for the charge.

The horses lumbered into motion, prompted by the
rowels of the riders' gilded spurs. Both men continued to
urge their mounts forward – with some difficulty, given

that each must hold the reins in the same hand that held the lance – but the horses knew the business well enough, and it was soon apparent that this would be a full-tilt affair. The gargantuan beasts accelerated steadily as they came together along their separate corridors, ducking their heads as soon as they were near enough to be hit. The riders turned in their saddles, each trying to drive the tip of his lance past his opponent's shield.

The simultaneous impacts produced a sound of cracking as both lances splintered – but both had nevertheless been turned, and neither rider fell. As they struggled to control their lumbering beasts, trying hard to pull them up, both men signalled that they were unhurt, and ready to take a second turn. It was for the judges to decide whether any man could be called the winner, but they had no hesitation in waving the contest on. There was a long pause before the two men could bring their horses back to the starting position, and take new lances from their attendants.

Emyr Siun was no longer at Thoron's side, because he had gone to make ready for his own turn with the lance, and the elf captain turned around in his seat to say: 'There is awesome power in those beasts. A battle-line of ten or twenty would be exceedingly fearsome, even if the men on their backs had no weapons at all. One would hardly need a lance with such a weapon beneath him, save perhaps to defend his charger from spears and sword-cuts.'

'That is true,' said Herla coolly. 'There is no infantry in the world which can stand against such a force.'

'And I am sure that none would try,' answered Thoron. 'But a company of bowmen might loose four or five shots while the horses were in motion towards them, and still have time to scatter.'

'Three shots at the most,' said King Coll. 'More likely two – and it needs a man of very powerful nerve to stand his ground while such as those come within his bowshot, heading towards him at speed.' He looked to Macalla for confirmation and received it in the form of a nod.

'Ah yes,' said Thoron reflectively. 'I was thinking of elven bowmen, of course. But still it seems to me that your cross-bows have the power to cut a swathe through such battle-lines, if only your crossbowmen are carefully arrayed. If you had three ranks of stout-hearted men, each man firing only two shots, could you not make the horses turn, even if you could not be sure of hitting the little men upon their backs?'

Herla could see that Coll was sorely annoyed by this observation – which was certainly true – and was about to intervene when the suave Macalla leaned forward to say that the combat was beginning again. Thoron turned to watch, and Coll subsided.

Again, both lances splintered, and neither man was unhorsed – but this time it was plain that while Sir Huw had deflected Meilir's blow cleverly, Sir Meilir had taken much more of the force of Huw's. Though the knight of Larne was quick to signal that he was unhurt, he must have understood that the judges would call against him, for he made no attempt to rein in his horse as if to take his place a third time, but let it run until it slowed and stopped of its own accord.

Lady Ceithlen heaved a sigh of relief, and her applause was half-hearted. Herla reflected that he had seen her in a much more enthusiastic temper five or six years before, when she had urged her husband on into every encounter. Now, with two infants to be cared for, she wanted her husband to survive far more than she wanted him to win.

Thoron turned around again, and looked quizzically at Herla – though it took the king a moment or two to realize that the elf captain expected an answer to his earlier question.

'It is not easy to persuade such horses to turn,' said Herla smoothly. 'A crossbow bolt is a powerful missile, but the force of its impact means little enough to animals as pow-erful as these – and from head-on it is very difficult for a bowman to find a vital spot at which to aim. In battle, the horses wear spiked helmets curved to deflect any bolts which would strike their heads – and the men on their backs, as you observe, provide surprisingly little targets until the charging horses are too close for comfort.'

Thoron nodded gravely, as though he were entirely satisfied with the answer. But Herla could read the thought that was left unspoken, which was that elvish bowmen – as Athdara had already demonstrated – were well able to hit very tiny targets, even at the full extent of human bow-range. Herla did not care to debate the point, which was purely academic. He knew – and Thoron knew too – that if ever there was a dispute between the elves and the men of Plennydd it could not and would not come to formal battle-lines. Siege and starvation would be the order of the day, and the stranded elves could not possibly prevail.

Herla gave his attention once again to the tournament, and watched two more of his noble knights charge at one another – then groaned as one was tumbled from the saddle like a booby, and lay gasping on the ground until his attendants came to carry him away.

More broken bones, thought the king. A wedding present I had rather done without. King Coll was cheering, having mistaken one man's misfortune and incompetence for the other's prowess – and thousands of those assembled were cheering with him – but Herla had not the heart for it. Already he wanted it all to be over: the tournament, the wedding-feast, and the wedding itself.

'Was that the man who fought Seremond?' asked Thoron, pointing at the victorious knight, who was acknowledging the acclamation of the crowd.

It was Coll who answered: 'Yes, that is Sir Moraint. He is young, but he might well be the best of all Plennydd's men. Alawn has none to match him in fencing, despite that your man beat him, and even I might be hard-pressed to unhorse him, although I was a champion with the lance in my day.'

Thoron accepted this information with all due seriousness, though Herla could not help but wonder when Coll had ever been a champion with the lance – or a competent judge of fighting-men without Macalla beside him. But Moraint's family was more closely related to the royal house of Alawn than Herla's own, and Coll was nothing if not partisan.

'He is a brave man,' agreed Herla tactfully. 'Not yet the best I have, but certainly the most promising.'

'Will he be your champion, then?' asked Prince Lin. 'Will he fight for Plennydd on the field of honour?'

Herla permitted himself a small smile. The prince was not much younger than Herla himself, but he was the youngest of three sons and the romance had not been knocked out of him in the cause of making him a future king.

'I dare say,' Herla replied, as diplomatically as before, 'that I would appoint him to perform that role, if ever it became necessary to name a champion for Plennydd.'

'What do you mean?' asked Thoron.

'When there are disputes between kings,' Lin was quick to explain, 'they are sometimes settled by means of trial by combat, in which each king appoints a champion to fight on behalf of his realm. By such means, wars are often averted.'

Far more wars have been started that way, thought Herla, than were ever averted. But he said nothing aloud – and even Coll had sufficient sense of protocol to refrain from making fun of the youth.

'That is good,' said Thoron. 'Honour means a great deal to elves, and the *Uranai* have similar traditions. Those who suffer most from wars are always the innocent, and it is entirely proper that men who live by a Code like yours should have better ways of settling their disputes. I am glad to find that fortune brought our boat to the shore of an exceptionally civilized kingdom.'

Herla saw Prince Lin's eyebrow twitch – the men of Gwron thought their own kingdom far more civilized than Plennydd – but the youth was not so callow as to pass any remark reflecting that opinion. In any case, the conversation was interrupted again by another crash of lances and another cheer, as Berwyn Aglavin cleft the shield of Owain Dene's younger son, to earn some compensation for his defeat with the bow.

'Fortune has smiled on us all,' murmured Herla, just loud enough for those nearest to him to hear. 'These are golden days.'

He wished that he could believe it – and that he could make others believe it too.

THE FEAST WEIGHED as heavily upon Herla's spirit as the tournament had. His stomach was so tense that he soon found it difficult to force down the food set before him, and he seemed to have lost all his habitual delight in sensations of taste. Before the long round of presentations had even begun he was wishing it over and done with, for he felt certain that the only thing which could soothe him was the sound of Trystan's playing. This august occasion was one of the few in which the great harp might be played purely for solace and pleasure, and he felt certain that Trystan would make the most of it.

It did not matter whether he could gladly tolerate the interminable catalogue of flattering praises and hyperbolic good wishes of which custom made him victim; they had to be endured regardless, and so he endured them, accepting each modest addition to his wealth with all due courtesy.

In point of fact, most of the gifts could not be reckoned to the increase of his personal wealth at all; rather they would become part of the family's treasury. That which was perishable would be consumed; some of the useful items would be handed down to his as-yet-unborn sons; some of the decorative ones to his as-yet-unborn daughters. As for the rest, they would go as they had come, as gifts to be presented at some formal occasion to kings and noblemen who had reached watersheds in their lives.

While he sat and listened, Herla was seized by a powerful sense of the futility of it all, but that was the tenseness in him straitening his thoughts; had he been of a more peaceful frame of mind he would have seen it differently. He knew full well the importance of gifts as tokens of amity and honour, and knew well enough how amity and honour might shrivel and die without such formal nourishment. He knew too that wealth which was not cycled from hand to hand was less apt to grow by addition and improvement. Miserly hoarding led to stagnation of effort.

He had almost forgotten that on this occasion there were to be more gifts than hallowed custom and the ordinary opportunism of flatterers would have awarded him. He felt a moment of astonishment when Thoron rose from his position half way down the high table to speak for the elves – and that moment of astonishment was compounded with a flicker of dismay, for he had thought the torture concluded. There settled upon the crowd a silence more profound even than that which had fallen when Coll of Alawn had made the opulent bequests which – as father of the bride – he had been duty-bound to offer.

'We of the *Uranai*,' said Thoron, without raising his voice at all, 'are proud and glad to have been invited to take part in these celebrations. Dire misfortune brought us to these shores, but that misfortune is balanced now by the luck which has left us in the care of such pleasant and honest folk.

'My people lost almost all that they possessed in the shipwreck which made us castaways, and such gifts as we have to offer are very humble ones. Nevertheless, I beg that you will accept them in the spirit in which they are given. They are three. The first is one of the finest of our bows, evidence of whose craftsmanship you have already seen today. The second is a crystal cup, wrought by a workman finer by far than any who were lost with me. The third is but a seed, but it is a very rare and special seed which was found by a captain of our people in a land farther from these shores than any human of the Old World has ever travelled; I do not know whether it can take root in your soil, but I hope that it can, for if it does it will grow into a tree which bears marvellous fruit

– and might, if cuttings are carefully taken, be parent to great orchards.'

Having said all this, the elf captain signalled to one of his followers who was waiting behind a curtained doorway, and the three objects which had been named were brought in, and laid with the rest of Herla's wedding-gifts upon the dais behind the high table. But Thoron had not resumed his seat.

'I have one more favour to ask,' said the elf, when the gifts had been laid down. 'I do not know your customs, but I understand that there will now be music, played by the man you call the Bard of the Realm. We do not have bards among the elves, but we are great lovers of music, and we will be greatly interested to hear this beautiful instrument' – here he pointed to the great harp – 'whose like we have never seen before. In return, we should like you to hear a little of our music, played by one among us who is truly a minstrel – which is a title we are not disposed to give to many. May I ask him to play, your majesty?'

Herla dared not let his impatience show – and he was in any case curious. All the world had heard of the prowess of elven minstrels, and it was unlikely that a man of Plennydd, even if he was king among his folk, would get two opportunities to hear such music played.

'You are very generous, sir elf,' Herla replied. 'We are honoured by your offer, and are delighted to accept it.'

Again Thoron signalled, and another elf came from the curtained doorway, carrying an ornamented lute – but instead of taking up a position where he could play the elf carried the instrument to the high table, where Kerewan sat with Trystan. It was Kerewan who took the lute and stood up. Herla was surprised by his own amazement – for was not Trystan a magician of sorts, as well as a musician? – and could not find adequate grounds for the thrill of anxiety which surged through him.

Why do I feel that I have been tricked? he thought. Why is this a dangerous thing? Will this cunning man spin some awful musical spell to entrance the entire court?

But when Kerewan began to play, Herla felt his fears ebbing away – and with them the tautness in his gut which reflected and embodied his deepest anxieties. Within minutes he knew that the reputation of elven minstrels had not been exaggerated; he would not have believed that such a seemingly resourceless instrument could produce such liquid notes, such delicate harmonies, and such compelling rhythm. And yet, it was only music – there was no obvious hint of strangeness or magic in it. It had only the ordinary power which music has over the human mind and the human heart.

As he listened, though, Herla realized how profound that power was, and wondered whether all music might be reckoned a kind of magic. Kerewan's playing had in it the kind of excitement which is an invitation to dance with joy; it had in it also the kind of sweet melancholy which brings fond memories floating up from the shadowed depths of forgetfulness to the surface of the mind; it had in it also a kind of plaintive lamentation that the world was not a finer and kinder place, and life a bolder and more joyous thing. As Kerewan's clever fingers plucked the lutestrings, his artistry touched the whole spectrum of emotion – not intrusively or rudely, but reverently and seductively.

And this is elven music, thought Herla. Can it be that these folk are so like to us that they feel as we feel, respond as we respond, are as we are, in spite of all our differences of manner and physique? Or does music such as this reflect a nobility of feeling which is constant in the elven mind, but which mere humans can only experience momentarily, as an elusive and fugitive thing?

Now that it had its hold upon Herla's heart, the music seemed to speak to his heart directly; it spoke of pleasure and sensuality, of the rhythms and harmonies of the flesh, of a pure ecstasy which might be the highest aspiration of human consciousness, whose attainment might be the only real ambition. As Kerewan made his patient way towards the crescendo of his improvised song, it seemed to

Herla that music was the only true reality, and that the solid world was only a shadow cast by the music of the spheres; he felt the music of his own heart, stirred to its first real awakening, singing a song of joyous hope, and hope in joy, which promised him that life had more to offer than he had ever been able to dream before...

And then the playing ended, and Kerewan bowed.

As the realization spread that the performance was ended, loud applause broke out throughout the hall. Kerewan looked up – not at Herla or Thoron, but at Trystan – and a slight smile played about his lips. Herla looked at Trystan too, to measure the effect of that sly look and that sly smile, and saw by the stoniness of the harper's expression that Trystan had reached the same conclusion as himself: this performance was no gift or mark of respect; it was merely one more competition, one more contest of abilities which the elves were very confident of winning.

Kerewan sat down, and Trystan stood up. The bard went to the great harp, and set himself upon its perch, reaching out with both his arms to caress and test the strings. A low ripple of sound came from the instrument, like a soft bubbling laugh. Thoron and Kerewan were watching intently, eager to know what Plennydd could offer by way of reprisal after their own display of artistry.

Trystan played, unhurriedly.

Because this was a wedding-feast, Trystan played the music of love, but he cast love in the form of a melody much gentler and more austere than those which Kerewan had used. There was little bounding joy in Trystan's love-music, but more affection; there was no promise of ecstasy, but there was a promise of calm and contentment. Just as Kerewan had laid down a melancholic counterpoint to his more exhilarating cadences, so Trystan did also; he did not play the music of grief, which would have been horribly out of place, but he played the music of time, the music of the passing of the days, of moments never to return but precious in memory. He played the music of lost youth, of responsibility accepted, of duty solemnly affirmed.

What Trystan composed was composure itself; what
flowed from his moving fingers was serenity, gravity and
poise. He did not deny pleasure, but what his music said
in the language of the heart was that ecstasy was not the
highest achievement, nor the highest aspiration, of the
human spirit. Instead, his playing spoke of a fusion of reason and emotion, a conquest of the divided self of man, a
marriage of contradictions which brought about a perfect
wholeness.

This was the ideal of Trystan's playing; the ideal of the
great harp itself. This was not the ceremonial music of the
seasons that the harper played – it was his own music, free
and unconstrained – but Herla could see how close this
was in spirit and intention to the music of the seasons; it
had the same acceptance in it, the same forbearance. It
spoke of knowing the world as it is, and men as they are,
of loving the Mother of All in all her many moods, and of
the love of men and women as a reflection of that kind of
patient, tolerant love.

Trystan's music was not as far-ranging as Kerewan's,
despite that he had an instrument of more elaborate
equipment; it did not span the entire spectrum of emotional potential, nor make any attempt so to do. The great
harp did not try to assail the same dizzy heights of delirium as Kerewan's lute, but by that very token was more
certain in its paces, more assured in its convictions, more
definite in its shape.

And when Trystan finished, the applause was much
louder.

Herla looked quickly around the room, wondering how
many of his subjects really had preferred Trystan's playing
to the elf's. There was not a human being in the room who
had desired to see Plennydd's bard outshone, and not one
who would ever admit to the opinion that Kerewan had
pleased him more; prejudice alone sufficed to explain the
storm of approval, and Herla knew it only too well. But he
felt a fierce desire to know what they really thought – all
the knights and their ladies, all the attendants and the

kitchen-maids. What was really in their hearts? Love of contentment, or lust for ecstasy?

Herla looked at Thoron and Kerewan, to see how they had reacted. He expected to see them calm, but perhaps a little resentful or crestfallen; he expected that they would have their own opinion as to who had played the better. He was surprised to see, however, that neither of them seemed in any way less enthusiastic than the other applauding guests. Indeed, Thoron's face was a picture of delight and captivation.

When the applause ended, Thoron remained standing. 'Your majesty!' he called, as Trystan made as if to rise. 'I beg you, do not let him go! This harping is a marvel, and the cheering says that there is no one here, elf or human, who does not want to hear more. For myself, I have no dearer wish than to hear your bard play the music of the storm as well as he has played the music of the calm. Can he do it?'

Herla looked at Trystan, trying to suppress a frown of anxiety. What Thoron said about the crowd being ready to hear more was certainly true, and what he had said about the music of the storm would appear to many to be a challenge which could not be refused – but Herla remembered what Trystan had said about his meeting with Bavian, and what anxiety it had caused him.

He has already played the music of tenderness, Herla realized. And now he is asked to play the music of the storm…

The harper caught the king's eye, and nodded, to say that he was aware of the other's disquiet, but that he was nevertheless prepared to go ahead. Herla nodded in his turn, and Trystan addressed the strings again, waiting for quiet to descend.

The sounds which flowed from the harp began slowly enough, capturing the rhythm of windblown waves and the scurrying of clouds, but they surged towards their crescendo with a rush, whipped into a fury that was all lashing rain and booming thunder.

The cascade of notes raced and raged, rolled and roiled in tempestuous confusion, filling the hall and promising to go on forever – but in fact, the piece was relatively brief, for Trystan had no other intention save to show what he could do, and what the great harp could do.

It was a demonstration rather than a performance – but it was no less wildly applauded for that, even by Thoron.

Only Kerewan, of all those in the hall, seemed disappointed – and if anyone but Herla noticed it, he must surely have drawn the conclusion that Kerewan was annoyed to be outshone. But Herla was sure that there must be another reason, and the thought came into his mind that Kerewan might have preferred to hear the musical image of a different kind of storm: perhaps the enigmatic 'blood-born storm' against which Bavian had warned the bard, or perhaps the colder storm born of the unassailable Chaos Wastes of the far north – the storm which was said to send the Storm Huntsmen galloping over Morien.

But still, thought Herla, as the tightness began to return to his body, here is a contest which men have won against the elves, at least in our own estimation. We needed one such, I think – I only pray that we may never need another.

It seemed a satisfactory end to a very trying day.

CHAPTER NINE

THAT NIGHT, TRYSTAN'S nightmares returned with a horrid ferocity. Again he fled through nightmarish darkness, pursued by shadowy horned daemons, while a blizzard raged about him and the wind sang to him in a fashion both eerie and mocking. Again he found release from this, and warmth and comfort, only to find himself beset by kindred daemons of another kind who sang a song of temptation and seduction – a song whose rhythms and cadences had nothing in common with the music of the storm, save that they too were ineffably strange and inexplicably derisive.

He awoke, when he was finally allowed to return to the world of man and time, in a virtual fever. That fever stayed with him while he washed and dressed, and its last vestiges still haunted him when the hour of Herla's wedding came.

The slow ceremony, full of pomp and formality, calmed him with its orderliness, and reunited him so fully with the world that he was able to put his own feelings aside and think instead of Herla, his sovereign and friend.

Trystan watched Herla very carefully during the early
part of the ceremony. The king's face was impassive; his
black hair and beard so dominated his features that all
expression was submerged and hidden. In spite of this,
Trystan thought that he understood very well the unease
which lay behind his friend's stern mask – the rigid knot
of frustration which was being pulled ever tighter by an
excess of dutiful conformity. Trystan knew that there were
many aspects of kingship which were not to Herla's taste,
and he knew what difficulties the young man faced in the
attempt to acquire new habits. Herla was strong and brave,
but neither strength nor courage was helping him to be
shaped and soothed by custom and tedious repetition into
a man fit for regal responsibility.

It was possible, Trystan knew, that marriage would help
in the forging of Herla the king, by making him a husband
and a father. Even the older knights, who thought Herla
still lacking in judgement and experience, held to the opinion that he might soon be tempered and finished by this
means. Trystan was not so sure, and feared that if Herla
should fail to make the most of his marriage, he might also
fail to make the best of his kingship.

He knew, because Herla had told him, how anxious the
king was about the the possibility that love might not grow
between himself and his wife – and Trystan feared that the
anxiety might itself become a barrier to such growth.

When the bride finally appeared to take her place by
Herla's side, Trystan was glad to transfer his attention to
her, for his contemplation of Herla's empty face had
become too uncomfortable to bear.

Princess Morgana of Alawn, youngest daughter of King
Coll and Queen Rhuannon, was a lovely woman. She had
eyes of blue and hair of gold, and delicate features. She
was perhaps a little too slim for the demands of conven-
tion, which asked that all wives – most especially royal
ones – should display hips of an appropriate dimension
for comfortable child-birth, but it was not a huge fault.
Trystan had seen her before, in the course of making

arrangements for the wedding, but had not seen her as she was now, brought to the peak of perfection by the art of her clothiers.

The mere sight of Morgana as she now was should have been enough to melt the heart of any virile young man – but Herla hardly turned to glance at her. Trystan, by contrast, could not take his eyes off her. Even when the ceremony had ended, he continued to watch her until custom swept the wedded pair away – and when that had happened, she remained in his thoughts. He could not get the image of her out of his mind.

As soon as he became aware that his preoccupation was becoming problematic Trystan tried to turn it into something else. He told himself firmly that his real concern was for his friend, and that his speculations about Herla's relationship with Morgana were merely a continuation of his earlier anxiety. Thus licensed, he allowed himself to pretend that it was Herla for whom he was concerned, and Herla alone in whom he was interested.

But that night, though no nightmares came, sleep did not come either, for his thoughts were entrapped by the idea of another bed, which would not be banished from his imagination.

Herla, he knew, was practiced to some degree in the craftsmanship of sexual intercourse, but Trystan also knew that both the king and the servant-women involved had been inclined to regard that experience as what it was – a matter of necessary education, in which authentic feelings were definitely not involved. Such play had, by logical necessity, stopped short of what Herla must do in making love to Morgana, which was to begin the work of turning a matter of duty into a steadfast loyalty of affection. Trystan found himself becoming gradually obsessed with the question of whether Herla could contrive that change in himself – and concealed from himself the fact that his true and underlying obsession was the fate and figure of Morgana, Queen of Plennydd.

In the days which followed, Trystan was careful to take every opportunity of lending assistance and moral support to his friend. He sang Herla's praises to the queen, and tried in every way he could to make her early days in Caer Plennydd pleasant. Herla was grateful for his efforts – and so was she. In fact, Trystan found that he enjoyed greater success in making her feel at home than he did in maintaining the good spirits of his friend. Herla found difficulty in amusing the queen, while Trystan found none at all; Herla's conversations with Morgana were underlain by an embarrassment which did not diminish with time, while Trystan's talk became effortlessly friendlier.

Because it was so utterly unthinkable, Trystan did not allow himself to consider the possibility that he might be falling in love with Morgana, let alone the corollary possibility that she might be falling in love with him. And because he maintained his own innocence, he was initially successful in maintaining Herla's; at first, Herla was delighted that the bard made such efforts to make his new wife welcome, and was equally delighted that the efforts were successful.

In time, though, the doubts began to creep in. A seed of confusion was sown by some trivial incident which made the bard and queen laugh together while Herla felt himself excluded. Then, for the first time, Herla saw the burgeoning friendship in a new light, which served only to amplify his own anxieties and embarrassments.

To make things worse, Trystan did not even notice when his friend began to cool towards him, and began to withdraw from their former intimacy. Trystan no longer needed the king for a confidant, now that his emotional needs were covertly nourished by the polite attentions of the queen.

It was as if an invisible worm had begun to gnaw at the very heart and soul of the kingdom of Plennydd.

TRYSTAN WAS SO satisfied with life, and his days were now so full, that he hardly noticed the trickle of unfortunate events which spoiled the lazy days of late summer for so many of the people of Plennydd. What should have been the best time of the year, with the harvest gathered in and the weather still warm, became in fact the most troubled of the year. Though the events in question were not confined to Caer Plennydd, Herla's castle was at the centre of them, as if they were in some strange fashion rooted there.

The chain began on the wedding-day itself, when there was an unsolved theft. Closely-guarded though they were, several of Herla's wedding-gifts disappeared from the display in the late hours of Lugnasad. Chief among them were a jewelled dagger presented by Prince Lin on behalf of his father, an ornate ring of locally-mined gold given by Emyr Siun, and the crystal cup given by the elves. The theft made little sense, given that none of these items could be traded in Morien without being instantly recognized, and this inexplicability made it difficult to investigate.

When sixteen days had passed without any of the objects being seen by anyone who was prepared to declare the fact, it seemed that the loss might be total. Herla was ready by that time to conclude that they had been smuggled away to Albion – but then the dagger turned up again, thrust into the back of one of Owain Dene's bondsmen.

The addition of murder to robbery compounded the offence, but did not help in the least to clear up the mystery, for it proved impossible to discover who might have killed the man or why. There was no evidence at all to implicate the dead man in the theft, and although the involvement of the House of Dene in the affair cast a certain shadow over the reputation of the family it seemed to King Herla and to everyone else that the shadow was no more than an unkind stroke of misfortune which might equally have fallen upon anyone.

Some twelve days later another dead man was found – this time a franklin whose small estate bordered the lands held by the Aglavins. He too had been stabbed in the back, though the deed had been done with a very ordinary weapon – and it might therefore have been considered an entirely separate incident, had it not been for the fact that the man's ring finger had been neatly severed at the root. There was, of course, no sign of any ring – and the man's labourers claimed that he had never worn one – but anyone with a sense of melodrama could easily be drawn to speculate that he might at the time of his death have been wearing the second of the three stolen artefacts.

In parallel with these distressing events there occurred an unusual confusion of curious triumphs and strange misfortunes. In the course of a great hunt fourteen days after Lugnasad – when King Herla carried and tried out the bow which Thoron had given him – two beaters were killed by a stag which turned on them and attacked with unprecedented fury; but Herla later killed the stag with a near-miraculous shot from the bow.

It later transpired that the stag must have been maddened by disease, for its flesh proved inedible and the herds about Caer Plennydd began to sicken; many of the yearlings died. Signs of the same sickness eventually began to appear in the neighbouring lands of the Siuns and the Gyreths.

Though Herla continued to hunt – and, indeed, became progressively fonder of the chase, as if possessed by an urge to get out of the castle and into the fresh air as often as possible – many of his followers became disheartened by the quality of the sport. It seemed to many that no one save the king could contrive to bring a chase to a successful end. The inevitable frustrations created by the series of poor runs spilled over by degrees into the daily life of the court, giving birth to frequent petty quarrels.

A quarrel of a much more serious nature blew up between the Aglavins and the Carlens, expressed in a dispute over various land rights which came back to Herla for judgement on no less than four separate occasions. On each occasion Herla reached a decision which, though not satisfactory to both contending parties, seemed fair enough to those uninvolved – but afterwards, some new document would be unearthed from the vaults of Caer

Plennydd by some over-assiduous scribe which would put the matter in a new light and give new hope to the losing side.

The whole court became heartily sick of the affair, but everyone was appalled when it came swiftly and unexpectedly to a gruesome climax. Beredir's younger son, Ivyr, fought a sword-duel with Ralf Carlen and struck him dead. Brought before Herla accused as a Codebreaker, Ivyr offered a spirited if not entirely coherent defence, which charged Ralf with attempting to rape his sister Aithe. Aithe, on being examined, gave evidence which agreed in substance with her brother's but differed in many points of significant detail – points which convinced many, including their noble father and elder brother, that they were lying.

Sir Beredir was quick to obey Herla's instruction that the Aglavins must pay compensation to the House of Carlen, but the Carlens were by no means satisfied. They remained so besotted with distress that it was obvious to all that there would have been further duels fought, save only for the fact that Berwyn and Ivyr were such fearsome fighters that the Carlens had none to match them.

None could find fault with Herla's judgements in these matters, but the fact remained that the king's justice seemed incapable of laying the affair to rest, and this inevitably reflected badly on Herla. But the picture was not entirely gloomy, for it did seem that one of Herla's decisions, doubted at first, now deserved to be hailed as a very wise one; this was his decision to let the shipwrecked sea-elves bide for a while within his borders.

Trystan's ploy of inviting Thoron to the wedding-feast seemed conclusively vindicated by the fact that even Godwin of Conwy soon began to speak of his new neighbours as though they were the best of all his friends. Far from expressing the doleful fear that they might never go away, he began to say with some regret that he would be sorry to lose them, and that his acquisition of the great stone house they were building would not fully compensate for the pain of never seeing them again. Though Lord Macalla, acting in King Coll's name, continued to forward messages from his spies reporting on the progress of the elven workings, together with letters indicating Coll's strong disapproval, it seemed that there was not a knight in Plennydd who held any longer to the opinion that the elves ought to be exterminated.

As if to symbolize this blossoming congeniality, the seed which had been the third of Thoron's gifts did indeed germinate in the soil of the small garden where Herla had directed that it be planted. Within days of its planting, and with the aid of careful watering, it had given rise to a healthy shoot which was a vivid green in colour, which burst into leaf thirteen days after Lugnasad. It seemed that the plant was in a hurry to catch up with the crops which had been sown in the spring and already taken up, determined to put on as much growth as possible before the autumnal equinox – when the nights would begin to draw in and the chilly winds would begin to blow.

By the time the equinox did come the tree was as tall as a man – though not quite as tall as an elf – and it had put forth blossom. The flowers were dark red speckled with brown, their petals entwining oddly to form a most curious shape like tightly-clasped hands which completely surrounded and hid the sexual organs.

The garden lay within the castle walls, but it was by no means secluded, and many of those who came back and forth through the gates of Caer Plennydd took the trouble to pass by it, in order to see this marvel for themselves. All were agreed that it was a very strange and beautiful plant, and wondered what fruit it might bear, if it could bear any at all after being planted so late in the year.

AS THE EQUINOX approached, Trystan was compelled to take himself off again, to join the druids at their ceremonies in the high mountains. He took with him a sorely troubled heart.

For a while, even when he had begun his journey, Trystan still laboured under the delusion that he was troubled on Herla's behalf, and that his deep regret was for Herla's worsening sorrow. But once he was alone, and Caer Plennydd was out of sight, a different understanding of his predicament began to dawn on him. Without the business of the court and the presence of Morgana to fill his mind and prevent him from a proper examination of his own feelings and motives, he could no longer keep the truth at bay.

As soon as she was out of reach, Trystan realized how dependent upon Morgana's company he had become – and how dependent on him Morgana had become in her turn. When that realization finally dawned, he saw clearly enough that he had made a fool of himself – and worse than a fool, a betrayer.

He tried for a little while to persuade himself that the love which he felt for the queen was brotherly, and that the affection she held for him was likewise innocent; but once the wall of self-delusion was breached it could not be shored up again. It was not until he was away from the castle, alone with the hills, that he discovered how deep and intense his love really was. Absence did not make his heart grow fonder, but the pain of absence made him fully aware of the force of his fondness.

That pain was added to the bitterness with which his liberated conscience accused him. He saw, at last, that while he had put on a show of aiding Herla he had been guilty of a serious treason. The king was not the only man who had a duty; the Bard of the Realm was no less firmly bound by the responsibilities of his office. Trystan saw now that while Herla had struggled manfully to come to terms with his duty, his bard had carelessly neglected his own, taking leave all the while to pity the unfortunate king! This dishonour was further compounded by his betrayal of the motto of his order – for he had signally failed to sieve the truth from the dishonest confusion of the world.

Pain and bitterness soon turned to misery when Trystan progressed from examining what had already happened to questioning himself about what he might – and must – do when he returned to Caer Plennydd.

On the first night of his journey – when he slept beneath the stars rather than display his anguish to any ringholder, franklin or peasant who might have given him shelter – he suffered a nightmare more terrible than any he had experienced since the eve of the wedding, and perhaps more terrible than any he had ever experienced in the haunted days of his childhood.

In the opening phases of this dream, as in many others, he believed himself hunted by dark riders who wore the antlers of stags mounted on their helmets. He fled from them through a stormy night. In this dream he could fly, but flying was no benefit to him, for those who hunted him were mounted on beasts which could take to the air themselves: on pegasi, or scaly things like ugly misshapen dragons, or monstrous eagles. The horned hunters themselves were but shadows, but they had some vestiges of identity nevertheless, and he struggled to recognize them; but he could not tell who they were – only that they were very, very old.

At the end of the hunt he found himself falling, first through the air and then through a curious whirlpool in the substance of the earth, which swirled about him like the circles on the badge which tied him to the Old Faith, to the Mother of All.

Beyond that unearthly vortex, as he knew already, was the realm of other daemons: daemons of lewdness and daemons of lust; daemons of desire and daemons of jealousy.

Because he feared to fall into the clutches of these daemons he struggled against the whirlpool, but felt that his soul was being torn apart by the circles which extended like ripples from the core of his being, and he finally consented to be drawn from the earth into the vault of heaven where mortality was set aside and there was an interface between the world of the gods and the world of the Mother's multitudinous children.

Once in this realm he had no choice but to heed the seductions of the daemons – which were not, for the most part, whispers to be heard or beautiful apparitions to be seen, but textures which touched him and moved through his quivering flesh, and tastes which dissolved upon his tongue to fill his being with exotic, ecstatic sensation.

He could see, though sight was not the most important of his senses to be engaged in this riot of temptation. He saw eyes and smiles, curved breasts and contoured haunches, jewelled bracelets and translucent shifts; he saw the delicate fingers which caressed him, and the engorged lips which brushed against his forehead, and the soft golden hair which fell in cascades about the faces and bodies of the succubi.

All the succubi wore the appearance of Morgana – as though every glimpse of her he had ever stored in his memory had become a separate instrument of temptation, a daemon in itself.

Nor was his hearing unengaged, though that sense too had lost its usual position in the hierarchy of immediacy. What he heard were not words, but music – as befitted the kind of man he was – but it was as though the music were very distant and unconnected with his own being. Though it echoed in his soul he did not feel that there was any sense at all in which he was composing it, or remembering it, or even understanding it.

It was wild music – wilder by far than any which harp or lute could produce; so wild that only daemons could ever hope to dance to it. Whatever quality was in it was alien to the human soul, and he felt that if he should find a way to take it into the rhythms and sinews of his being... if ever he should find strings in his own fibres to play such paradoxical threnodies... then he would be changed in form and nature, to become something other than what he was and desired to be. He hated that music with all his might; it made him nauseous... and yet it was, in its own fashion, a kind of temptation. It had in it some kind of promise, though he could not tell what it was that he was being promised, or why he should ever want it.

When he had resisted the daemons long enough they abandoned him yet again before the throne of their god, who was the same that he had seen on the night when he slept with the elves.

'Be true to yourself,' said that horned and two-sexed god. 'Only be true to yourself, because you are all that you are, and if you forsake yourself out of loyalty to some other, or some ideal, you betray and hurt yourself, and pervert your soul. You are lost, my little one, and fiercely determined to be unfound – but if you cannot find yourself, you will have naught in life but darkness, and naught in all eternity but regret. Satisfy your heart, dear harper, for the heart cannot lie, and only when the heart is satisfied can the true music of the soul be played and the true harmonies of existence enjoyed. Be true to the commands of your own fair flesh, lovely boy, and know the relief of knowing that you are truly mine, and that I am the only truth – for only I am you and only I can help you to be yourself.'

Not until this had been said did Trystan finally succeed in breaking away, and in returning to the solid world – though the solid world presented itself to him, in that moment of awakening, as darkness so cold and earth so hard that he was forced to recognize life for the sharp and uncomfortable thing that it was.

And the love for Morgana which obsessed and consumed his heart was a dreadful pain coursing through his being, killing and cleansing at one and the same time.

CHAPTER TEN

TRYSTAN'S ABSENCE FROM Caer Plennydd allowed Herla pause for reflection too, and he saw a new opportunity to become more fully united with his wife.

On the day of the bard's departure, there seemed reason enough to be optimistic; Morgana was more inclined to take pleasure in his company on that day than she had ever been before. But when night fell, her spirits fell too, and Herla saw that she had valued his company only as a temporary and ultimately futile distraction from her disappointment. Then he too became bitter, and asked himself why he should play the comforter when his lawful wife was sad for the lack of another's voice and another's presence. Instead of persisting in his attempt to draw Morgana closer to him he became deliberately cold, and thus accentuated her sense of loss.

The next day, Herla went hunting on the forested slopes to the north of Caer Plennydd. The thrill of the chase filled him up as no other activity could, driving everything out of his mind but the excitement of the moment. His new

bow was such a lucky weapon that he hardly ever returned
empty-handed.

The party with whom he rode out was not large, including only three knights – Meilir Larne, Huw Peredur and
Hywel Heilyn – and two squires, but it was an enthusiastic
group. Late in the morning the riders found a stag at the
peak of its power, which showed no trace of the sickness
which had come into the herds, and they pursued it fer-
vently for many a mile.

All the knights had fine coursers, Herla being mounted
on his favourite black stallion, and they stayed close
together for more than an hour, racing through the undergrowth, ducking beneath low branches and hurdling fallen
trees. It was not a race, but it felt like a race, and every
clever turn or bold leap which moved one rider ahead of
his fellows brought exhilaration to the one and dismay to
the three.

In any ordinary matter, bound by Code and custom,
politeness required that every man must defer to the king,
but in the hunt it was different; it was as though the hunt
took place in a world which was slightly apart from the
kingdom, where there were no kings or knights or commoners, but only hunters and their prey. Here, if nowhere
else, it was acceptable for men to outdo their lawful liege-
lord – and because it was the one arena where such
endeavour was permitted, it was one where effort to do so
was never lacking.

In ordinary times the outcome of a chase was determined by tricks of fate which favoured no man: the jinking
of the stag in its flight, the unfortunate footfall of a horse.
But the times had not been ordinary since Lugnasad Day,
when Herla's hunting had seemingly fallen under the spell
of a lucky star; his black stallion never stumbled, and even
though a stag might run directly at another man it was
always Herla's arrow which brought him down.

Herla never questioned the source or nature of this good
fortune; he was content to enjoy it – and enjoy it he did
with a fervour of exhilaration finer than any feeling he had

ever known in his life before. While he galloped through the green-clad glades he could forget that he was a king at all, let alone a king with a diffident wife and a doubtful friend. In a way, he forgot even that he was a man, and became simply a seamless web of sinew and sensation, all strength and boldness, ambition and rapture. It was a feeling full of luxury, which seemed to him the finest experience which life had to offer, all the more so because it was unalloyed with any matters of duty and expectation.

The chase eventually fell into the familiar pattern which had been established of late. The two squires had poorer horses than their betters, and nothing like the skill in riding; they were left far behind. Then, Hywel Heilyn's horse landed badly after a jump and he was forced to dismount, leaving three to pursue the stag to its final stand. Huw Peredur's horse had begun to tire, and though it kept to its work as best it could he fell gradually behind, so that only two were left with a chance to be in at the kill.

As the stag reached the limit of his endurance Sir Meilir was on the right and King Herla on the left. Sir Meilir, having suffered more than one dire disappointment in recent days, rode as though he were possessed, and when the stag made a sharp turn to his side, he let out a loud cry of triumph. Though Herla's black stallion came swiftly about, the stag's turn gave Meilir an advantage of forty or fifty yards, and it was clear that the hunted beast could run no further. The moment when the knight could rein in and notch an arrow to his bow could not be more than three or four minutes delayed.

And so it proved: the stag was forced to pause and turn about in the centre of a grove of oaks, presenting a clear shot to its pursuer. But even while the head of the House of Larne drew back his bow to take careful aim another arrow sailed past him, coming as if from nowhere to take the stag behind the neck, and bring it instantly to its knees.

Meilir, who must have felt as certain of the kill as he was of the fact that he deserved a change in his luck, could not help but howl with anguish. Nor could he forbear to shout

that he had been cheated, although he must have known
that only his king could have shot the stag from the greater
distance. That was an unfortunate insult; the hunt was over
now, and men had resumed their proper stations.

Herla, when he heard these protests, knew that Meilir
could not actually have seen him shoot; but he knew that
the knight must have known who had fired the shot, and
when he reached the fallen animal he was sorely annoyed.

'Sir Meilir,' he called out intemperately, as their two
mounts converged, 'the Code bids you to be courteous
even to those you do not love – and courtesy implies that
you should not call another man a cheat because his shot
overtakes your own.'

Sir Meilir seemed quite amazed by this rebuke, and
Herla knew that the man must be telling himself in self-
justification that he had not seen the king, and could not
rationally be held guilty of any insult – and that this was a
hunt, after all, where all men were entitled to do their best,
and none had precedence of rank when it came to the
shooting.

'Would that the Code instructed young men to respect
their elders, whatever their ranks,' Meilir muttered, as he
dismounted – just loud enough for Herla to hear.

Herla might have allowed the remark to pass, save for
the fact that he suspected Meilir of taking a leading part in
the talk which questioned his suitability to sit upon the
throne, and he replied in kind with a more churlish murmur to the effect that it was a great pity that Meilir had not
taught such discipline to his own son.

Meilir, inevitably sensitive about the shame brought
upon his house by the banished Hallam, could not help
but react angrily to this low-toned slur, and opine in his
turn – again, as though he spoke only to himself – that it
was a great pity when men could not trust their own wives
not to flutter their eyes at innocent boys.

Precisely what Meilir meant by this, Herla could not be
sure, and he certainly did not dare react to it as if it were
an aspersion cast upon the queen, when Meilir might only

have intended to refer to the wife of Berwyn Aglavin. Nevertheless, the implication hurt him very deeply, and when the two men finally came together to stand over the corpse of the stag there was no politeness at all in their bearing.

Herla stared at his noble subject with open hostility, while he took out his knife to cut the antlers.

'A fine shot, sire,' said Meilir, loudly enough to be clearly heard, and in a voice quite devoid of any enthusiasm.

Huw Peredur had by now ridden up to join them, and he echoed the sentiment much more honestly – and then looked curiously at his two companions, clearly unable to understand what had happened between them.

'In fact,' added Meilir, 'I am beginning to think that your new bow is enchanted, for it is the only weapon in the realm which can hit anything during these wretched days when the herds sicken.'

'At least,' said Herla, still staring bleakly at the older man, 'this was a healthy animal, and a worthy quarry.'

'I fear not, sire,' murmured Sir Huw.

Herla looked down to see what he meant, and he was amazed to see that the stag's hide – which had been flawless while it ran – was now covered in sore patches like huge ulcers.

'Mother of All!' exclaimed the king, as surprise drove away his anger, 'I never saw such a thing before.'

'Enchanted,' said Meilir Larne, letting his voice fall again to a mere murmur, 'or accursed.'

And Herla, looking down at the knife in his hand, was suddenly reminded of another hunt, when he had killed a very similar stag, and had refused to give the antlers to one who asked for them. Who had that man been? he wondered. Who could have been the master to whom he referred, who did not like men who clung too tightly to the letter of the law, and loved to test their mettle?

Well, he said to himself, I am tested now; there is no doubt of it. Sinister elves make camp on my shore, my wife likes the bard of the realm far better than its king, and

Meilir Larne is but one of those whose doubts are being turned to active dislike. Even the hunt which was ever the last of my refuges, has now begun to turn sour.

He put his knife away, and turned back to his horse, convinced that fate had set its hand against him.

ON THAT SAME afternoon – perhaps at the very same moment – Trystan Harper walked into another grove of oaks, with his eyes lowered and his thoughts far away. He did not see until Bavian called to him that he had once again stepped outside the proper course of time; until he looked up he had not noticed that the oaks, despite that Samain was not far away, had green acorns still young upon the bough.

'Did I not warn thee, blood of my blood?' said Bavian sorrowfully, coming into being with the words he spoke. 'Did I not tell thee to beware the blood-born storm, and the music of tenderness?'

It was not until the magician spoke those words that the prophecy returned to Trystan's mind, so that he could see its meaning at last.

How stupid I must have been, thought the bard, not to know before that he spoke of love. Why did I not see the implication of his words, and take better care to guard my feelings?

Miserably, he confronted the bearded man who might be his ancestor, and shook his head in despair, saying: 'Why did you hide your advice in a riddle? If only you had made yourself plain, I would have been far better equipped to follow your advice.'

The magician did not answer immediately, and Trystan heard the wind toying with the rejuvenated boughs, as though delighted to discover them out of season.

'Would you have me tell you in simple terms what to do?' asked the ancient, with a plaintive sigh.

Trystan could not help but wonder whether this man was anything more than another tormenting daemon sent to hurt and harry him. 'Why not?' he asked. 'It would save you the disappointment and displeasure which I hear in your tone.'

'Do not waste time in grieving,' said Bavian tiredly. 'What is done is done, and destiny is not so easily moulded. Alas, I cannot foretell in any simple way how the course of history is to be hewn from the cruel profusion of possibility, for the way in which that hewing is done is not simple. No man can speak plainly of the Mother of All when she is not plain in feature or scheme. The world is a fevered and troubled place, Trystan Harper, and no matter how men try to suppress its richness with codes and faiths and dogged demands, circumstance will not long yield to them.

'The blight has come as I foresaw – unopposed as yet by the hearts and minds of the men of Plennydd. There are those in the realm who have drunk from the cup of avarice; there are those who have seen their king hunt with the bow of envy; there are those who wait hungrily for the tree of confusion to bear fruit.'

It took Trystan a moment or two to fathom the implications in this pronouncement, but he saw the meaning soon enough. 'You speak of the gifts of the elves,' he said sourly. 'But you told me when last we met, as plainly as you told me anything, that the elves are not our true enemies.'

'They are not,' answered Bavian, with a groan of impatience. 'The elves could not harm you at all, were you not so very eager to harm yourselves. Those who are without avarice may drink of the cup with impunity; those who are without envy are not stirred by the power of the bow; those who do not yearn gluttonously for the satiation of desire will not overburden the fruit of the tree with sweetness. Had you fallen upon the elves and slain them all you would be worse than you are, for they who choose the way of slaughter forsake Slaanesh only to run to the savage arms of Khorne, just as those who choose the way of treachery become the champions of Tzeentch, the Changer of the Ways. The ways of Chaos are many, and the way of Order itself may only be another of those ways, and perhaps not the best. If there is an answer, it lies in Agam's Code – but it is hidden there, as all answers are hidden in this vexing world of ours, and it is ever the fate of men to be too stupid to discover what they already know, until it is too late.'

Trystan had been utterly overawed by this mysterious person on the occasion of their first meeting, and perhaps would have stood in terrified awe of him now had his heart not been stretched by his unfortunate love, but he found himself looking at Bavian with a strangely jaundiced eye.

'Thou art a cheerless fellow, art thou not?' he said, lapsing momentarily into formal speech as the other seemed wont to do. 'Hast thou nothing to bring to the druids and bards of Plennydd but doleful lamentations and promises of injury? If not, perhaps 'twould be best to stay in thine appointed place, and cease to trouble thy unfortunate and thankless child.'

For a moment, Bavian looked at him thunderously, but then the broad man's eyes grew softer, and the tangled beard quivered with what might have been a suppressed laugh.

'That is good, Trystan Harper,' said the wizard. 'That is very good. Confront the worst and do not yield. Look into the abyss of darkness without dizziness, and into the eye of the monster without fear. You too will be tested, as Herla will be tested, and your test may in the end be the harder. But remember this, my son, I beg of you: whenever nightmares come to claim thee, dreams may also come; whenever the music of Chaos enters into your soul, the Mother's lullaby may enter too; whenever the Storm Huntsmen of Slaanesh ride on the wind of doom, hope may also soar to heights unknown.'

When the sentence ended, Trystan was not surprised to find that the waking dream had ended too. Bavian was gone and the brown acorns had already begun to fall to the earth, where they would rot into the soil, or be carried away and hoarded by the busy squirrels.

'Nightmare and vision,' said Trystan softly. 'Temptation and warning. Dusk and dawn. To every thing there is a season, and though there is no straight and narrow path of Order, there is a balance to be found. I think I begin to see, my lord, what you mean to say to me – but thou'rt a cheerless fellow ne'ertheless, and thy riddles will take a deal of fathoming… and at the end, what will I be but a poor fool in love with his liege-lord's lady, and a harper with a broken heart? What dost thou expect of me, father of my kind? What can the likes of Trystan Harper accomplish, when even mighty Bavian can do no more than weep and wail and play with mysteries?'

He did not think that Bavian could hear him any longer, but he said it all aloud, as carefully as he could. And then he rode on towards the Great Circle, and whatever destiny was mapped out for him in the Book of Fate.

CHAPTER ELEVEN

TRYSTAN RETURNED TO Caer Plennydd with his heart full of uncomfortable contradictions. The thought of seeing Morgana again was both thrilling and threatening. Aware as he now was of the degree of his infatuation he could foresee nothing but turbulence and torment in the prospect of future meetings with her. He did not know how he could face Herla, and continue to face him in the day-to-day routines of their existence. Nevertheless, Herla had to be faced, and Morgana too, and he knew that if he could conceal his feelings from both of them he must do it.

In addition to these personal troubles he had other news to bring to the castle from the stone circle – warnings given by the druids to supplement and amplify those given to him in veiled form by Bavian.

When first he came face to face with the king he felt that his guilt must be written clearly in his features, so that Herla would instantly see and understand it – but Herla gave no overt sign that he could see any such thing, and it was written clearly enough upon the king's furrowed brow that he had troubles of his own to preoccupy him. Little time was wasted in the greetings appropriate to their reunion, and Trystan was grateful that there was a certain stiffness in the king's manner.

'Dissent and mistrust are spreading like an infection through the land,' said Herla grimly. 'In the highest ranks of the court there is a constant tension, expressed in scores of petty quarrels. And somehow, I am blamed for it. Because I am the king, it seems, the malaise in my realm is my responsibility; it is up to me to quell it.

'You know how little I like sitting in judgement at the sessions, but I had always thought my decisions just. Now the number of petitions to be heard is increasing so rapidly that I must soon appoint other judges to deal with the lesser of them, and every judgement which I hand down becomes a focus of grievance. In the past, those who lost their cases received no sympathy from others, but now it is different – every resentment feeds the general opinion that Herla's justice is no justice at all. You are the Bard of the Realm, and these difficulties are yours as well as mine; advise me, I beg you, as to how I am to save my authority from crumbling away.'

'Winter is coming,' said Trystan, swallowing a lump in his throat as he tried to put on the mantle of friendship and wisdom which was required of him. 'Winter brings hardship, and hardship makes a common cause between men. After Samain, it will not be so bad, and by the time Imbolc comes there will be snow on the grounds and the ringholds will be closed. Rumours die in snowdrifts like homeless men.'

Herla was eager to accept the reassurance – perhaps a little too eager. 'No doubt you are right,' he said. 'But this is still the first year of my reign, and I had hoped that my people would love me for a while longer. I am not a bad king, Trystan – I hold to the Code as unswervingly as any. What is wrong with my knights, who were so loyal to my father?'

'I have seen Bavian again,' Trystan told him, evading the question. 'Though he repeated his claim that the elves are not our true enemy, he took care to imply that the gifts which Thoron gave to you are in some way tainted. The cup is already gone, but I think you might do well to put the bow away and never use it; should the strange tree in your garden bear fruit, no one should be permitted to eat it.'

'The elves again!' said Herla bitterly. 'And yet, as my star fades, theirs is in the ascendant. I never hear a bad word spoken of them – and Godwin Conwy, who was once their most resentful critic, has become their most fervent champion. Are they evil magicians all, do you think? Have they used insidious means to split me from my people while repairing their own reputation? Is it their intention not merely to make a home in Plennydd, but to rule the kingdom?'

'I cannot tell,' answered Trystan. 'But I heard two rumours from the druids at the equinoctial rites which may put the situation in a worse light still. There were holy men there who had travelled as far as l'Anguille where the ships of the elves often make port; they had heard a story there that a company of elves had been outcast by their clan and set to drift in a small craft, as a punishment for turning to a kind of worship forbidden among that folk. One man repeated to me a phrase which he had heard used – "the sin of the *druchii*" – but he was not certain of its exact meaning; he was only sure that the *druchii* are elves regarded with horror by their own kin: the dark elves of legend.'

'So they were not shipwrecked after all,' said Herla bitterly. 'If they were cast out by their own kind, they certainly do not intend to use that ship which they are building to rejoin their clan. Perhaps they do plan to make their own safe harbour in my land. But what was the other rumour which you heard?'

'It was said that evil and forbidden worship has come to Plennydd too,' said Trystan, licking his dry lips uneasily. 'The druids of Morien say that men are turning away from the true faith, tempted by some dark cult whose worshippers hold luxury to be the only good and the only ambition. My lord, I believe that they are right – for my own dreams have been invaded by such temptations, and had it not been for my education as a bard, which allowed me to know them for what they were, I might myself have taken them for truer visions. Have you had such dreams yourself, sire?'

Herla looked at him curiously. 'It is not like you to address me so formally,' he observed. 'But no – my dreams have been little troubled since you went away. Before that…' He paused in order to force a small laugh, and said: 'Do you think that men still dream when they cannot remember what they have dreamed? If that were so, perhaps I have been tempted after all, but have put the temptation so completely from my mind that I do not know it.'

Trystan could not match the laugh, for he suspected that Herla might speak more truly than he knew.

'What can we do?' asked Herla softly, when the silence became unbearable. 'What can we do to halt this blight?'

'The druids will make their own magic,' Trystan told him. 'I do not know how, for those things are held secret even from members of the order, but they will add their prayers to the weight of the Mother's love for her children. As for ourselves, we must issue a summons to all the noblemen of Plennydd to attend the Samain celebrations, and there we must try to heal the rifts in our community. When I play the great harp on Samain Day I must use my magic, such as it is, to apply the balm of music to all the wounds which have opened since Lugnasad – and we must use ordinary means, too, to speak of friendship and loyalty, to make all those who have nearly succeeded in forgetting Agam's Code to remember its authority. There must be story-telling, and perhaps a play. A play, I think might be a good idea – let us see Agam himself parading upon the stage, putting down his enemies and giving succour to the weak. And let us not…'

The sentence which he had begun would have ended with the words 'invite the elves' – and he would have added more, too, had he not been interrupted. But he was forced to stop, because Herla's steward had hurried into the room, fervent with anxiety.

'Your majesty,' he said, 'there is an elf at the gate, begging the favour of an immediate audience.'

'Thoron!' exclaimed Herla – but the man shook his head.

'Not Thoron,' said the steward. 'It is the one called Kerewan.'

'The wizard?' said Herla, as though he might rather have faced the captain himself.

'He is not attired as a wizard,' answered the servant. 'He is dressed colourfully, but as a herald.'

'As I was when I went to their encampment,' said Trystan, in a low tone. 'He is playing the bard – as I suppose he is entitled to do, for it does seem that these elves can turn their hands to many tasks.'

'Bring him to me,' said Herla dully. 'His audience is granted.'

Within minutes, Kerewan appeared. He was, indeed, attired in what seemed a kind of parody of the tunic which Trystan had worn when first he went to study the elves. It was quartered and brightly coloured, though what the colours meant Trystan could not begin to guess. He noticed, however, that the elf's cloak was the same one that he had worn before, grey and decorated with the down-ward pointing arrowhead picked out in silver thread.

Herla said nothing to indicate that the elf was welcome or unwelcome, or whether it was pleasing or annoying to see him – he simply waited for the visitor to speak.

'I bring you greetings from your grateful guests the elves, your majesty,' said the elf, in a very polite fashion, 'and from their captain, Thoron. I bring you an invitation, to attend the house which we have built on your shore.'

'An invitation?' said Herla, in some surprise. 'With what purpose?'

If Kerewan was aware of the impoliteness of the question, and the suspicion which it implied, he gave no sign.

'Two purposes, your majesty,' he replied smoothly. 'Firstly, that you should see what kind of dwelling we have erected, and understand that it poses no threat to you or to any of your landholders. We know that your people have been uneasy in their minds, and we are determined to allay their fears and demonstrate our friendship.'

'And secondly?' asked the king.

'Secondly,' said Kerewan, with a smile, 'to return the great honour and compliment which you were kind enough to extend to us; we invite you to attend the wedding-feast of Shipmaster Thoron.'

The elf must have anticipated the astonishment this announcement would cause, for he rocked back on his heels after declaring it, his smile turning into a broad grin.

'Wedding-feast!' exclaimed Herla, doomed to play the echo because he was all too obviously at a loss for words.

'May I assume,' said Kerewan, in a leisurely fashion which ill-disguised his haste, 'that the invitation is accepted?'

Trystan felt an awkward feeling inside himself such as he had never felt before, as though every fibre of his being had been seized by the conviction that Herla must not accept this invitation – and yet, how could it possibly be refused? What reason could Herla give, not merely to Kerewan, but also to his own court? If resentments were building up against him, and the elves had become popular, it could only be the height of folly to issue such an insult.

'When is this wedding-feast to take place?' asked Herla gruffly.

'The feast will be seven days before the festival which you call Samain,' said the elf smoothly, 'and the wedding itself the following day. We had anticipated that you would like sufficient time to return to Caer Plennydd for Samain, but we feared that if we left the occasion until afterwards, inclement weather might make travel difficult. Our house is finished and the match is made – we are eager to repay the generous hospitality which you have afforded to us, and to express our gratitude for the way we have been received in your realm. There will be no competitions, I fear, but I think you will find it interesting. You may, of course, bring as many of your knights as you wish – and servants to attend to them.'

While he had been speaking, Herla had had time to think and make his decision – but Trystan understood only too well that this was a situation which permitted only one decision, no matter how wrong and perilous that decision might be.

'I will come,' said King Herla. 'I will bring with me as many men as Thoron brought to my wedding – that is a fitting number, and I would not like to burden your company with a retinue of body-servants and men-at-arms. Expect us on the eve of the wedding. Now, do you require accommodation here while you rest before your homeward journey? If so, I will ask the steward to find a room for you.'

'That is most kind,' answered Kerewan. 'We elves are only mortal, after all, and time to rest would be most welcome, before I convey the gladness of your acceptance to my master.'

Herla ordered that the steward should arrange matters, and Kerewan left the council chamber with the servant.

Herla turned immediately to Trystan. 'So much,' he said, 'for all our plans for Samain; we are pre-empted, it seems. Is this a trap, do you think?'

'I think it is,' said Trystan, 'though it might be hard to find others who believe it. We must forewarn those who travel with us – but we do not know exactly what kind of trap it is, for I cannot imagine that they mean to slaughter us. That would undo at a stroke all the cunning work which they have done, and bring a wrathful army to their doors just as winter sets in.'

'I would rather they did mean to fight us,' said Herla dully. 'A fight is something which I understand far better than any gentle trap intended to seduce us. If all that you have heard and said is true, they have already made covert shifts to divide and corrupt the realm – now they intend to strike at its head. Why, Trystan? Why has the Mother of All decided that I am such a poor son? Why has such a fearful flock of troubles descended upon me? So soon, Trystan – so soon!'

Trystan, remembering his dreams, thought that he had some notion of what manner of seduction the elves might attempt. 'Courage, my friend,' he said, with all possible sincerity. 'The Mother has not deserted us, we may be sure of that. And we have the Code to defend us as we defend it. We are not elves, but we are men – and the strength of men is not a negligible thing. Bavian promised me that we would both be tested, though he did not tell me how – but he would not have come at all if he had not believed that we might meet our tests adequately and somehow win the day. The secret, he said, is in Agam's Code. If we can only uphold the Code, Herla, I am sure that we can win this curious war.'

If we can only uphold the Code! Trystan echoed in the privacy of his own thoughts. Fine words for a man besotted with his friend's wife!

Herla said only: 'Go to Kerewan, Trystan. Stay by his side, if you can, while he is within these walls. Try to tempt him, in his haughtiness, to reveal more than he ought.'

It was a sensible ploy – but as Trystan moved to obey he could feel his heart sinking yet again, for it was not a duty he could relish.

LATER, TRYSTAN AND Kerewan went walking in the castle grounds, and Trystan took the elf to see the tree that had sprung from the seed which Thoron had given to the king.

'Why,' said the elf – who had shown no inclination at all to be secretive, and if anything tended to the loquacious – 'it has done far better than we ever could have expected! Who would have thought that a seed from half way across the world could take root so cleverly in the soil of Morien?'

'Who indeed?' replied Trystan. 'But we must not leap to conclusions, for Morien's winter can be a very testing time, and many a bough which now seems healthy must wither when its time comes. I have heard that the great island of Ulthuan – where the elves live – is always summery, and this plant may not relish the cold at all.'

'It is not from that island that we brought it,' said Kerewan, with a slight hint of disdain which implied that he did not altogether approve of the island's inhabitants.

'Oh,' said Trystan airily. 'That is a pity – for the legends which we humans hear about Ulthuan say that the sweetest fruits in the world are grown there.'

'I do not think that you will find the fruit of this tree lacking in sweetness,' said the elf, recalling to Trystan's mind what Bavian had said about those who were gluttonous for the satiation of desire finding the fruit of the tree of confusion overburdened with sweetness.

'But it will not be quite the same,' said Trystan, with a sigh. 'You will think us foolish, no doubt, but we humans know so very little about elves that we have a very romantic idea of you and your island kingdoms – perhaps exaggerated here in Morien by the fact that we too are islanders of a kind. You know what Ulthuan is really like, but to us it is the stuff of moonshine: marvellous pastures where all live in luxury and none need toil; where life is entirely given over to the pursuit of pleasure and the cultivation of every sensual delight. The makers of our own legends have designed their own imaginary places of a similar kind – like the one which the northerners call Mag Mell – but we cannot believe in any human realm as gorgeous and delightful as the elven one.'

Whether Kerewan knew or not that he was being offered a baited hook, he was quick enough to take it. 'The elves are more austere than you imagine,' he said. 'They are great believers in pleasure, or so they say, but they are also great believers in moderation. You might have more in common with them than you think, for that music you played when last we met had something of the same half-hearted attitude in it. The elves know too much of discipline and too much of restraint to take a proper part in the affairs of the world. That is why the some had to quit their company in order to carry forward the great quest which their cousins had all but abandoned.'

'And is that why the *druchii* turned against their own kind also?' asked Trystan.

'I know as little of the *druchii* as you do,' answered Kerewan serenely. 'Which is to say that they are little more than a word to be whispered about. But I dare say that they too became impatient with the idleness of the elves, and tried to recover the true ambitions and destiny of our race.'

'I dare say,' echoed Trystan. 'And I dare say that we men are wrong to think of the elves in such terms as we do. I confess to some disappointment that they are not, after all, the pursuers of perfect luxury which we imagine them to be.'

'If you envy them so much,' said Kerewan, 'I am surprised that you do not devote more effort to the pursuit of luxury yourselves.'

'Ah,' said Trystan softly. 'This is a hard land with stubborn soil and too much rain. Luxury is out of place here, even in our palaces. Oh, we dream of it... we feel its warm temptations... but we know in our hearts that we were made for different lives. Our richness is the richness of Agam's Code and the Old Faith – of honour and strength and Mother-love, and capitulation with the stern rule of the seasons – and we are a proud people after our fashion. In the end, we always contrive to remember that perfect luxury is but a dream, which cannot possibly take root in our soil.'

'I am sorry to hear it,' answered Kerewan smoothly. 'I am an elf, after all, and cannot judge your human nature. But you are great huntsmen, are you not? Does your king not find a special ecstasy in the chase and the kill, which might truly be called luxurious?'

Trystan saw that a curious smile played briefly upon Kerewan's lips, and knew that the elf sought to play with him, and tantalize him with mysteries. 'The king is a great and enthusiastic huntsman,' he agreed.

'And generous, no doubt,' added the elven wizard softly. 'As all followers of your Code of Agam are asked to be.'

Trystan could not understand what the elf was saying – or even what he might be implying. 'There is no more loyal follower of the Code in all Morien than Herla of Plennydd,' he said, uneasily.

'I do not doubt it,' answered Kerewan. 'And yet, if what I have been told of your Code is true – for I was not present when you recited it to my companions – there must be many situations to which two different commandments might apply, urging in opposite directions. Sometimes, surely, there arise circumstances which test the Code to near-destruction. Is it really possible to defend the weak against their oppressors while holding to the rule that one should not harm those who have not harmed you? And can you really bear arms for all of Albion against its enemies while also being courteous and mild with those you do not love?'

'It is in the nature of things,' said Trystan, as coolly as he could, 'that a man's duty is sometimes problematic, and that he must sometimes balance one hurtful course of action against its hurtful opposite. The path of right is not always an easy one to follow.'

'Indeed not,' said Kerewan, with some satisfaction. 'In fact, there are those, even amongst the *Uranai*, who claim to have similar difficulties. One such was a kinsman of mine – whose name, I recall, was Senduiuiel. He also found it hard to follow what you call the path of right.' There was a certain flirtatiousness in the elf's manner, which suggested that he did not altogether care whether Trystan knew what he truly was – but Trystan did not feel that the questions he had so far asked, or the teasing reference to this mysterious Senduiuiel, had brought him any nearer to the heart of the matter.

'We are all instruments of those higher powers which guide us,' Trystan said. 'It is possible, is it not, that what the Mother of All deems to be right, another god – perhaps the god which you follow yourself – might deem to be wrong.

Your code of *kerrmieryon* is no doubt less contradictory than our merely human Code, but still there will be differences of opinion as to where perfection lies. From what you have told me, your kinsman Senduiuiel would, at least, agree.'

'I feel sure he would,' replied Kerewan dryly. 'Certainly there are such differences, even amongst elves. But only those who have experienced perfection can know it for sure – and those who have not found it often believe wrongly that they have.'

'Such ecstasy as a man has chanced to know,' said Trystan, 'may easily seem to him the finest thing of which the human mind is capable – but how can we measure one man's feeling against another, in order that we may know for sure which of our many pleasures and pursuits is the finest of all?'

'A man who philosophizes thus about ecstasy,' said Kerewan slyly, 'must be in love. But you have music in your soul, sir bard, and the means to weave that music into a power to influence the souls of other men. You are a minstrel, of sorts, and a magician too – as am I. I know that you would not sell your soul for any ordinary ecstasy, but I think you might sell it for a finer kind of music. Am I wrong?'

'You are wrong,' said Trystan, knowing that he had brought the elf close to an admission of his true nature, but quite unable to feel any sense of triumph in consequence. 'My soul is my own, and not for sale.'

CHAPTER TWELVE

HERLA DID NOT find it easy to select the knights who would accompany Trystan and himself to the elves' house. There were many who wanted to go, and were displeased that he would not agree to take more than six; there were also many who believed that they were entitled by rank to be included. Herla dared not say openly that he believed the invitation to be a trap, nor did he dare to confine his choices to those men he considered the most steadfast in their loyalty.

In the end, having tried to balance all priorities, Herla decided that those who would go with him would be Emyr Siun, Owain Dene, Meilir Larne, Moraint Heilyn, Berwyn Aglavin and Huw Peredur. The first three he could not exclude, because of their high standing – though he trusted Sir Emyr and Sir Owain well enough; the second three he deemed most likely to support and obey him in a crisis.

There was some talk among the company of going mounted on the tallest warhorses the castle could provide, to provide a spectacle, but Herla ruled that they must take coursers instead, and go very lightly armoured. He gave his companions leave to carry spears if they must, but told them to put pennants beneath the heads so that they would serve as colour-displays. Axes he forbade, and heavy broadswords, but he said that each man ought to wear a light fencing sword like the ones which the elves had brought to Caer Plennydd, and might also carry a bow and arrows.

Herla had also to select gifts to take with him, which he did very carefully. He found an ornate broadsword in his armoury which would match the bow which Thoron had given him, a silver plate to match the cup, and a pup from the litter of one of his best hunting-dogs to match the seed.

He counselled his men to be on their guard, and would have said more save that they were so dismissive of the warning. All of them, it seemed, had been infected with benevolence to the extent that they could no longer imagine that the elves might be their enemies. Herla began to wonder whether his own suspicions might not be unworthy ones, and whether Trystan's visions of Bavian were anything more than the productions of an uneasy mind.

As the day of departure approached, the king's unhappiness deepened steadily, and he felt very much alone. Though Morgana and Trystan now avoided one another, it was plain that both found the avoidance uncomfortable, and neither drew any closer to Herla in consequence. The king felt as though he was consigned to a peculiar void, cut off from the nourishment which his relationships with other men should have provided. He had put the elven bow away, but he could find little enthusiasm for the hunt while he could not carry it, and his only opportunity to forget his cares was provided by his fencing sessions with Moraint. He threw himself into this pursuit with typical single-mindedness, bringing his artistry to a peak of perfection after a fashion which he thought worthy of the name *kerrmieryon*.

Herla was glad when the day came when the seven rode forth to their appointment with fate. The bright surcoats of his followers showed the blue and silver amid the riot of their own colours, but Herla did not know any longer how much that signified. Some chose to wear helmets, though some did not, and some wore gauntlets, though none had any mail beneath their coats – but neither Herla not Trystan carried any armour. The king had no weapon but his light sword, and Trystan had none at all.

The weather was still good – better in fact, than it had been during the drearier part of the summer, which had been spoiled by heavy falls of rain. Emyr Siun played the part of guide, having hunted this land more frequently and more thoroughly than any other, and his cleverness made the journey as short as it could possibly be. Even so, they took longer than Trystan had, for they had not so many spare horses and could not drive on so quickly.

They stopped overnight at the same unringed house where Trystan had stayed on his return journey, and had to listen while the franklin Dewi Lwys – inspired by the stating of their eventual destination – repeated rumours he had heard about the benevolence and generosity of the elves. Diplomacy demanded that the account be generously spiced with comments as to the wisdom of the king in permitting the elves to make a temporary home in his realm, but the farmer's mind was slow enough that it failed to conceal his acquaintance with the wisdom of hearsay which said that Herla deserved little credit for his actions.

Included among these rumours were awed comments about the magnificence of the house which the elves had built; but it was not until the travellers came within view of the house, late in the morning of the next day, that they were able to judge for themselves how little the natural exaggerations of rumour had been forced to add to the tale. The house was by no means as large as the citadel of Caer Plennydd, but that fortress had taken three years to build. This house had been raised in the space of a single summer, and could hardly have seemed much more miraculous had it sprung up overnight.

Its walls were jet black, and astonishingly smooth,
though the blocks which comprised them were far huger
than those with which human stonemasons could comfortably work. It had three towers, the tallest of which
stood on the seaward side of the house, with a beacon-
light in its turret which must be visible for many an
ocean-mile; that one was slender, while the other two
were twice as broad, but all three were very neatly
rounded. The crenellated walls between the towers followed the contours of the hulking headland. There
seemed to be no open courtyard, the space within the
walls being filled by a jumble of slated roofs slanting
hither-and-yon according to no discernible pattern. There
were more windows than were usual in human houses,
and most were much broader, but all were carefully latticed and glazed as well as shuttered. The doors were
uncommonly broad and tall.

The house had more than a dozen chimneys, but only
four were smoking now – those presumably the kitchen-
chimneys where cooking fires were permanently kept. If it
was, indeed, a house where no more than sixty people
might abide for a year or so, then it had certainly been
constructed with reckless opulence.

'If that is to be Godwin Conwy's when the elves leave,'
murmured Huw Peredur, 'it's no wonder that we have not
seen him recently in Caer Plennydd. With his ringhold no
more than a dozen miles away the temptation must always
be strong to ride over here, to pass the time with his good
friend Thoron.'

'If I know Godwin,' added Sir Meilir, 'he'll be here when
the first heavy snows of winter come, unable to reach
home again until the thaw.'

'But he would surely miss his beloved Lady Lynette,' put
in Sir Moraint. Godwin's wife had been a beauty in her
day, but she had never produced a son and the inference
drawn by most men was that she must thereby have
proved a sore disappointment – though her two daughters,
Melicent and Morwen, were reaching the age when they

would soon become objects of fierce competition among the bachelors of the court.

'How soon will we see the rest of their camp?' asked Herla, who was not disposed to take any notice of the jesting.

'When we come to the next rise,' Trystan told him. 'We will see the roof of the great hut then – they must have laid the keel further out, though they will need to dig prodigiously to turn that tiny stream into a canal which can bear the vessel to deep water.'

'Digging prodigiously appears to be one of their best virtues,' said Herla. 'Unless their magic fashioned that black stone from thin air they must have hollowed it from the hill. A thousand men with picks could not have done as much in thirty or forty years, nor a battalion of druids intent on raising one of their rough-hewn circles. That is mighty work for sixty, given that most of them have not laid claim to be magicians.'

'There may be more artistry in it than power,' said Trystan, 'but even so, it is an astonishing achievement.'

They went on, in order that they might inspect the marvel more intimately – and they did not find it one whit less marvellous even at the closest range.

WHEN GREY-CLAD ELVES had taken their horses to be stabled, the knights were led to the hall of the house. Three long tables had already been set for the feast, arrayed along three sides of a rectangle. Trystan counted the places and found that they numbered eighty-two – which implied that there were to be other guests besides those from Caer Plennydd, unless their previous estimates as to the number of the elves had all been low.

The furniture in the hall was well-made but plain, and the walls were quite bare of hangings and other decorations, their smoothness being interrupted only by alcoves and brackets for oil-lamps. Although the stone had been reddened in some way to make it much lighter in tone than the grim black which it presented as its exterior,

Trystan judged that it would be a rather gloomy place once the sun was down.

They had been waiting for three or four minutes when Thoron emerged from a screened doorway at the back of the hall. There were two others with him. One was Kerewan; the second was Godwin Conwy. Despite the remarks which had been made earlier, several of the visiting knights stiffened with surprise to find Sir Godwin here. Trystan was not so surprised, for the possibility had come into his mind when he counted the places set at the tables.

'King Herla!' said Thoron, bowing in a slightly exaggerated fashion. 'You are very welcome to my temporary home. I fear that the poverty in which our shipwreck left us is still evident here, but our neighbours have been extremely kind in helping us to prepare for this feast. Sir Godwin wanted to hold it at his own house, but I could not let him do that – and he has insisted instead that he must provide a full staff of servants to wait upon us all.'

All eyes were on Godwin, and Trystan was not the only one whose perplexity was mingled with sheer astonishment. It was not simply that such generosity was untypical, but that Godwin stood so haughtily beside his elven friend, looking at King Herla as though he were his equal – though the House of Conwy was not even counted among the great houses of the realm.

'I am sure that we are all most grateful to Sir Godwin,' murmured Herla, with careful courtesy. 'And to yourself, Captain Thoron.'

'You must be tired and thirsty after your journey,' said the elf captain. 'I will have you shown to your rooms without delay, and will have hot water sent so that you may bathe. Please ask for anything you might require.'

Having said this, Thoron turned abruptly away – but his two companions remained. Kerewan greeted Trystan as though the harper were an old friend, but Trystan's attention remained divided while he watched Godwin and Herla.

'Thank you for coming, your majesty,' said Godwin, in a tone whose attitude was quite unfathomable. 'It means a good deal to me to have you here.'

Herla frowned. 'I am sorry, Sir Godwin,' he replied, 'but I cannot quite see why it should be a matter of importance to you.'

There was no mistaking the expression of surprise which passed over Godwin's features then – nor the gathering embarrassment which followed it. From the corner of his eye Trystan saw Kerewan smile, as if the magician had anticipated this moment with some amusement.

'Why, sire...' Godwin began, though he had then to break off and begin again. 'Sire, were you not told...?'

'Told what, Sir Godwin?' demanded Herla, as impatient with his own embarrassment as with the other's.

'That my daughter... that the elf captain is to wed...'

Trystan heard Huw Peredur gasp in amazement, but he had little difficulty in controlling himself – for he had half-guessed it when he saw Kerewan's smile. The elf had never given the name of Thoron's intended bride, and no one had thought to ask. All had assumed that she would be one of the handful of female elves which were with the castaways.

But this makes no sense, thought Trystan. It is no more reasonable to think that an elf might wed a human girl than to think that a human might give his daughter in marriage to an elf. What purpose can this marriage possibly serve? Even if Godwin's dearest ambition is to inherit this house when the elves leave, he surely need not barter his daughter away in order to secure it!

More elves were arriving, having been appointed to lead the knights to their quarters, and it seemed that Herla was by no means anxious to delay. The king clearly needed time to think, and to consult with his friends. But Trystan was not in such a hurry; he turned back to Kerewan.

'Why did you not tell us this?' he asked, in a low tone. He felt that he had the right to be less than polite.

'My captain asked me to avoid the issue if I could,' replied the magician straightforwardly. 'Had I been asked, I would have told the truth, but I was content to leave the question unasked and unanswered, lest your king's anxieties should make him refuse the invitation. That would have hurt Sir Godwin, and would have disappointed us. Our one desire is to befriend your people, and we felt that this was one way to make our intentions clear – yet we feared to be misunderstood if the news were to be hastily broadcast. You know well enough, I suppose, how rumours can distort matters.'

Trystan found the elf's effrontery astonishing. The last thing he required was a homily on the sly corruptions of rumour. And yet, he thought, what an irony it was that in all the rumours they had been forced to hear while they rested at the franklin's house, there had not been the least inkling of this.

'If King Herla and the knights of his court bear witness to this marriage,' said Trystan slowly, 'there is not a man in Plennydd who can complain of it. It will be as though it had his consent and approval from the beginning. That is what you have sought to obtain – and yet you have been careful to obtain it by trickery.'

Kerewan was unabashed. 'Perhaps,' he answered. 'But you are a clever man, Trystan Harper. You know that the best result is one which must often be gained by stealth and cleverness instead of brutal honesty. It is the way of the world. Your king knew that when he sent you to summon us to your own wedding – which he did not do because he wanted us there, but because he wanted to bind us with the obligations which are assumed by those who accept hospitality. Can you blame us for wishing to do the same?

'Try to look at matters from our point of view, sir bard. We are little more than sixty strong, cast away among strangers who are regarded by most of our kind as untrustworthy barbarians. We have certain kinds of shaping magic to aid us, and the strengths and skills which elves normally have, but we know full well that should your people turn against us we would be overwhelmed.

'We have found you to be pleasant folk, to be sure, but we have heard it rumoured that some men suspect that the ill luck which has recently descended upon the kingdom was caused by our curses, and that your priests and magicians have whispered warnings against us. We are afraid, Trystan Harper, that we might not be given the time which we need to build our ship. We are afraid for our lives. We have seen, thanks to you, how your own folk deal with such anxieties; we have witnessed marriage used as a means of demonstrating – and thus securing – amity between nations. Why should we not seek to use the same means? We only seek to do that which will be best for all of us.'

This speech threw Trystan into utter confusion. There was cunning in it, but there was also truth. Had not Herla's invitation to the elves been as cynical and self-serving as the elves' invitation to him? And was it not also true – how sharply Trystan was aware of the fact! – that there was no more honest affection between Herla and Morgana than there was likely to be between the elf captain and Godwin Conwy's pretty daughter?

It occurred to Trystan that he still did not know which daughter Thoron was to wed. No one had thought to ask. How much genuine concern could the king and his courtiers be said to have for her?

'This is a trap,' said Trystan, unable to keep the anguish out of his voice – though no one but Kerewan was left in the hall to hear it. 'We have known it from the start, and yet we have allowed ourselves to be drawn into it. Do you have the magic of shaping spiderwebs as well as fortresses of stone, sir magician? Have you brought the skill of seducing men to the same perfection which you seek in all your other arts?'

Kerewan smiled, and in that smile Trystan read the kind of predatory satisfaction which a cat shows while it plays with a mouse.

'We are your friends, Trystan Harper,' said the elf. 'We only wish to make your friendship secure. Be friendly to us, I implore you, and to our purposes. That way lies reward.'

'And what lies in the other direction?' demanded Trystan sharply.

'Dishonour,' answered Kerewan. 'Remember your Code. You may not injure or violate the privacy of another man's house and property. You must respect all the ties and obligations of lawful marriage.'

'As you pointed out yourself,' said Trystan bitterly, 'there are times when the items of the Code conflict. We are commanded also to bear arms for Albion against its enemies, under the command of its king and his appointed generals. *And we are commanded to stand firm against the temptations of daemons and all foul magic!*

'Why did your own folk cast you out, Kerewan? Why did the clan reject you, and give you to the mercy of the violent sea? Was it not because your company has turned to the worship of daemons, and courted the rewards of the dark god of luxury? Is it not those rewards which you offer to us like oversweet fruit?'

Trystan would have given much to see Kerewan frown in annoyance, but the elf's expression was perfectly steady.

'You talk easily of daemons, harper,' he said, 'and more easily still of the one whom you term the dark god of luxury. And yet it is true that there are those amongst the *Uranai* who are attracted by that which such powers may offer. Long ago in Ulthuan, that kinsman I spoke to you of earlier, Senduiuiel, studied daemons.' The elf smiled and went on silkily: 'But we took very different paths, Senduiuiel and I, and I swear to you, Trystan Harper that my companions and I mean you no harm. Amity is what we seek, not enmity. If you intend to make us your enemies, you will have to break your own Code to do it, and you will fully deserve the penalties prescribed there for Codebreakers. Again I implore you: only be friends with us, and all Plennydd will be the happier for it.'

Trystan, lost in his confusion, could only ask to be taken to his room. He could not win this duel of wits with Kerewan, and he knew that Herla must be desperate to speak to him.

He only wished that he had some sensible advice to give.

CHAPTER THIRTEEN

TRYSTAN FOUND HERLA alone, staring down through the latticed window of his room at the cove beneath. There they could see the keel of the ship which had been laid, and at least a dozen elves busy around and about the timbers and decks; the vessel was a long way from completion, but the work was progressing well.

'It will be a fine ship,' said Herla tiredly. 'Will they take Melicent away with them, do you suppose – or will they leave her here as Thoron's steward?'

'It is to be Melicent, then?' asked Trystan quietly. 'You have spoken to Godwin about it?'

'Indeed I have,' replied Herla. 'He has explained to me at great length how delighted he is with the match, and how proud he and the Lady Lynette will be to see their daughter wed to a captain of the elves. He has told me in no uncertain terms what excellent fellows the elves are, and how much their friendship will mean to the kingdom.'

'Have you seen Melicent herself?'

Herla shook his head. 'I believe that she will be at the

feast,' he said. 'It is not our custom, of course, but Thoron
has told Godwin that it is theirs. Godwin has not told me
about her delight, of course – but I dare say that not a
word was ever spoken about Morgana's delight in being
offered to me.'

'Morgana's pleasure in her marriage need not be
doubted in the slightest,' said Trystan, too quickly and with
far too little conviction.

'You think not?' asked Herla bitterly. 'I had thought that
the coolness between my wife and myself was not entirely
on my side. Perhaps it is only an illusion, but sometimes I
think she is wistful. Do you think, perhaps, she had
formed an affection for some handsome squire at her
father's court?'

Trystan knew by the king's sarcastic tone that his guilty
secret was partly discovered. It had been inevitable. But
how much the king knew – and how much he might suspect in addition that was not true – he could not guess.

'No, sire,' he said doggedly. 'Your queen loves you, as you
will come in time to love her.'

'As the Lady Melicent will come to love her elf lord, no
doubt – if she does not love him already. Captain Thoron
might find it more difficult to engage his affections, but he
will be no worse a husband than I am if that be the case.'

'Herla,' said Trystan abruptly, 'we must stop this marriage. At the very least, we must leave before it takes place.'

'Why?' countered the king, with equal abruptness.

'You know why,' said Trystan. 'If you stay, that will signify
consent. Godwin is your liege-man, and Melicent – however remotely – your ward. If you condone this, you accept
the elves into your realm. You extend to them the full protection of the Code. What could you then say if they decide
that they will not leave? What could you do if they make a
permanent base here, on the landholding of Thoron's
father-in-law?'

'And why should they not?' asked Herla defeatedly. 'Is
Godwin wrong to say that trade with the elves could only
increase the prosperity of the kingdom?'

'They are outcasts from their own kind,' Trystan said. 'They have turned to the worship of forbidden gods. I said as much to Kerewan, and he did not deny it.'

This was stretching the truth just a little, and Herla might have refused to accept the implication, but the king was in a strange mood. 'What right have the worshippers of one god to forbid the worship of another?' he said, angrily. 'What business is it of ours how these castaways stand among their own kind? Should we not judge them for what they are, on the basis of what they do? Would that not be more just, at any rate, than hating and fearing them on the basis of your mad dreams of long-dead Bavian and the malice of unattributable rumours?'

'My lord,' said Trystan uncomfortably, 'we must not allow ourselves to be tricked and used in this manner. If you will not forbid the marriage – as you have a right to do – then at least let us ride away from here before sundown.'

'If you want to go,' said Herla, 'go.' Then, at last, he turned away from the window to look his bard in the eye.

When Trystan had first returned to Caer Plennydd from his long years away, he had greeted Herla as a steady friend – the king had not seemed to be in any way a stranger. Now, by contrast, he felt himself completely set apart from the man he had known all his life. Herla was overwrought and distressed, and Trystan knew that he was as much to blame for that as anyone, but he was still the king's adviser and the Bard of the Realm.

'This is a trap,' said Trystan earnestly. 'I am sure that the elves mean to take our reason prisoner, and will try to turn us to the worship of their dark god. The kingdom itself is in danger.'

'You begin to sound like the phantom Bavian yourself,' said Herla. 'Dire warnings and doleful prophecies spill from your lips, but you cannot say exactly what you mean. Captain Thoron walked willingly enough into my house, trusting that there was no trap to detain or harm him – how can I be less courteous? And if all the interested parties desire that this wedding should take place, why should

I listen to the voice of a druid's acolyte who calls it unnatural? When so many of my own subjects have begun
whispering about me behind my back, why should I not
trust the elves, who have never done me any harm?'

Trystan might have objected that he had not used the
word *unnatural*, but it seemed a mere quibble. He was
more anxious about the king's description of him as a
'druid's acolyte' and the implication that the whispers
which had cast doubts on the king's justice might have
something to do with other whisperings about his wife.

'You intend to stay,' said Trystan flatly. 'For reasons of
your own, you have decided that you have no right to
object to this marriage, and hence must tolerate it, so giving it your blessing. You are determined to ignore my
advice, because you have ceased to trust me.'

'What reason could I have for not trusting you?' asked
Herla cuttingly. 'Have you not always been my truest friend?'

'Aye,' said Trystan quietly. 'That I have. That I am.'

And having said that, he went away, to wait for the
wedding-feast to begin. He went because he could not
bear to stay – and because he knew that if the evil destiny which had them all in its grip could still be cheated,
the opportunity had not yet come.

WHEN TRYSTAN WAS finally summoned to the hall by one of
Godwin Conwy's servants he found himself descending in
the company of Berwyn Aglavin. Sir Berwyn's manner
seemed cold, and Trystan thought at first that he was angry
with Herla – but then he realized that the knight had come
to a different understanding of the situation.

'Why did you bring us to this?' muttered Berwyn, as they
descended a gloomy stair.

'I?' answered Trystan, wounded by the apparent injustice. 'How am I to blame for this?'

'Was it not your advice to make friends with these folk
when first we heard of them? Was it not you who came to
inspect them, and liked them well enough to invite them
to Herla's wedding?'

Trystan could hardly deny it. 'I have urged the king to go,' he said defensively. 'He will not do it. He thinks himself bound by obligation.'

'So he is,' said Berwyn, in a low voice. He touched the hilt of his sword, and went on: 'Though I am armed against the kind of treachery which I understand, I fear that this affair is too deep for me.'

Trystan dared not say: Me too.

A curtain was drawn aside to let them pass into the hall, and both men drew in their breath. Berwyn might have been surprised to see the assembled host – for the elves had put on much gayer clothes than any which the humans had seen before – or he might only have been astonished by the food and wine piled high on the tables; but Trystan was surprised by one thing only, which eclipsed all else from his sight.

In the middle of the hall, within the area three-quarters surrounded by the tables, the elves had set a harp.

The instrument was not nearly so ornate as the great harp of Plennydd; its frame was not gilded, nor was it set upon a decorated plinth. Nevertheless, its construction demonstrated considerable craftsmanship, and its rim was intricately carved into a delicate pattern inset with the same downward pointing arrowhead symbol as on the wizard's cloak.

Kerewan was already hurrying to meet them, and while Sir Berwyn was led away by the servant to a place on the right-hand table close to Sir Owain and Sir Huw, Kerewan took Trystan to the head table where two empty places waited, with an elf to one side and the Lady Lynette to the other.

Trystan moved as though to take the seat beside the lady, but Kerewan was quick to indicate that it was the other which had been reserved for him.

'You are doubtless astonished to see the harp,' said the elven player, 'but I was astonished myself when I heard you play at Caer Plennydd. I had no thought in my mind when I returned here but to build a similar instrument and learn to play it. Alas, I have not had time to practice as much as I could have wished, for the magic which we use to work the stone is very tiring. I will show you what I can do when the time comes, but I know that you will far outshine me when you take your own turn, for your fingers are so much more nimble than mine.'

'You want me to play?' said Trystan stupidly.

'It will be the high point of the feast,' Kerewan assured him. 'When you played at the king's wedding, you set our very hearts afire. I beg you not to refuse.'

Trystan set his mouth thinly, and thought about the magic which was in the music of the bardic order – his magic, which he held in trust for all the men of Plennydd – and he suddenly saw a ray of hope that this situation might be saved.

'I will be pleased to play,' he said softly.

Trystan sat down and took up the knife which had been set by his place. He began to take meat and bread on to his plate, while a servant came to fill up his cup with some kind of liquor. He began to eat, but his mind was so busy that he could hardly notice the warmth or the taste of it. The first sip of the liquor suggested to him that it was no stronger than ale or watered mead, but it was unfamiliar and he decided that he must not take too much of it if he was to make magic.

Once or twice he tried to make conversation with Lady Lynette, being anxious to discover what she really thought of the prospect of marrying her daughter to an elf, but Kerewan was always in the way.

The lady showed no obvious inclination to make any complaint – indeed, she seemed so flushed and bright-eyed with excitement that Trystan wondered whether the entire House of Conwy had been thoroughly bewitched by elven magic.

From time to time Trystan looked long and hard at the place where Thoron and Melicent sat, with Herla between them, but it was difficult to see because they were on a level with him, with a dozen others in between. Herla was stony of face by comparison with Thoron, who seemed in an expansive mood, but Trystan found it impossible to judge whether the girl was in the same frame of mind as her mother.

As he sipped the liquor, Trystan felt a feeling of calm and well-being creeping upon him – and became even more suspicious of it. The intoxication still seemed gentle enough, but he was afraid. He pushed the cup away, and ate more bread in the hope of soaking up a little of what he had already quaffed.

It was easy to see that the six knights were by no means so cautious. Having found the spirit smoother to the taste than those which they knew they had assumed it to be innocuous, and were gulping it back very freely. Only the king, who seemed to have no appetite, seemed not to be raising his cup to his lips at all.

Three of the elves began playing music almost as soon as the affair had begun. One played the lute, one an array of panpipes and the last a tambour and a drum. Other elves began to quit the tables, two at a time, in order to take their turn with one instrument or another. Eventually, other pairs got up to take turns at dancing, which they did very gaudily, leaping about the space between the tables like gymnasts – loudly applauded as they leapt by their seated compatriots. The Conwys joined in this applause from the beginning, and it was not long before the other knights began to join in too.

When two female elves got up to dance, Trystan could not help but be astonished by their manner, their dress and their agility. Previously he had only seen the females of the company dressed like the males, working alongside the males; now they had shed their working clothes for brightly-coloured skirts and embroidered slippers, for painted faces and ornamented hair. The steps of their dance were wild and yet perfectly balanced, and the two dancers mirrored one another's movements very precisely as they leapt soaringly and pirouetted with flowing grace. They continued much longer than the pairs of male dancers who had preceded them – to the evident delight of the watchers, who called out encouragement to them and grew steadily more excited.

Trystan recalled the stubborn dullness of Herla's wedding-feast – the interminable stale flatteries, the slowly-cooling food, the gathering impatience.

Despite that he had eaten frugally and had stopped drinking altogether Trystan could not help but feel the vivid pulse of the occasion – the sheer joy of it – as though it were something tangible in the air. That the six knights had surrendered to it already he could not doubt, for he could see them laughing with delight, cheering with the crowd and talking animatedly to their neighbours.

While Trystan watched he saw Sir Moraint and Sir Berwyn separately approached by the two female elves who had danced, and saw them blushing with the force of their attraction as they spewed out their hurried compliments.

Unnatural! he thought, recalling the word which Herla had unjustly charged him with using. Why, what could be more natural than the love of human for elf? They are so very beautiful, and – when their haughtiness and reserve are weakened by liquor – so very friendly. What man would not marry his daughter to an elf, if he only could, in order to ally his blood with folk who are so very clever in what they do, so very civilized in what they are, so near to perfection in all their aspirations? But what could these elves want with crude and vulgar men? How could they possibly put away their sense of self-importance in order to worm their way into our affections? What can they possibly intend, save to make fools of us, and use us in some fantastic game?

Trystan looked again at Herla, but Herla would not look at him.

Turn your stony face away, said Trystan silently. I am glad to see it, for while your face is stern your mind is not addled, and you may yet have a part to play in this.

'Do not be so gloomy, my friend,' said Kerewan reproachfully. 'You are treating yourself unkindly. There is pleasure here, if only you would condescend to let it into your reluctant heart. A man should take pleasure when it is there, for there are many times in life when it is harder to find than buried treasure.'

'For ordinary men,' said Trystan spitefully. 'But not for us, friend Kerewan, for we have our music, to which we can always turn for solace and joy.'

'Ah,' said Kerewan, with the air of one who has come belatedly to an understanding. 'You are apprehensive! You fear that if you surrender to the moment you might play badly. I assure you that you are wrong – this wine will not make you dizzy or dull, but will favour you with a thrill which will improve your playing immeasurably. There is no finer music, I assure you, than the music of pure ecstasy. If only you could play it once, my friend, you would know what I mean. Drink deep, Trystan Harper, and forget your fears.'

'No doubt I will hear the music of ecstasy,' said Trystan, 'When you go to play yourself. If this wine is as clever as you imply, its effects will surely compensate for your lack of practice.'

'If you require a demonstration,' said the elf, with a smile as wolfish as Trystan had ever seen upon his face, 'I will be happy to give you one.' So saying, he stood up, and went to the harp. By the time he had arrived there, the other musicians had stopped playing, and there were no more dancers in the empty space between the tables.

For the first time, a momentary silence fell upon the company as every eye was turned expectantly to the player.

Kerewan took up his position, flexed his fingers, and caressed the strings of the harp with what seemed to Trystan to be a parody of his own habit. Then the magician looked up and ahead, allowing his gaze to scan the cross-table from end to end. He did not pause to look at his captain, or Herla, or Melicent or Godwin Conwy, but

when he reached Trystan he paused for a single fleeting
second.

No competitions! thought Trystan. He lied about that,
too, for this is certainly a challenge, and there may be more
at stake than I know.

Then Kerewan began to play.

When he had played before, in Caer Plennydd, there
had been no magic in his music save for the magic which
was inherent in all music; this time it was to be different.
From the very first note, Trystan knew that this was
music full of magic, and he guessed that this was what he
and his companions had been brought here for. This was
the trap into whose jaws they had been so smilingly
invited.

The shock which surged through Trystan's soul as the
music took form was more terrifying than he could have
anticipated. He had not thought that any sound could hurt
him, nor any music captivate him. He had braced himself
to hear something like the wild music of his dreams – the
supposedly-alien music which his imagination had sup-
plied to be a seduction and a threat to him. That, he had
thought, must be the nature of the music of Chaos, the
music of the god of wicked luxury. Now he realized how
completely his dreams were his own, and how that which
he had thought of as distant and alien was really his own
invention.

This was the real seduction.

This was the real threat.

It was not wild at all; it did not soar as one might have
expected ecstatic music to do. There was nothing insistent about its rhythm, nothing ambitious about its
melody. It was low and sweet, deep and welcoming and
somehow full of light. Though he had been determined
to keep it at bay, as though to fend it off with armour
and shield, Trystan found that he had no armour against
such sweetness, no shield against something which
seemed so utterly benevolent. It was as easy to take in as
the air he breathed, and it seemed to answer a hunger

which he had nursed forever without ever knowing what it was that he hungered after.

Trystan let the music in.

He let it into his soul, of which it took possession with an absurdly easy grace.

He felt that he was no longer in the red-hued hall of the elves' dark citadel; he could not see its lamplit walls or the guests assembled for the feast. He could see nothing, in fact, but the image of Morgana, which filled the world with its beauty – and though he could hear nothing save for the music of the harp, her thoughts were perfectly clear to him, as though they were his own.

Her thoughts were these: I am in the world for such a brief interval, and I have the gifts of youth for a briefer one still. Though I have lived nineteen years I have never been myself until this moment in time, for I have been a mindless babe and a stupid child and an ignorant girl, only growing and unfolding into my true and present being.

How long it will be until age corrupts and destroys me I cannot tell, but I know that the worm is already at work in the bud, for I began the business of dying long before I ever emerged from the womb. Now I am what I am, but tomorrow I may be less, and in due course I will be nothing at all; if I am truly to live, it must be now and tomorrow. I must be what I may be now and tomorrow, or never, and if the name Morgana – if the thought Morgana and the soul Morgana – are to be anything at all, they must be what Morgana desires, what Morgana needs, what Morgana truly is… not queen of Plennydd, not Herla's wife, not Coll's pawn.

One thing matters in all the world, and that is to be Morgana, beloved of Trystan Harper and lover of Trystan Harper. All else is loss and treason of the soul; all else is betrayal of self and negation of being. The gods gave us love, and it is sacrilege to spurn that gift; the gods have made us what we are, and if we cannot honestly be what we are then nothing has meaning and there is no good at all. Love is the one truth and the one joy; love is the one existence. Beyond love there is nothing but pain and disease and age and death, and if love is denied there is nothing in life but the hell of loss and suffering and self-betrayal.

Not for an instant did Trystan doubt the truth of it. Morgana loved him, and needed him, and would be bitter throughout her life if she could not follow her heart.

His own heart was aching with a fierceness which he had not thought possible. His throat was burning with thirst, and he reached out with his trembling hand to the cup which sat on the table before him. He lifted the cup to his mouth, and drank. He sipped, and then he drank more deeply, and felt enormous relief as the cool liquid's gift of peace flowed through him, easing his pain.

He did not become aware, until he had set the cup down, that the music had stopped. Kerewan was no longer playing; he had stood up to receive the acclamation of the crowd. Trystan could not understand, for a moment or two, why their applause was so unstinted. It seemed bewildering that music addressed so intimately to him should have evoked such a reaction in other listeners. It was only by slow degrees that he realized that others must have been invaded just as comprehensively, just as intimately, by phantoms of their own desires.

He looked quickly around, and saw Owain Dene weeping with happiness, and old Meilir Larne smiling like a prisoner redeemed. He saw Berwyn Aglavin illuminated like a man possessed, and Moraint Heilyn shaking with some intense fever of conviction. The applause itself seemed suddenly to resemble a disease – a tremulous palsy setting the entire company a-quiver with malaise.

O Mother, Mother, Mother! cried Trystan silently. Look upon these, thy children, and weep bitter tears!

Then he looked at the empty cup before him, which had been full only moments ago, and he knew that he had hurt himself, and made himself weak. When he stood, in order to make his slow way to the harp which the elves had made for this moment, he turned so as to face his king – and for the first time, his king turned too, so as to look at him. But when their eyes met, Trystan could not read the other man's expression at all; he simply could not tell whether Herla too was lost in some private dream of final fulfilment, or whether those eyes were accusing him with all the fury of hate.

He took his seat anyway, and touched his senseless fingers to the strings.

CHAPTER FOURTEEN

As Trystan stroked the harpstrings, trying to judge the quality of their sound, he brought forth a strangely languorous glissando which left him in no doubt about the power which was incarnate in the harp.

He was amazed by what the elves had done in making the instrument; Kerewan had had only the briefest acquaintance with the great harp at Caer Plennydd, and only once had the elven magician heard the music which it made, yet on that meagre experience he had reached a full understanding of what the harp was supposed to do, and how. Not only that – with the help of other elf craftsmen he had built a device of the same kind, which would bend the same kind of magical power to the ends of his own god instead of the ends of the Mother of All.

Pausing for a moment to compose himself, Trystan looked along the faces assembled at the cross table. Herla remained monumentally stern, and Thoron carefully impassive, but there was a certain anxiety as well as curiosity in Kerewan's face. It was none of these faces which

momentarily caught his eye, though; it was instead the face
of Godwin's daughter Melicent, which he saw squarely for
the first time. There he saw a much odder combination, for
her features spoke of laughter and gaiety, while in her eyes
there was a shadow of alarm which seemed to echo his
own fearful feelings.

Her soul has been made prisoner! thought Trystan. She
is seduced, but not yet utterly lost. There is something in
her still which seeks escape – from Thoron, and from the
daemons which he serves.

While he paused he felt the subtle intoxication of the
liquor working in his gut. He was aware that he had
already yielded much to the temptations which Kerewan
had laid before him, and he knew full well that the harp
was supposed to complete the task of his seduction.

He was perversely pleased to realize how much the elves
and their patron daemons wanted him; they knew that he
was more vital to the health of the realm than the king.
The kind of conquest which they sought in Plennydd was
not a matter of bloodshed and seizure; they had no intention of deposing Herla. What they wanted was to spread
the worship of their new-found god, and to make a base
for him in the Isles of Albion. The opposition which they
feared most was not the opposition of arms and armies,
but the opposition of druidic and bardic magic and the
opposition of Agam's Code – once those were corrupted,
Chaos was truly come to the realm. The elves intended to
use this night to attain dominion over the minds and
hearts of Herla and his knights, but their most important
objective was to obtain command of Trystan Harper – and,
through him, the great harp of Plennydd.

Trystan began to play the tune of an ancient popular ballad. It was simple and delicate, with a smooth swaying
rhythm. There was not a human in the hall who would not
recognize it, and put the words to it; it was redolent with
nostalgia, and he knew that it would break the hold which
the moment had upon the knights, dampen their eupho-
ria, and remind them of youth, home and hearth.

He saw Kerewan frown, and knew that the magician had hoped that he would play a very different kind of song. But it was only a grimace of petty annoyance; it had no conviction of defeat in it. Trystan understood why when he felt the harpstrings plucking at his fingers, trying with all their might to draw him into a very different rhythm, a very different melody.

The harp had daemonic power in it, and was not content to be mastered. It wanted to produce music which could speak directly to his soul – which could *possess* his soul – and through his playing could bring its own fervour to the souls of all the humans there. He was the Bard of the Realm; his was the authority, the duty, the trust. What Kerewan had so far done to them all was superficial – without consolidation it would eventually fade away, like all intoxications and illusions. But if the music which the harp was avid to play could possess Trystan, then Trystan's playing could break through their last reserves of moral strength – the strength which bound their souls to the kingdom, to Morien, to Agam's Code and to the commonwealth of all mankind.

His resistance of the will of the harp soon brought pain and stiffness to his fingers. There was nausea in his belly, churned up by the effort of his resistance to the will of the wine.

He suppressed the reflexes which urged him to let his fingers flow with the current of the harp and to let the wine soothe away the tenseness of his thoughts. Instead, he tried to use the pain to keep his mind sharp, focused and defiant.

When the ballad ended he began to play a nursery song – a lullaby which the mothers of Plennydd used to rock their children to sleep. On such an instrument, in such a place, on such an occasion, the choice was grotesque – but as he looked about him he saw that the six knights had become puzzled and disoriented, no longer quite so willing to throw themselves wholeheartedly into the revelry. King Herla's face was as white as chalk, and the face of the

Lady Melicent was full of terror, her eyes brimming with tears.

Thoron and Kerewan were scowling, and again there was anxiety in the magician's features.

Trystan now knew why that anxiety was there. In making and empowering this harp the elves had taken a risk. They had given themselves a means to seduce him to their cause, but if he would not consent to be seduced, they had given him a weapon. If the power which was in the harp could not subdue his resistance, it would remain available for him to use. He could break the spells which they had so cunningly woven about their victims: about Godwin Conwy and his family; about the knights of Herla's court; about the realm itself. It was all in the music of the harp – all he needed to do, and all he needed to know.

His fingers were bleeding now, and so stiff that he could hardly avoid false notes. There was nothing flowing and graceful about his playing, and had he not been playing such a simple tune he would surely have lost it. The sickness in his stomach had become an awful grinding which threatened to make him faint, if not to kill him.

He heard Thoron's voice ringing in his ears. 'Away with this childishness! Play the music of the storm, sir bard. *Play the music of the storm!'*

To his astonishment, he heard others shouting likewise, human voices mixed in with those of the elves. The knights did not understand what he was doing – they only knew themselves to be discomfited. Herla was not shouting, nor Melicent either, but the words seemed to boom and echo in his head, breaking up his chain of thought... and his fingers began to play a different music, louder and more lively.

He heard the sound of the new music assert itself within the hall, and a new sensation assert itself within his fingers – and, with a great rush of relief, the stiffness and the pain were suddenly gone. The horrid tearing in his belly was replaced by a golden tide of well-being, which swept him away.

He was no longer his own man; he was the harp's.

He was lost.

He was so completely swept away that he could not tell whether that which followed his capture by the music of the harp was really happening, or whether it was merely a dream conjured up by the fever of the music – but it seemed to him that the entire company rose to dance with mad abandon, hurling themselves about as though they had no will of their own, capering and cavorting without reason, without modesty, without self-awareness.

If this was dancing it was not of a kind which he had ever seen or heard of before; if it was a kind of madness it was a kind which he feared.

It seemed that there now came into the hall a new guest, more regal by far than Herla or Thoron: a huge person who was both male and female, who wore armour of delicate coloured crystal, who carried in his right hand a sceptre of jade, whose face and hair and curving horns were very beautiful, and whose expression was at one moment utterly loving, and at another contemptuously cruel.

To Trystan this new and most welcome guest spoke, saying: Come to me, my pretty one, and be my beloved. I promise you joy without limit, and suffering too – for without the desperate and dismal pain of suffering, joy cannot properly be savoured. Be mine, dear one, and be my toy to be cherished and caressed. I promise you ecstasy and all the keenest peaks of possible experience, and frightful despair too – for without the blackness and negation of despair, that heady rush to the peak of bliss cannot be steep enough to bring transcendence. Play the music of the storm, my darling songbird, and know what life is like when it has burst the confines of that dull and tawdry thing which men call the world. Play the music of the blood-born storm, and *be*!

It further seemed that Trystan's sight was no longer bound and confined by the solid wall of the elves' dark

house. Outside, in the gathering night, flocks of flying
daemons were eclipsing the two moons, and the galloping
of monstrous steeds was setting the hillsides a-quiver. The
riders on those steeds were huntsmen who wore antlers
mounted upon their helmets, and their faces were transfigured by the unmatchable thrill of the chase. Their
quarry was a flock of human souls.

Trystan saw all this by virtue of the marvellous music
which swelled inside him and flowed from his fingers into
the strings of the harp.

In the music, the cold north wind began to howl, but
instead of striking fear and dismay into the hearts of those
who heard it, it became a fervour urging them to seize
their bows and spears and mount their horses in order to
join the Storm Hunt. Black clouds boiled in the sky,
exploding into cataracts of snowflakes, which filled the
world with lightness – but the clouds and the snowflakes
were nothing more than rhythms of the mad dance which
had consumed the folk who were in the hall, elf and
human alike. These dancers were crying out to their god to
give them pleasure or to give them pain, to caress them or
lacerate them as he pleased, but above all else to grant
them fierce sensation and the raw power of life...

But then Trystan, liberated as he was from the stiffness
and the sickness which had almost prevented him from
playing at all, began once again to intrude his own will
into the music. The power of the song was relentless, but
in some curious fashion it had lost possession of itself,
had lost its particular identity within its own wildness.

Whenever nightmares come to claim thee, Trystan said
to himself, as though the words were his own, dreams may
also come; whenever the music of Chaos enters into your
soul, the Mother's lullaby may enter too; whenever the
Storm Hunt of Slaanesh rides on the wind of doom, hope
may also soar to heights unknown.

The music, Trystan realized, was not in itself evil. The
power which was in the harp was daemonic, but that did
not mean that it could not be turned to better ends than

the daemons had. He realized that the God of Luxury to whose worship these outcast elves had turned should not be seen as an embodiment of pure evil any more than the Mother of All Things should be seen as an embodiment of pure virtue – he knew that he, as a Bard of the Realm, must understand that even if other men could not.

Storms there were, in the world and in the blood, and their force could not and need not be denied – but they had to be recognized for what they were: mere disturbances. Life must be lived in spite of them, and not because of them. In life, they must be contained, so that their fury did not overflow to spoil everything.

Understanding this, Trystan set out to contain the fury which was in the music of the storm. He set out to divert and dissipate its wildness; he accepted that he must bend before it when bending was enough, but resolved to stand firm when standing firm could be achieved. He set out to be master of the storm, not by preventing it but by diverting its energy to his own devices. He set out to bring harmony out of the assertive thrust of the notes, melody out of each violent crescendo.

Into the music of the thunderheads he brought the music of the sun – the steady light which could be hidden but never quelled. Into the music of the blizzard he brought the music of the earth – the soil which could be frozen and soaked and baked and turned to dust, but never forbidden to bear life, to give birth to the Mother's children. Into the music of the tumultuous god of ecstasy he brought the music of the patient Mother, whose love survived her many moods without ever being sated or diminished, and which could never be turned by a whim or a hurt to hate or lust or blind savage nihilism.

When he looked up again, with his fingers thrilling to the grandiosity of it all, and with his heart beating bravely in his breast, he saw that no one was dancing. No one was moving at all. Everyone in the hall – and the god which had briefly been summoned was not here now – was rapt with attention.

There was no fear, no anxiety, no sternness and no wrath in any expression which he could read.

When he was sure of that, and of his own power of command, Trystan began to play again the song which he had played before so awkwardly – the cradle song which every child of Plennydd knew. This time, his fingers did not stiffen and his stomach did not churn; this time, the music flowed from the unresisting harp liquidly, naturally, and beautifully. The storm wound down, and consented to become the lullaby, so neatly that it seemed entirely natural.

Then he finished, and in the silence which descended he looked directly at Melicent – seeing for the first time the shiny texture of her brown hair, the softness of her eyes, the delicate contours of her rounded face.

She was beautiful. She was also innocent. There was the possibility, now, that she might be saved from those who would hurt her.

'My lady,' he said clearly, 'is it truly your desire to be wedded to this elf, or will you ask us to take you away from here? You have only to say the word, and Herla your king is honour-bound to take you, whether to your father's ringhold, or to Caer Plennydd – where I would gladly wed you myself if you feel the need of a husband.'

In the pause which followed there was not a sound to be heard.

Then the Lady Melicent said: 'In the name of the Mother of All, I swear to you that I have been bewitched, and I beg you to take me away from this dark and horrid place, if you can.'

But even before she had finished, Thoron was on his feet, and his sword was in his hand, and he joined in with her final words loudly and sneeringly: *'If you can!'*

HERLA HAD COME to his feet also, and was quick to position himself at the point of Thoron's sword, challenging the elf captain to run him through. The king had not touched his own weapon.

Every eye in the room was upon the two, and for a moment it seemed to Trystan that the elf might strike, thus provoking a bloody scramble which could only end with all the humans dead and at least some of the elves hurt. But that, Trystan knew, would only be a prelude to the real war which would follow, when all Morien would rise against the elves and destroy them.

Nor was Trystan the only one who knew when weakness was a kind of strength, for Kerewan was quick to move to his captain's side and touch him on the shoulder. The touch was enough to make Thoron lower his weapon instantly, and it displayed clearly for the first time the fact that the real authority here was not the captain's.

'Captain Thoron,' said the magician, when the immediate threat of violence had been suppressed, 'you must not forget that we consented to be bound by the Code which is this land's law. We are bound to do no harm to men who have not harmed us, just as our guests are bound not to injure or violate our house and property. There are more universal principles at issue here, in any case, for these men are our guests, and it is acknowledged everywhere that hosts and guests must respect rights of hospitality.'

Thoron licked his lips, and said: 'I cannot remember the precise words of their Code, but I remember that it commands them to deal honestly with all men in commerce, and to respect the ties of marriage. The girl is betrothed to me, under agreements made with her father and sealed with more than mere promises. If they take her, they do so in violation of their own law.'

Herla turned to Godwin Conwy, who was white in the face and trembling.

'What do you say, Sir Godwin?' he asked, his voice like a whiplash.

'It is true,' said Godwin haltingly. 'She is promised.'

'And do you stand by the bargain which you made?'

All eyes were on Godwin now, as he shivered before the cold wind of the king's wrath. Trystan could not be sure exactly what was going through the man's mind. Was it a

massacre he feared, or was he already committed to the forbidden worship which the elves practiced? Was it only that
his life was under threat, or was his soul already forfeit?

'I... cannot revoke it,' said Godwin finally. 'I am
bound... by the Code of Agam.'

Melicent, who had not believed that her father could
abandon her, gasped with alarm. She was no longer
englamoured. But the Lady Lynette, her mother, made no
move or sound. She too, it seemed, was of the elves' party
now.

'You cannot have her,' said Herla steadily. 'I am King of
Plennydd, and all my subjects are my wards. You will not
prevent me from taking her without killing me – and the
knights of my realm will stand with me.'

There could be no doubt of the strength of the answer.
Beguiled the humans might have been while the elves
danced and Kerewan played, but Trystan had upset all that.
No voice was absent from the cry of consent but Godwin
Conwy's.

Kerewan did not waste time in suggesting that a battle in
the hall could have only one end. His plan was unravelled
now, and he wanted that battle no more than anyone else.

'If you choose to take her,' said the magician coolly, 'we
will not raise a hand to stop you, for we are honourable
folk. But we will name you Codebreaker if you do it, and
Sir Godwin will testify for us. We are in a human land, and
must do what the humans would have us do – but we will
not be ashamed to cry foul if we are treated unfairly. We
will demand justice, King of Plennydd, from the opinion
of your own people – and if you do this thing, your reign
will be irreparably tainted.'

Trystan saw immediately how clever this threat was.
Already there were doubt and dissent in the kingdom; the
seeds of sedition had already been sown. The possibility of
an armed uprising against Caer Plennydd was so remote as
to be hardly imaginable, but a king disliked and distrusted
by his subjects was a king who could not maintain the
well-being of his nation. If Herla rode away now the elves

would still be here, and their magic would be as strong as ever, and their ability to corrupt the realm might hardly be diminished at all.

'This marriage is unnatural,' said Herla steadfastly, 'And it cannot be permitted. I can justify my actions to my people, and they must support me. I am defending the Code, not breaking it, and I am prepared to argue that case here and elsewhere.'

'When first I heard the terms of your ten instructions,' said Kerewan, with an exaggerated sigh, 'I deemed them badly framed, for I could see all too easily how men might disagree about their application. You are the king, of course, and the highest judge among your own people – but I dare say that kings in Morien who use their position unjustly are hated as tyrants, like bad kings everywhere. But there is a way, is there not, of settling such disputes more honourably? Your customs permit that disagreements of this kind be subjected to trial by combat, and your men are carrying weapons of an adequate sort.'

Trystan drew in his breath sharply as he realized what Kerewan meant to do – and realized also what Herla's reply would be. Every human here had seen Sir Moraint narrowly bested at the fencing by the elf Seremond, and every human knew that Herla was a better swordsman than his friend – and that the elves could not know it. But no one among the humans could possibly know whether Seremond was the best of the elven swordsmen or the least.

It made no difference to Herla – that much was obvious. He leapt into the trap with alacrity.

'You would agree to such a trial?' he asked swiftly. 'One man against one, with the result to bind all – and the trial to be fought with light swords like the ones we are wearing?'

'We would,' said Thoron, equally eager. 'Should your man win, I will surrender all claim on the girl, and you may take her away with our consent. Should your man lose, the rest of you will be free to leave with honour, but the girl must stay.'

'No,' said Herla resolutely. 'I demand more than that. Should my man win, I will take the girl away – and then I will send messengers to Gwron, to buy a ship, which I will present to you as soon as I can take delivery of it. You will take that ship and sail away, never to return to the shores of Morien.'

Kerewan was evidently startled by this extra condition, but did not react angrily to it. 'We have always said that we would leave when we could,' he replied. 'We are sorry that you should treat us as enemies, when we have done everything within our power to be friends, but we will agree to that – nor do we make any extra demands of our own. If you win, you are free to ride away from here with the girl.'

Trystan knew immediately that there was some covert malevolence concealed within this promise, but Herla saw only that the elves seemed perfectly confident of victory.

'I agree,' he said. 'Name your champion.'

'I am the aggrieved party,' said Thoron lightly. 'Among the elves, it is not customary for one man to ask another to fight for him. I will fight your man, whoever he may be.'

The captain said it so negligently that Trystan wondered whether the elf might have made an honest mistake. He was clearly challenging the king to match him, and it seemed probable that he did not know that Herla would have nominated himself in any case. Was Thoron assuming, wrongly, that Herla must inevitably be a poorer swordsman than Moraint?

'I am the man,' replied Herla, drawing his own sword and unbuckling its ornamental scabbard so that it would not get in his way. 'If you will have someone take away that infernal harp and make a space for us, we may begin.'

CHAPTER FIFTEEN

WHILE THE HARP was being moved Trystan went to the lady Melicent, and took her by the shoulders to reassure her that all might yet be well.

She was looking at her father in frank dismay, while he – well aware that he had abandoned her – was staring blankly at the littered table.

'Courage, my lady,' whispered Trystan gently. 'The elf thinks that he is invincible, but Herla has right on his side, and if the gods do indeed consent to take a hand in such trials as these, he will surely win.'

'That depends,' said Kerewan disdainfully, 'on which gods deign to take an interest, and which is stronger among them. But you should hope that Thoron will be victorious, my lady, for he will be a better husband to you than any man of your own race ever could be. You have been offered a rare honour, and your father is wiser than you think.'

Melicent turned away from this assault to bury her head in Trystan's shoulder.

'Do not mind him, lady,' said Trystan softly. 'He is annoyed because I played better than he thought possible, and now he is anxious lest he has mistaken Herla too.'

'My annoyance can be compensated,' answered Kerewan. 'But you too should hope that your friend fails, Trystan Harper, for you do not know what the consequences might be of his winning.'

'I know that you will be thwarted,' Trystan replied.

'You must not mind *us*,' Kerewan told him. 'It is for yourselves that you must be concerned. Do you really think that a man can triumph by betraying the true desires of his own heart? Do you think that the music of the storm which you conjured up in order that you might turn its strength to your advantage can be so easily put away again? When you come to face that storm, sir bard, remember that it was you who called it, not I. When you discover how you have hurt yourself by self-denial, you will regret that you were so miserly with your own soul that you would not let it taste fulfilment. The Code which you seek to uphold is flawed, as all Codes are flawed which try to subdue the desires of the heart.

'Do you imagine that there ever was or could be a land of human beings where the laws were so just and good that they would never be broken? Do you imagine that there ever was or could be a human nation where all men worshipped at the shrine of righteousness? I am a better friend than you know, Trystan Harper, and I will trust you with a great truth which is known only to a few of the wisest creatures on earth: *We make our own gods*. Whatever gods are made by reason, justice and liberty, and whatever authority they claim, there are gods made also by those fierce desires of the heart which care nothing at all for reason, justice or liberty, but only for joy and fulfilment and the slavery of sensuality.

'Those are the gods to whom all must turn in the end: the god of luxury and the god of wrath, the god of change and the god of decay. Men, elves, dwarfs and monsters alike must turn to them – the arrogance of some and the stupidity of others can make no difference at the last. There is desire, and there is denial of desire, but there is no fulfilment save for passion. You cannot win, sir bard, whatever your king may contrive to do with his prickly sword.'

There was no time for an answer, even if Trystan could have shaped one. Herla and Thoron had touched blades, and their duel was begun.

Like Moraint and Seremond on the earlier occasion, the two combatants began carefully. Each wanted to measure the other, neither to commit himself. Their blades flicked out teasingly in strokes which were more flourish than thrust – they challenged one another to react, to mimic, to parry.

The blades touched a dozen times in the space of a minute, but the contacts were light, producing tiny clicking sounds like those a man might make when indicating displeasure with small clucks of his tongue. Herla took two paces back, then came one forward. The shift from their starting positions meant nothing in terms of real advantage.

Thoron made the first true thrust, feinting with a small false movement of shoulder and arm before changing his balance and trying to flash his blade beneath the defensive stroke which Herla was preparing – but the king was equally quick to change his move, and brought his blade down upon the other with alacrity, making a sharp ringing sound which echoed around the hall, informing all who were there that a true beginning had been made.

Then Herla attacked, moving lightly on his feet and trying to brush the other blade aside by a combination of grace and power. It was a bold move, given the advantage of reach and muscular strength which the elf had, but Herla's movements were very precise and skilful, and Thoron had to move hurriedly in order to evade the combination.

The elf captain stretched more effortlessly, taking care to position himself in such a way that he made full use of his reach – but his sword was not an inch longer than Herla's, and Herla made no attempt to imitate him, moving instead to be able to sweep more forcefully.

Seeing a chance to make a cut, Thoron whipped the point of his weapon through a labyrinthine sequence of threats and postures, then stabbed at Herla's forearm with the intention of pinking him. Herla's strategy was equal to the ploy, though, and the elf's blade was simply battered aside as soon as his arm was at full stretch, so that he had again to dance backwards out of harm's way.

Trystan saw that the captain moved very lithely; he had seen enough of the elves to know that he must have considerable powers of endurance too. Herla, who was more solidly built, would surely tire faster if the contest were protracted. It was difficult to think of any advantage at all which the king held, and which he might seek to exploit while he still had the power to take his turn in dictating the moves of the contest.

In fact, Herla seemed very patient, as though he were studying his opponent with meticulous care. He occasionally essayed a tentative combination of thrusts to test a particular hypothesis as to the other's reflexes and powers of response, but did not seem disturbed when his gambits came to naught. The expression on his face was one of total concentration, and though Trystan had seen it many times before while the king was sparring with Moraint he felt that he had never properly apprehended what intensity and determination there was in that stance.

Kerrmieryon, he thought. The pursuit of perfection. This is no mere exercise in the art of slaughter, but a test of what the human mind and eye can do, in combination with an iron blade.

There was a gasp then as Thoron attacked again – this time using a curious combination of wide thrusts which recalled the pirouetting of the elf dancers rather than anything which Trystan had ever seen in a fencing match. But Herla's reaction could not be faulted – it was as though he had known such a move was coming and was prepared for it. Wherever Thoron's blade was, there was Herla's, not merely to parry but to block it hard enough to jar the wrist which bore it. Strong and supple though Thoron's wrist was, it could be jolted like any other wrist, and made to ache.

Thoron's face flushed with annoyance, though Trystan could not tell whether it was because of the strain in his far-reaching arm or the total failure of his extraordinary ploy.

Thoron thrust again, more orthodoxly this time and more forcefully, trying to drive through Herla's stubborn defence. As Herla moved backwards he seemed for an instant to be unsteady on his feet, and Thoron redoubled his assault. Herla went further back, but there was no longer the ghost of a stumble in his retreating paces. When the attack ran out of ingenuity, and consequently faltered, Herla was ready with a clever riposte, which instantly turned the tables and had the elf back-pedalling, fearing to stumble.

They paused again, and stood still for a moment to breathe. There was nothing at all to separate them in the eyes of those who were trying to judge their chances. Thoron was as good as Seremond, and perhaps a little more daring – but Herla had his measure. It seemed that this was indeed a trial which lay in the lap of the gods to be decided – a contest which either man might win by virtue of some slight trick of fate.

Thoron came forward yet again, endeavouring to drive Herla back to the limit of the space allotted to the duel. But Herla was too wily to be trapped with no further retreat behind him; he turned away, then moved quickly inside Thoron's guard to engage him at close quarters. For the first time the combatants came within reach of one another, so that they might use their left hands if they could – and it was Herla who tried to do so as the two blades were briefly caught by their shaped guards, reaching out to grapple with Thoron's sword-arm. But Thoron was quick enough to respond in kind, and he had the longer and wirier arm. For a moment, all was confusion, and there was a violent collision of bodies – but which man had checked the other it was impossible to say.

Thoron recovered more quickly, and tried to take advantage by hurling himself into a wild attack, his feet and blade dancing in curious precision. Herla struck back, too boldly, and for a moment neither man had an adequate defence. Thoron took a cut across the cheek, while Herla was scored across the ribs – but both men retreated from the wounds as one, and came effortlessly apart again.

There were cheers from both sides, but Trystan knew that the cut which Herla had taken would extend pain to the muscles of his shoulder, and hence work to his direct disadvantage, while the cut on Thoron's cheek would only flood the corner of his mouth with blood.

Thoron knew it too, and tried to keep the blades high so as to test Herla's strength to the full. He tried a little too hard, for he gave Herla space to come in beneath a fancy flourish and cut at his leg, raising his own spare arm to block any downward slash. The downward slash came, and cut Herla's left forearm, but Herla contrived to dart the point of his own sword into Thoron's thigh, very close to the knee.

It was a light wound, but Trystan knew how vulnerable the knee of a man was to pain and to the convulsive seizure of the muscles; he could not believe that an elf was much different in that respect. So it proved; though Thoron did not immediately react to the cut at all, it only needed an instant's disruption caused by internal bleeding or delayed shock to make him falter. Herla was hurt in his turn, but the slender blade had rebounded from the bone, and Trystan judged that no significant muscle or ligament had been cut.

The two fighters paused again to breathe and count their losses, and it was Thoron again who broke the pause by unleashing a fierce attack. He drew now upon every reserve of his strength and skill; it was obvious that he was stretched to the utmost. Again Herla was driven back,

almost to the limit of the arena, and again he twisted and
turned in a desperate attempt to avoid being trapped.

The blades clashed fiercely, and Trystan could not have
been the only watcher who quite lost sight of them in the
melée. But then the fighters cut again at one another's
bodies, and again both strokes went home. Thoron was
touched on the upper part of his swordarm, but Herla
was struck again about the chest, this time nearer to the
shoulder.

Neither man wanted to rest now; with only the briefest
of pauses to recover his stance, Thoron attacked furiously,
certain that he could now beat Herla's defence despite his
own limp. But Herla would not yield, and every attacking
thrust was somehow met, until Thoron impatiently closed,
so that their bodies came crashing together again.

The impact could not have been intended by either man
– it was a collision rather than a check, misjudged by both.
But Thoron had his legs wide apart and braced, while the
king – who was shorter – had perforce to maintain a
straighter stance. In the confusion of the moment, as each
man sought to bring his sword into lethal play, Herla
could not quite step back as he had intended, and he
stumbled.

Thoron was quick to move forward to stand above his
opponent, trying to thrust him further down. Herla par-
ried desperately as he tried to recover his position, but for
an instant all was lost for the human and the elf seemed
certain to prevail. Then, when it seemed inevitable that
Herla must fall and sprawl, Thoron was forced by his own
efforts to throw all his weight on to the leg which had been
pricked, and the knee suddenly seized up.

The leg did not instantly collapse, as it might have, but
Thoron's sword-stroke was turned almost at a right-angle,
and for a moment his limbs seemed completely without
co-ordination.

Herla, almost down, put all his strength into one last
upward thrust, which went explosively home into the elf's
exposed breast. Although the blade did not go in very

deeply, it must have gone between the ribs and punctured the heart, for Thoron was never able to collect himself, or bring his sword back for a counterblow. His limbs jerked again, and then he fell on top of his opponent, driving Herla at last to the floor, where both men sprawled in most ungainly fashion.

But one was dead, and one was alive, and one only rose unsteadily to his feet, having rolled the other over and away.

King Herla of Plennydd raised his sword high, and claimed his victory. His knights cheered wildly – as wildly as might have been deserved, had the kingdom truly been saved.

HERLA WASTED NO time in gloating. He sent Moraint, Huw and Berwyn to see to the saddling of the horses. Then he came to where Trystan stood with the Lady Melicent, and took her to stand within the protection of his own arm. He recovered his scabbard and sheathed his sword, but paid no heed at all to the blood which seeped from his wounds to stain his shirt and surcoat. He did not look at Trystan or Kerewan, but turned instead to Godwin Conwy.

'Will you come with us, Sir Godwin?' he asked.

Godwin had ceased to tremble, but his face was more ashen than ever. He shook his head.

'That will not do, sir' said Herla sharply. 'I ask you again: will you come with us?'

Godwin drew his lips tight for a moment or two, and an ugly light flared within his eyes. 'No!' he said loudly. 'I cannot – I will not! Do you suppose that you have won? Poor fool, you could not win! Do you imagine that these are men like you and me? They are not – they are dae-mons! We were damned, one and all, the instant they set foot upon our soil. You do not know them, sire, or you would have listened more carefully to their words before you accepted their bargain.'

Herla could not quite contrive to remain impassive, though he was well nigh drained of all emotion. 'I made the bargain which I sought to make,' he answered defensively.

'Aye,' said Sir Godwin, lowering his eyes. 'But it was one they were glad to make.'

Trystan looked at Kerewan, who had not the slightest difficulty in retaining his own passivity. 'What does he mean?' asked the harper.

Kerewan shrugged his shoulders. 'I said the same to you myself,' he replied lazily. 'In winning, you have lost. My kinsman, Senduiuiel, doubtless learned that bitter lesson long ago – as you will also. The hour will soon come, Trystan Harper, when you will wish that you had taken what we had to give instead of refusing it. But we are elves, and we keep our bargains. We keep them very well. We will depart from this land as soon as we can – there are other tasks for us to accomplish, other places where we may prosper. You will never see us again in Morien.'

No one attempted to stop King Herla as he led his men from the hall, taking the Lady Melicent with him. The elves watched, but the expression in their dark unhuman eyes was unreadable.

Outside, it was still dark – but the sky was clear and star-lit, and Trystan judged that dawn would not be long in coming. As they mounted up, Kerewan came out behind them, carrying two oil-lanterns in his hands, each with a rod and hanger so that they might be carried. One he gave to Trystan, the other to Owain Dene.

'To light your way,' he said.

Herla might have refused the gift had either of the lamps been offered to him, but he was lifting the Lady Melicent into the saddle of one of the spare horses. Neither Trystan nor Sir Owain was too proud, and Owain moved promptly to take the lead, pausing only to ask: 'Which way? Do we take the maid to her own home?'

'Godwin's ringhold is no home to her now,' replied Herla. 'We can reach Dewi Lwys's house today, and rest there awhile. Then, if we ride hard, we might reach Caer Plennydd on the following day. Let us make haste to do it.'

And so they rode off. The two lanterns gave them light enough to find their way until the sun rose – and when it did both Trystan and Sir Owain were quick to throw them away. They rode as hard as they could, and did not stop at all, though their mounts quickly grew tired.

As they rode inland, they came into a region afflicted by a light fog which was slow to clear. They saw the sun for less than half an hour before it was hidden from them again. They had no difficulty in picking their way through the valleys; even where the mist was densest they could see for ten or fifteen yards – but they shivered with the cold. When they were able to ride along the ridges of the hills conditions were better, but still the mists were about and below them and the sun was no more than a pale yellow nimbus in the white vapour which hid the sky.

Owain Dene had led them unerringly while it was dark, and for a while the fog did not confuse him, but when noon had come and gone he became gradually more perplexed. Trystan and Emyr Siun rode forward to join him, and asked what was amiss.

'I do not know,' replied the old knight. 'I recognize the contours of the land well enough, and I think I know where we are – but does it not seem to you that we have somehow come out of season? It is not yet Samain, and yet the land has the hand of deep winter already upon it. Does not the grass seem to have withered since yesterday? Are not the trees barer than they were?'

Trystan remembered only too well that he too had stepped out of season while on his way from the elves' camp to Caer Plennydd, and he wondered whether Bavian might be about.

'Perhaps it is only the dreary mist which makes it seem so,' Emyr answered. 'I confess that I am confused myself, though I thought I knew this land well enough. It is familiar, after a fashion, and yet... wrong. I do not know why.'

They had come to the crest of a rise while they spoke, and were about to descend again into a rift where the fog was huddled. Owain stood in his stirrups while he tried to take a bearing before descending – and then he cursed in a startled fashion.

'Why,' he said, 'I must have missed my way after all, for there is a farmhouse down yonder, where no farmhouse ought to be! Can you see the smoke, and the chimney from which it comes?'

Trystan squinted, trying to make out what Owain was pointing at – and he saw, aided by a sudden swirl of the mist, that the old man was right.

'But that is not possible,' he said, in a low tone. 'However we had missed our way, we could not have come to such a place. Dewi's house is at least three hours away by my reckoning, and that is certainly not Godwin's ringhold. There is nothing bigger than a shepherd's cot for a dozen miles and more.'

They had reined in, and were quickly joined by their fellows.

'What house is that?' asked Sir Owain of Sir Emyr – but Emyr could only shake his head and say: 'There is no such house. I know this land, and there is no such house.'

'It could not have raised itself overnight,' said Herla impatiently. 'Even elves could not have done that. If you think it a mirage, let us ride down and see.'

So they rode down, with Herla now taking the lead and Emyr Siun beside him. The house remained as clear and solid as ever to their eyes – and when they had come within a furlong two men came out to watch them approach, the one carrying a pitchfork and the other an axe. They were father and son, to judge by their appearance. Both men eyed the riders with suspicion and distrust, despite the colours which the knights wore to show who they were.

'Who are you?' demanded the older man, when the knights brought their horses to a standstill. 'What do you want?'

'That is no way to speak to your king,' said Sir Emyr gruffly.

'King!' exclaimed the farmer, with an anxious laugh. 'There is no king in Morien!'

Emyr was angered by this impolite and unreasonable response, but Herla raised a hand to tell his loyal friend to be quiet.

'What do you mean?' he asked. 'There are three kings in Morien, are there not?'

'Nay,' said the farmer scornfully. 'We are free men here, who live by Agam's Code. What need have we of kings? The last of them was long gone before my great-grandfather was a babe. Have you come from some foreign land, to be shipwrecked on the isle's wild western shore?'

Again Emyr made as if to speak, but Herla silenced him with a gesture.

'This is surely the kingdom of Plennydd,' said the king mildly, 'And its monarch is Herla, is it not?'

The farmer shook his head. 'I know not where you heard that,' he said, 'but Plennydd was what the land was called long ago, and the king named Herla figures only in its legends. Someone has told you a nursery tale, my friend, and you have taken it for news. *There are no kings in Morien!*'

The words were insult enough, but the derisive tone of the last sentence was too much for Emyr Siun, who took no further heed of his king's gesture, and jumped to the ground with the obvious intention of punishing the man for his temerity.

But as soon as his boot touched the ground it seemed that his body turned to shadow, and within the blink of an eye he was gone as completely as if he had never been.

The farmer and his son let out a cry of terror and dismay, and the older man dropped the pitchfork. The knights were not one whit less alarmed, and even their horses had taken fright. Of Emyr Siun there was not a trace; in the space of an instant he had ceased to be.

'Ghosts!' cried the farmer's son. 'Father, they are ghosts come from the mists to haunt us!' He grabbed his father by the arm, and pulled him backwards towards the house.

Trystan stared dumbly at the spot where Emyr had been. The knight's riderless horse whinnied and tossed its head, and might have bolted had not Moraint Heilyn taken hold of its rein.

Ghosts! The word echoed in the harper's mind, as he knew it must be echoing in Herla's.

'We are enchanted!' said Moraint, more wrathfully than fearfully. 'The elves have cursed us. They have not kept their word!'

Herla turned to look at him, strangely unalarmed, and said: 'Alas, they have! They promised us that we should be allowed to ride away, without hindrance. They did not say where we might or might not ride to. That is what Godwin meant when he said that I had not won.' He looked back again at the farmer and his son, who were still hesitating in the doorway. 'I am sorry, good sirs,' he said. 'I know not whether I am the ghost, or you, but you are right to say that we do not belong here, and we must go.'

'Where?' asked Moraint sharply. 'Where must we go? Where *can* we go?' While he spoke he was looking at the treacherous earth which had swallowed up his fellow knight.

Herla looked at the ground too, and then at Lady Melicent, who was uncomfortable in her saddle. 'Do not step down, my lady,' he said. 'Whatever else you do, do not step down.' Then he looked at the other knights, to tell them that the warning was meant for all of them; but they had seen what had happened to Sir Emyr, and there was none who was anxious to risk the same fate for the sake of an experiment.

Melicent Conwy looked back at her king and saviour gravely, and nodded. Trystan thought that she seemed no more fearful than any of her companions, perhaps because she trusted the king better than the rest. Herla had delivered her from an earlier bewitchment, and from Thoron; she read his composure now as an indication that he could and would deliver her from this new and mysterious plight.

Trystan read the king's mood rather differently: the man was simply too numb to display any further shock.

'We are lost,' whispered Owain Dene sadly. 'If we are not dreaming, we are lost. Tell me, sir bard, is this a dream?'

'It is a dream of sorts,' Trystan assured him. 'But I fear that it may be a deadly one.'

'Where?' demanded Moraint, for the second time. 'Where can we go?'

'To Caer Plennydd,' answered Herla emptily. 'We must ride to Caer Plennydd, to see what has become of my castle and my kingdom.'

CHAPTER SIXTEEN

CAER PLENNYDD WAS in ruins. The town which had surrounded it was derelict and deserted. The inner wall of the fortress still stood, but its battlements were broken and its towers crumbling. The outer wall was breached in a dozen places, no more than a tenth of it retaining the height which it had had when Herla and his knights rode away. The gates through which they had ridden were heaps of rubble now, but they had no trouble finding a way through to the inner precincts.

The only inhabitants of the citadel which congregated there by day were sparrows and jackdaws; no one sought shelter among the buildings. Whatever had been here to be looted had been carried away long ago, and the fact that no one lived here now could only mean that the place was considered unlucky or accursed.

'Was it haunted, do you think, before we came?' asked Trystan bitterly.

It was not the first time he had spoken to Herla since the episode at the farmhouse, but on the previous occasions

Herla had looked away. Now the king looked the harper in the eye, and answered him: 'Perhaps we are visible to the people we left behind here, though we have been snatched out of their time. Perhaps our image echoes back through the years and the centuries. Perhaps…'

But there were too many fancies which might be proposed; nothing now was impossible to conceive.

'What now?' asked Meilir Larne. He spoke as one who had grown accustomed to hopelessness. They had been riding for many hours, but darkness had not fallen. Grey clouds obscured the sun, but they did not need to see it to know that – for them – it did not move at its natural pace.

Herla did not answer.

Trystan surveyed the wasteland of stone and slate. For a minute or two he thought that nothing grew here at all, but then he saw the tips of tree-branches above the topmost stones of a half-fallen tower. He walked his horse around the tower, and saw with a shock of alarm what the branches were.

The tree was vaster than any he had ever seen. Its trunk and bare boughs were extravagantly twisted into ugly shapes. Nothing else grew in this place, but the tree had thrived; its roots ran in every direction, projecting above the surface for twenty or thirty yards. Though bare of leaves its huge crown did not seem lifeless, for its branches moved in slow and sinuous fashion. It seemed to know that Trystan was near. The harper had no doubt that the tree stood alone because its presence had poisoned the ground against all other life.

It was the tree which had sprouted from that seed which Thoron's elves had caused to grow in Herla's kingdom: the tree of confusion.

Trystan was about to call out to the others when a sudden wave of dizziness struck him. The tree burst explosively into leaf while the harper was forced to shade his eyes against a deluge of bright sunlight. Within two seconds the sky above him was turned from grey to deep blue, with the sun at its summer zenith. The tree was now a gargantuan blaze of unearthly green, and among the myriad leaves were countless pendulous fruits, pink and luscious like monstrous peaches.

The branches moved like lazy snakes, but they seemed incurious now, and less threatening.

'I did warn thee, Trystan Harper,' said the man who was standing beside the gnarled trunk. 'I did warn thee, but I could not prevent any part of it.'

'Nightmare and vision,' said Trystan, remembering. 'A balance to be found. I thought I understood, when I sat by the harp, what was required of me. Now, I find that it was all in vain.'

'Do not say so,' answered the magician sharply. 'You did well, when you played the harp. You did well to resist their spell of temptation, and you made me proud to be the father of your kind. But Chaos is not so easily thwarted or thrown back. There is a battle yet to be fought, more terrible than that trial which Herla contested in the elves' hall – *but it can and must be fought.*'

'I have had enough of riddles,' sighed Trystan. 'Will you tell me plainly – is there a way back to the world which we left? Can we return to our own time and place?'

'Aye,' said Bavian, in a way which was less promising than Trystan might have wished. 'There is a way back – but it must be found, and won.'

'I'll wager that you will not tell me how,' retorted Trystan churlishly. 'Or you'll put it so subtly that I cannot hope to unravel it in time, but will see well enough when I have failed what I should have done?'

'The future is yet to be made,' Bavian told him. 'I cannot say what it will be, or how it will be forged. But I can and will say this: Agam's Code is not flawless, but it is a better guide to action than any I know. Do right, and do it bravely.'

'Is it safe to dismount now?' asked Trystan sourly. 'Can you tell me that, at least?'

'No,' replied the other sharply. 'You must know by now that there is no need. While you are outside time your hunger will not increase, nor your thirst, nor any other of your needs save the need to sustain your courage and your hope. For the horses, it is the same. In the trial which is coming you must ride, and ride as you have never ridden before. Only when the sun rises again will it be safe to dismount. I fear that the dawn will be a long time coming, but it will come, Trystan Harper, that I promise!'

'You seem uncommonly comfortable beneath the canopy of that evil tree,' said Trystan suspiciously. 'The tree of confusion shelters you as if you were a friend.'

'I too am outside time,' said Bavian, with a sigh. 'Such life as I have brings me closer to the tree than I might desire, but it is the life which I chose. I will admit, if you insist, that I am a creature of Chaos, with the daemon-taint about me – but Chaos is not itself evil, no matter what evil consequences may flow from its intrusions into human affairs. If there are powers in the Realms of Chaos whose pleasure it is to torment and trouble humankind we must bear at least a part of their guilt ourselves.'

'We make our own gods,' said Trystan. 'That is what Kerewan told me. Is it true?'

'I do not know,' said Bavian. 'But this I know and know full well – we choose the gods which we worship and the daemons which are hungry to bargain for our souls. We do not make the wind which blasts us, or the snow which chills us, or the winter which follows in the footsteps of every summer, but we must choose whether we will suffer these things nobly or not. The dark elves are defeated, Trystan – what remains to be seen is whether you can defeat the forces which you harnessed and used in defeating them. I will help you if I can, but you will have to find a way to free me in order that I might do it. I am a man and not a god, but I have power here, if only I have the chance to use it. Those against whom we must contend are more daemon than man – *but they can be defeated*, and their dark master too. The gods themselves have neither omnipotence nor omniscience to help them shape the destiny of the world.'

As the words faded, so did the leaves upon the tree. By the time that Herla rode up to stand beside his bard the branches were bare again, and there was no one beside the twisted trunk.

'What is it?' asked the king, looking up at the leafless crown of the monstrous growth. He was alone – the other knights were out of sight, for the moment.

'The seed which the elves planted,' answered Trystan.

'We should never have set it in the soil,' said Herla bitterly. 'Or else we should have destroyed it when first it showed a shoot.'

'Perhaps,' said the harper. 'But the confusion was already in our hearts and in our souls, and would have found its expression anyway. The elves did not bring confusion to Plennydd – they merely helped it to flourish and bear fruit.'

'Meilir asks *what now?*' said the king. 'He speaks for all, and I have no answer to give him. Have you an answer, my good and faithful friend?'

'I am your faithful friend,' replied Trystan. 'I think you know that, in your heart. No matter how strong my love for your wife became, I would never have broken the Code. I regret now that I did not confess my feelings to you at the very beginning, and ask for your help – but I was greatly disturbed by that which blossomed in my soul, and so in her turn was Morgana. But I am no Codebreaker, and nor is she.'

Herla looked at him angrily for an instant, but the anger faded quickly now that the matter had been declared aloud. 'I never doubted it,' he said eventually. 'I only envied you, because you had what should have been mine: love in your heart for the queen, and the queen's love in return. It is myself I despise, not you.'

'There is no need for that,' said Trystan. 'And though I have no proper answer to Meilir's question, I can say this: it is not over. Cursed we are, but we need not step down into oblivion as Emyr did. There is hope for us all, if we can only weather the storm which is coming.'

Herla looked up at the cloud-filled sky, and lifted a bare hand to feel the pace of the gathering wind. 'Yes,' he said, 'there is a storm coming. It will be a bad one, I think – it is coming from the north, and may bring snow.'

What he left unsaid was the more important part of what he meant. Trystan knew it too.

'Whenever the huntsmen ride on the wind of doom,' he murmured, 'hope may also soar to heights unknown.'

Herla smiled wryly. 'When we were boys together, playing in the wintry wood, did we not wish that one day we might see the Storm Hunt ride by?'

'Aye,' said Trystan. 'That we did.'

HERLA AND TRYSTAN rode back to the company of knights. Trystan told them that he had seen Bavian – not for the first time – and that the father of the bardic order had promised that they were not yet lost. They were by no means content with this, and demanded a fuller account; but when he gave it they were impatient with the mystery of it all and suspicious of its import.

'What does it mean?' demanded Berwyn Aglavin.

'It means,' said Owain Dene sadly, 'that our harper has been dreaming.'

No one else said anything aloud to agree with this judgement, but Trystan saw by the way that Sir Berwyn and Sir Moraint looked away from him that they could not and did not trust his word. It was the Lady Melicent who sprang to the bard's defence, saying: 'Were it not for Trystan we should never have escaped from the house of the elves.'

This did no good. The lady was only a lady, and unwed – and thus had no voice in a company of noblemen; and there were evidently those among the knights who wondered whether they might not have done far better to conserve that comfortable intoxication from which they had been startled by Trystan's music. Now that they were ghosts, condemned to ride through a bleak and alien wilderness, their resistance to the seductions of the elves had come to seem foolish.

Then the king spoke. 'We have no other hope. Trystan says that there is a way back to the world we have lost, and we must believe him. If we have Bavian's help too, so much the better – but if we have not, still we must do what we can, and hope that dawn will bring a new day.'

This speech should have had an effect on the knights far more profound than the lady's, because of its reasoning as well as its source, but as Trystan looked around he saw that the king's authority was no longer strong enough to compel belief.

'No doubt you are right,' said Meilir Larne, in a tone which implied that he had doubts enough, 'but I say again, sire, to you and to your bard: what now?'

Trystan did not know how to answer, but it seemed that neither he nor the king would have to, for the sky was growing darker by the minute and the wind was beginning to howl about the jutting points of the shattered walls and towers, frightening the birds into hiding. In the north, darkness was gathering – darkness made of clouds and shadows.

Lady Melicent's face was stricken with terror, but she did not scream. Instead, she took a tighter rein upon her horse and looked directly at Trystan, as if to say that she trusted him, and would follow him wherever he decided to go.

'Mother of All,' whispered Owain Dene, staring into the fast-approaching mass of seething cloud and shadow. 'It is the Storm Hunt, come to claim our souls!'

'Ride away from the buildings!' cried Herla, forced to shout in order to be heard above the keening wind. 'Go down the hill and into the vale, where there is shelter. Ride with all your might, and pray for the dawn to come – and whatever else you do, *never dismount!*'

Trystan reached across and caught the bridle of the Lady Melicent's horse, intending to draw it close to his own so that he might guide it – but she shook her head, and he released it again. He nodded and began to pick his way through the ruins, going towards the forests of mid-Lorien, which had been the hunting-grounds of the kings of

Plennydd since time immemorial. She followed him, while the rest of the company fanned out.

As soon as they were clear of the precincts of the ruined castle they spurred their horses into a gallop and fled south-eastwards as fast as they could go.

As they went, Trystan looked away to his left, and saw the racing shadows which rode upon the clouds take on form and substance, until they had assumed the shapes of a host of ghostly riders, eighty or a hundred strong, bearing spears and bows. Their helmets – all but a few – were decked with spreading antlers, and their surcoats were all black as night, with not a hint of colour about them. He heard several cries as the others caught sight of them, and more than one of his companions veered away as if to flee directly southwards – but then Herla turned the other way, and reined in to await their coming.

Trystan had no doubt that the king intended his followers to run on, while he faced the oncoming host alone; but when the others saw Herla turn, they turned too. No matter how they mistrusted the king, they would not flee while he stood his ground. Trystan reined in, and so did the Lady Melicent; the bard did not try to send her on, because he understood only too well how terrible it might be were she to find herself alone in this dreadful night.

The knights brought their mounts back, and positioned them as though to form a ragged battle-line. The horses neighed and tossed their heads, because they did not like to have the fierce wind in their faces, but they yielded to the commands of their riders.

For half a minute Trystan thought that the Storm Huntsmen might actually ride them down – and, indeed, that the force of the wind was so powerful that they could not refrain from so doing – but as the host approached its leaders slowed in their tempestuous paces, and began to form their own lines, three or four deep.

Trystan half-expected to see Bavian among the ranks, but the magician was not there; these men were of a different breed – warriors all. Some had pale and ragged beards as thick as Bavian's, but most were clean-shaven. Almost all were leaner men than the father of the bards, and their sunken eyes were lost in shadows; these men had long since quit the land of the living. Many bore the scars of battle, which showed up lividly white against their grey flesh, as if they were shining with starry light. Some of their horses were enormous, lending credence to the myth which said that the Storm Huntsmen always claimed the souls of the best of Morien's warhorses, but the rest were lean coursers, black as night or white as mist.

When they had stopped, as high on the hill as Herla's smaller company, one pale horse came forward. Its rider was by no means the tallest or the broadest of his crew, and he carried no weapon other than a spear, which he held high as though it were a flag. He was one of the few whose helmet had no antlers.

'Hail to thee, dutiful Herla!' he called, when he paused some twenty yards away. His voice was no more than a sigh upon the wind, but the words were clear. 'We thank thee for bringing so many bold men to our ranks, and we promise each and every one a royal welcome.'

'Have you come to claim us then?' called Herla, in his turn. 'Is that the fate to which the elves have sought to condemn us?'

'Thine own generosity brought thee,' replied the herald of the Storm Hunt. 'Thou hast brought thy company out of time, to serve our loving master and join with us in all the hectic passion of the hunt. Come with us now, and ride o'er land and sea, to hunt those phantoms of the mists and clouds which Chaos makes for our pleasure and our prey. Come with us, and praise the happy fortune which has made thee one with us!'

'We are not here by choice,' shouted Herla, 'nor by any chance which we could deem fortunate. I know you now, huntsman, and I know why your master has condescended to play with me, but I say now as I said before when you asked me for the antlers of that deer that was mine by right – I have the law with me. We have been cast out of time, but may yet return to it, and to the kingdom which we left behind.'

It seemed then that many of the huntsmen laughed, but it may only have been some trick of the wild and zestful wind. Trystan saw the knights exchanging puzzled glances, and wondered with them exactly when and how Herla had encountered this hornless huntsman before.

'Poor fool,' replied the herald, 'there is no way back to time. Has none of thy company tried to set foot upon the earth? Hast thou not seen that thou art one with the phantoms of the wind? If thou dost not ride with us, there is one fate only to which thou canst be brought – to become smoke and shadow, and vanish into nothingness. Step down, King Herla, if that is what thou seekest – if not, come with us, and be a creature of eternity. Earn a fine pair of antlers, and be a joyous member of the Storm Hunt forever.'

Trystan wondered how much of a temptation this might be to a king who loved the hunt more than anything else in the world, and had only the word of a harper that there was any alternative to be found.

'I will not step down,' replied King Herla, 'nor will I join with you. I have my own path to find.'

This time, there was no possibility of error. There was laughter among the huntsmen – callous laughter, which held a curious thrill of anticipation.

'There is no other path,' the messenger replied. 'For thou art in our world now, where those who are not huntsmen must be prey. If thou wilt not unite with us, we are bound to pursue thee, and to cast thee down. All thy men must know that we are the Storm Warriors of Slaanesh, from whom there is no escape.'

Herla turned to look at his men, who were perturbed by what was happening. Suddenly a voice could be heard from the company of huntsmen, crying: 'Owain of Dene, I am blood of thy blood, and bore thy name a thousand years ago. Come join me, man, for there is nothing else to do. Be a Storm Warrior, I beg of thee, else I must weep to see thee die!'

There followed a cacophony of other cries, which made poor Trystan flinch – but when he looked around he seemed to be the only one who was deafened. He alone could hear the entire profusion of voices. Each of his companions was bolt upright in his seat, hearing only the voice of one who was – or claimed to be – his kinsman.

Trystan tried to cry out, to say that this was temptation and must not be trusted, but the wind caught hold of his words as they were formed, and snatched them away into the raging storm where they could not be heard.

Another unhorned rider came forward from the ranks of the Hunt, and Trystan recognized the face of Emyr Siun, unnaturally pale but otherwise unaltered.

'For me,' cried the phantom of Sir Emyr, when he drew level with the messenger, 'there has a been a reprieve. Because I knew not what I did when I stepped down from my horse, I have been taken in by the Storm Warriors. But they have commanded me to say that no such mercy can be extended to another, now that you know what you are and what destiny awaits you. I beg you, my friends, to join us. Ride with the Storm Hunt and not with the hunted! Be warriors now and forever, or be quarry tonight and dust thereafter!'

Trystan tried to shout out that this was a trick, and that the man who wore Emyr's face and spoke with Emyr's voice was not Emyr at all, but his own doubt combined with the wind to ensure that no sound was heard by any other.

'Who rides?' cried the messenger, raising his spear higher. 'Who rides with the Hunt to glory?'

Meilir Larne was the first to answer, and to quit the line which had formed beside Herla. Then Owain Dene went after him. But Berwyn Aglavin, Moraint Heilyn and Huw Peredur stood still, looking at one another, and then at their king.

Then Berwyn Aglavin shook his head wearily, and rode away across the hillside, without a backward glance.

But Moraint Heilyn's lips formed the words: 'I will not!'
– though the wind would not allow them to be heard.

Huw Peredur's horse pranced as though to measure the
progress of his indecision – but in the end, Huw bade it be
still. He, too, tried to call out an answer, but whatever he
said was lost in the triumphant howling of the storm.

When Herla saw that three of his men had gone, and
that the other two were fearful in their hesitation, his own
face clouded over with dreadful doubt, and he turned to
Trystan as if to ask what point there was in refusing to go.
Trystan shook his head, but he could see as he did so that
mere stubbornness was not enough.

Herla turned again to the messenger, who stood alone
now, because Emyr – or his simulacrum – was riding back
to the ranks with those who had so far been seduced.
'What of the lady?' demanded the king. 'Must she also join
the Hunt?'

'Nay,' called the messenger. 'There is no place here for
such as she, and she is pledged to our master. Cast her
down, good Herla, or let her loose – we will not harm her,
but she must find her own fate.'

Trystan wondered whether the three knights would have
ridden away to join their pretended ancestors had they
known of this – but they had not waited to hear the question put, and probably did not care. But Huw Peredur still
stood firmly by his king, and Moraint Heilyn too; and
Trystan knew that Herla could not and would not go. The
king had fought once to save the girl, and had pledged his
life for her safety. He could not abandon her.

'I will find my own path,' called Herla. 'I free those who
remain here from any bond of fealty which they owe me,
so that they may choose as they will – but I will not join
the Hunt.'

The herald laughed, and said: 'Then we will have bold
prey to pursue, and all the more pleasure in its capture. But
what sayest thou, Sir Huw of Peredur? Wouldst thou be
hunter or hunted? And what of thee, Sir Moraint? I give
fair warning – I cannot ask again!'

Trystan noted that his own name had not been called. He, like the Lady Melicent, was not included in this invitation. He would not have accepted, but the knowledge that he must be the Storm Hunt's prey no matter what sent a stab of bitter anger through his gut.

'I think not,' replied Huw Peredur, with affected disdain. 'In my heart of hearts, I have never loved the hunt as much as honour.'

'Nor I,' said Moraint, seemingly pleased to borrow a little of the other's boldness. 'And I would not care to hunt my dearest friend and noblest lord.'

'All who will not become one with us must run before us,' said the messenger ominously – but he paused for just a moment more before he lowered his spear. There seemed to be a genuine reluctance in his manner when he finally said: 'So be it.' He turned his horse, and rode away, but looked back over his shoulder as he went, and shouted: 'In that case, Herla the Deposed, begone – for thou mayst expect no mercy now!'

The host of the Storm Hunt, greater now than it had been before, surged forward. Herla and his four companions turned their mounts to the south, and spurred them to the gallop without delay.

CHAPTER SEVENTEEN

THE INVITATION WHICH had been offered to Herla had
seemed for a moment to be tempting – more tempting by
far than any of the cruder inducements which had been
tacitly offered at the elves' banquet. It promised him an
infinite extension of a kind of paradise – a veritable warrior's heaven, all hard riding, furious pursuit and
bloodlust – and the fact that it was offered to him by the
same dark god to which the elves had sold themselves
was not important. But he could not yield to the huntsmen's entreaties because he was not, in spite of the way
he had been tricked into the dark god's game, an ungenerous man.

What he did now he did for another – for Melicent,
daughter of Godwin Conwy. His sense of obligation to her
was not lessened by the fact that she was no more to him
than a technical ward. He did not love her, he was not married to her, and he had hardly spared her a glance in all the
time that he had known her father, but he felt that her fate
now rested on his shoulders.

And so he refused to be a Storm Warrior, and elected instead to be the Storm Hunt's prey.

As the five fugitive riders turned away from their adversaries the glowering clouds began to discharge great quantities of snow, whose huge flakes fell fast and dense. The snow was instantly whipped into a blizzard by the howling wind, swirling madly about the riders in such a way as to rob them of all sight of the landscape and of one another.

Within seconds Herla found himself cut off, and though he shouted an instruction to Trystan to keep close to the Lady Melicent he could not hear any reply. The possibility that he might become separated from his companions did not unduly distress him, though, for he was sure that the Storm Warriors would deem a king's soul a very precious trophy. If he could draw the Hunt away from his companions, that might be the best chance they had to survive the night.

He was worried at first in case his unsighted horse might stumble and send him to the ground, condemning him to ignominious vanishment, but he soon realized that whatever magic had transformed the fabric of his own person had wrought an equally wondrous transformation in the flesh of his mount. The black stallion ran as he had never run before, as though sharing his master's exhilaration in the moment, and though Herla could hear the sound of his hooves striking ground of some kind he was certain that this was no ordinary course of rutted roads and creviced hilltops. He could easily have believed as they galloped into the blizzard that he was outside space as well as outside time, in some uncoloured realm where there were no mountains and no forests, nor any honest soil or sea, but only looming clouds forever threatening to take on shape and substance.

Behind him, the sound of the wind dissolved into the baying of a pack of dogs, the drumming hoofbeats of the Storm Warriors' horses, and the eerie trumpeting of their hunting horns. The sounds were much closer than he had anticipated, and it seemed that the pack was nearly at his heels. He drew his sword, and ducked lower in the saddle for fear of arrows – but no arrows came yet, for this was sport and not slaughter.

He felt rather than saw the presence of the first hound to draw level with him. The warmth of the beast's breath on his right leg was tangible before the ugly head reared out of the confusion of snow and shadow, and Herla was already cutting backwards with his weapon as the huge wide snout and the jutting teeth emerged from the gloom. The cut caught the beast in the eye, and brought a scream of pain which sounded more human than canine – and made Herla wonder whether all the human souls adopted by the Storm Hunt were privileged to serve as riders.

A second hellhound drew level on the left, where it could not be cut so easily. Herla did not try to reach across with his sword; instead he lashed out with his boot, trying to catch the dog's head with the spiked rowel of his spur – but his stirrup was too tightly-leathered to let the blow land, and the jerk upon it made the courser veer leftwards. The combination of movements defeated the dog's attempt to close its jaws on Herla's leg and it disappeared into the storm, perhaps caught by the stallion's hoof, but within seconds it was coming again.

This time Herla turned in the saddle – to the right rather than to the left – so that he could slash down over the horse's rump without his own arm getting in the way. It could only be a blind and hopeful cut, but he felt the tip of the blade collide with the hound's head, and heard again that harrowing scream.

Herla urged his mount on, but tried to use his spurs sparingly lest he should cut the horse. He succeeded in drawing a little way ahead of the hounds again, and then attempted to change direction, curving away to his right so that any dogs which caught up would be more likely to leap into the scope of his sword-arm. He was jerked up and down as the stallion leapt a ditch of some kind, and felt glad that the animal's night-vision was far better than his own.

For the first time, as he veered away, he saw the shadow of a rider nearby – and instead of trying to straighten his course so that he would draw away he exaggerated the turn to draw him closer. The huntsman had already seen him, but was handicapped by the heaviness of the ponderous spear which he carried. Herla had no difficulty in evading the clumsy probing of the spearhead, and was able to slash backwards with all his might, sending the edge of his sword horizontally into the huntsman's unprotected neck. Had the weapon been heavier the man would have been decapitated, but there was no need of any such spectacular achievement – the spearman fell backward in the saddle gouting blood from his wound.

That crimson was the first hint of colour which Herla had seen in this drear grey world.

The two horses collided shoulder-to-shoulder, but the huntsman's mount was a light one, and had been badly unbalanced by its rider's unwitting acrobatics. There was never any doubt as to which would come off worse. As soon as he had appeared the huntsman was gone again, and Herla wondered what happened to the undying when they were struck a mortal blow. Would the man be healed tonight, or must he be remade to ride again next time the howl of the north wind called the Storm Hunt forth?

The man he had struck down had been robbed of a throat with which to howl or scream, but Herla shouted with the triumph of it, crying defiance of the Storm Warriors who thought him easy prey. With every kill which he made – hound or huntsman alike – he seemed to grow in strength, and his mount too. Violence was the currency of this world outside time, though it was an artful kind of violence rather than a wrathful kind. This was sport, not war, and it had the rewards of sport along with all the luxuries which mere earthly hunting had to do without.

Herla saw a barrier looming ahead amid the dancing snowflakes, and instantly asked his mount for a prodigious leap – which the horse, having also seen the obstruction, was very ready to make. They soared together

into the air, and Herla felt his breath caught with the sheer
grandeur of the moment – and it seemed that they never
came to earth again beyond whatever wall of darkness they
had jumped, but continued to fly into the sky and ride the
clouds themselves as the Storm Warriors did.

Herla could still hear the baying of the pack and the
moaning of the horns, but as his mount surged ahead it
seemed that the sounds grew fainter and more feeble –
and he could easily have forgotten, then, who was supposed to be the quarry in this marvellous adventure.

FOR TRYSTAN, IT was utterly different. He did not need
Herla's shout to tell him to stay as close as he could to
Melicent's horse; the one thought in his mind was to guide
the lady out of the path of the approaching horde. As he
spurred his own horse to a gallop he tried to steer a diago-
nal course which would take him over the crown of the
hill; he felt sure that Sir Huw and Sir Moraint would rather
go down, and he knew that their best hope lay in splitting
up.

For a moment he thought that the huntsmen might stay
tightly together, intent on chasing down their prey one
man at a time, but as he came to the crest of the hill in a
gale of stinging snowflakes he knew that there were at least
a few riders coming directly after him. The two horses
seemed to be aware of what he was trying to do, and to
have every intention of co-operating, but he was nevertheless fearful that he might easily lose the lady in the swirling
snow. He called out to her to stay with him, and she called
back to him that she could do it.

At first, they were adrift in a maelstrom of confusion,
and all they could do was ride as hard as they could –
but the bard heard the thunderous hoofbeats of his pursuers drawing closer and closer, and knew that they
would be caught and overwhelmed within minutes
unless he could bring some kind of magic to bear. He
wished briefly that he had some other kind of magic
than his own – a kind of magic which could make war

by striking men down or blinding them, or a kind of magic which could control the violent air and swirling snow, or a kind of magic which could whisk them to some distant and happier place in the blinking of an eye. Such magics did exist, he knew, and had been mastered by the greatest of the great; but he was only Trystan Harper, not even a druid, and all the magic which he had was contained in music.

For a second or two he wished that he had a harp to play, but the sheer absurdity of the wish made him laugh at himself. The image of a man on horseback in such a storm as this, wrestling with a vast and unwieldy instrument while trying to woo the music of calm contentment from its strings was irresistibly funny. But then, in all seriousness, he remembered that he was not without instruments which had a kind of music in them.

The first source of all meaning in music, he reminded himself, was the rhythm of the heart; that was the beat which connected the sound of music to the emotions, uniting slowness with sadness and quickness with excitement. There was music in his body and his soul, and if he had the talent to draw upon that resource, there was potential for making magic.

Then again, he reasoned, there must be music in the storm, too – for how else could there be such a magical thing as the music of the storm? How could music come to signify – and thus to anticipate and influence – the many moods of nature unless the turbulence of wind and cloud had in it some intrinsic musicality and magicality?

Of all this he *knew* nothing, but the magic of music, like music itself, had more to do with feeling and inspiration than what could be written in books.

As the hoofbeats of his pursuers rose in volume Trystan suddenly ceased to hear them as hoofbeats at all, but heard them instead as racing kettledrums – and the howling of the wind became, *in truth*, the sound of some strange and barely imaginable instrument, its voice mere art and artifice.

Trystan made no attempt to *play* the storm as if he were playing the music of the storm upon the great harp. Control of such a power was far beyond his abilities. But he listened to the storm in a new way, searching its cacophony for hints of pattern, of structure, of composition. He searched, not for the music of all storms, but for the music of this particular storm – for its flourishes and momentary rhapsodies as well as its underlying rhythms, for its identity. And he found, as he did so, that he was growing to know and understand the storm – even that astonishing motif which was the Storm Hunt. He felt and understood its appalling exuberance, its amoral joy in its own phenomenal power, and the curious seductiveness of its uninhibited dancing.

This, he knew, was Chaos; here was that same insidious god which had filled his dreams with lewd caresses and taunted him with mockingly affectionate whispers. Despite that it was called Chaos, it was not without its own curious order, its own orientation; whatever raw and primal power underlay the storm had been channelled through the focusing art of some other power – the power of the god which some called Slaanesh – so that it was something very different, whose wildness was in part illusory.

He understood it, he knew, because there was a sense in which he had been familiar with this kind of music all his life. It reflected – or was a reflection of – what Bavian had called the 'blood-born storm': the storm in the human heart which was the source of reckless infatuation and the careless cruelty of the hunt. He had always known it, and though he had never learned to control and suppress it, he had learned how to live with it, how to escape from its worst excesses.

He could not yet strike out at those who were hunting him, but he could read the music of the storm well enough to navigate within the snow-sheeted gloom, to guide his flight and to evade those who were coming to destroy him.

He guided and spurred his mount, turning it this way and that as though threading his path through an invisible labyrinth, going up and going down. All the while, Lady Melicent and her brave horse kept pace with him, never flustered by the intricate cunning of his moves.

Sometimes the bare branches of trees brushed his head and shoulders; once or twice he heard splashing sounds as the two horses capered across a ford or along the course of a shallow brook. He even contrived to find occasional coverts where the snowflakes were not so densely clustered, and where the wind was shadowed and quiet – and by degrees, the drumbeats behind him became more distant and less certain, until their rhythm was entirely broken and they faded into inaudibility.

He dared not stop, lest the pursuers pick up his trail again, and he dared not hope that dawn might be near, but he began to believe that he had found the possibility which Bavian had promised him – the possibility of escape. He dared to believe that the Storm Warriors could not track him, or capture him, or steal his soul, and that he might win his contest against them.

HERLA, POSSESSED BY a fierce fervour for the sensation of flight, drove his mount upwards and onwards. The snow died away as he soared above the clouds from which it came, until at last he burst free of the clouds themselves and came into clear air again.

The snowless air was bitterly cold and sharp, and he felt a shock as it entered his lungs. The stars above him were abnormally luminous and unnaturally profuse, as though some barrier to their sight had been removed in order that he might look upon their true glory. The black stallion galloped on tirelessly, its hooves falling soundlessly on an uneven carpet of dark grey vapour which was somehow adequate to support it. This strange surface appeared infinite, and in its further reaches the gentle undulations became invisible to the naked eye, so that it seemed quite flat. The sound of the wind was gone now, and he rode on in silence.

Herla did not rein in at all, though he believed himself to be quite alone upon the plain of clouds. The necessity was still in him to drive himself to the limit, and so he went on at speed; but he sheathed his blood-stained sword and gave both hands to the reins.

He did not know, when first he saw it, how long the face of stars had been looking down at him.

Once he had accepted the incredible fact that the stars should have patterned their uncanny light in such a way as to form a beautiful face, it did not seem at all remarkable that the eyes of starfire should be looking directly at him, and studying him closely – for was he not the only visible entity in this featureless world-above-the-world? Nor did it seem particularly strange that the face should speak to him, with a voice redolent with music – for what would be the point in appearing to him thus if no such communication were intended?

'Herla, my beloved,' said the face, 'have you come to ask me for a better destiny than the Storm Hunt? Have you come to pledge fealty to me, and to appoint yourself my champion? I would be glad if it were so, for I think that you are one who might survive all trials and travails, to become a mighty daemon.'

Herla understood enough to know what it was he was being asked to do.

'I pledge fealty to no one,' he answered, 'for I am a king in my own land, and a hero, bound only by Agam's Code.'

'But I am a god,' replied the other, though his lips of starfire did not move at all, 'and even a king may bow down his knee to a god without shame. Many kings have pledged themselves to me, dear Herla, sometimes without their even being aware of it. It is not given to all to see my face, even in dreams. I can answer all your desires, my beloved, if you will only pledge yourself to me.'

'I could have done as much in Thoron's hall,' answered Herla, 'or when the Storm Warriors called on me to join them. Do you think that you can frighten me with a face of stars? Do you think you can make me feel so tiny that all ambition and pride will shrivel within me? Take on firm flesh, my friend, and come to meet me here on this great grey plain, with bow or sword in your hand, and I'll fight you like a man – but I will not fall down and worship you, even if you defeat me.'

As Herla spoke the god began to laugh, as if with genuine good humour at the boldness and temerity of the king – and as the face of stars dissolved, a wind sprang up between the stars themselves, which whipped their light into a coruscating cascade and stirred the plain of cloud into a mass of waves and vaporous surf.

From the roiling cloud, surging up from beneath, came a great host of warriors, not only behind and before King Herla but all around him, in a huge circle. Emerging within the circle, trapped as Herla was, were two other riders, whom he recognized instantly as Huw Peredur and Moraint Heilyn. Sir Huw was bloodied about the head, as though he had been struck by the flat of a sword, and Sir Moraint's leg was badly torn as though by the teeth of a great hound, yet both were still alive and in the saddle, and both had contrived to drive their mounts up into the stormy sky to reach this final battleground.

When they saw the predicament they were in, both knights reined in and turned their horses uncertainly. Huw's reared up and nearly threw him, but he controlled it and kept his balance.

'To me!' cried Herla. 'To me!'

While they came, Herla unslung the hunting-bow from his shoulder, thoughtlessly regretting for a moment that it was not the magic bow which Thoron had given him for a wedding-present. He drew an arrow from the quiver which hung from his saddle-horn. He sent the arrow flying at the nearest of the Storm Huntsmen, and saw it strike home in his breast – but that was taken by the huntsmen as a signal, for they took up their own bows and began to fit arrows to the strings.

Sir Huw and Sir Moraint formed up into a triangle with the king, and unslung their own weapons – but Herla did not need to see their eyes to know what dismay must be written upon their faces as they stared at the opposing ranks. There were at least a hundred men surrounding them, and in spite of the agitation of the clouds on which they rode there was no possible cover to shield them.

Moraint fired, and then Huw. Herla heard the twanging of their bowstrings though he could not see where the arrows went – but then the answer came, and the air was full of humming sounds. The three men at the centre of the circle ducked as best they could, but there were too many arrows and the range was too near. Huw Peredur was struck three times, and his horse twice; Huw screamed as they fell, and the scream died slowly as man and mount vanished into the cloud which no longer consented to contain them.

Moraint too was struck, but only in the upper arm, and the one shot which hit his horse grazed its withers but did not bring it down. Only Herla and the black stallion remained untouched, but both men knew that one more volley of arrows would be the end.

Herla realized, belatedly, what a fool he had been to allow the intoxication of the hunt to draw him up into the clouds, into the territory which belonged exclusively to the Storm Hunt. Down below, among the trees and the ravines, there might have been a chance to evade the huntsmen, but up here there was none. He had been a fool – and it made things worse rather than better to know that his two remaining friends had been similarly seduced by folly. They, too, had discovered that in their present state they could fly, and had not paused to wonder where flight would take them.

Moraint did not wait for the next volley of arrows. Throwing his bow aside, he drew his sword; holding it before him he charged full-tilt at the nearest point in the encircling rank of the huntsmen. They could have shot him down before he reached them, but they did not. Instead, one of the grey-faced huntsmen cried, 'Mine!' and rode to meet the boy, with a spear extended before him.

Herla watched, giddily, as the two figures converged –
and saw, agonizingly, that Moraint's face became suffused
with alarm before the meeting was contrived, and that the
youth actually snatched back his sword at the last
moment.

It would probably have made no difference, because the
spear was the longer weapon, and it was used to deadly
effect. Poor Moraint was spitted beneath the breastbone,
and the spear broke with the force of the impact, so that he
rode on – dead in the saddle – with the bloody point projecting from his back and the splintered end of the shaft
from his belly.

As the spearman followed through, Herla saw his face.
The eyes were sunken and shadowed, and the features
unnaturally thin, but Herla saw what Moraint must have
seen, and recognized the man. Once, he had been Berwyn
Aglavin, knight of Plennydd – now he had offered himself
to be the kind of fiend who could hunt his erstwhile friend
to death's door, and strike him down.

Had Herla fired another arrow then, he might have
achieved some petty vengeance against the traitor – but he
wondered again what good it could do to slay those who
had already died, and had become immortal after their
own dire fashion.

'I will fight any one of you!' he yelled. 'I will fight any
three, if they will come one after another like honourable
men in the lists!'

The huntsmen laughed to hear him, and the one who
had earlier been the herald of the Hunt called out: 'There
are no lists here, noble Herla, for this is no tourney. This is
the Storm Hunt and thou art the prey!'

'I am a man,' cried Herla, furiously. 'I claim my right as a
man, to face an honourable opponent, be he man or daemon or petty godling. I will bear any trial, but I will not be
butchered like a hog!'

But the huntsmen only went on laughing, and put up
their spears as though they were indeed about to stick a
wild boar; and then they charged.

CHAPTER EIGHTEEN

WHILE TRYSTAN LEARNED to listen to the music of the storm it became increasingly clear to him, and having long since eluded his pursuers he began to seek for a way which would take him out of the storm altogether – or, at least, to a part of the storm where its violence was greatly muted. This quest ultimately led him to a dark forest whose clustered boughs, though bare of leaves, kept the mist and snow at bay. It was very dark therein, but Trystan did not need his eyes in order to see, so closely attuned was he to the magical and musical patterns which were all around him.

As he rode through the forest, with Melicent still beside him, he felt as though his ghostly self were putting on new substance, undergoing some kind of miraculous metamorphosis as the power of the storm flooded his soul. He felt power building within him – the same power, no doubt, which formed the clouds into those huntsmen of the storm who styled themselves Storm Warriors. In Trystan, that power was turned to a higher ambition, and was gathered into some limitless inner store, filling and transforming him.

He too was a warrior of the storm, but no mere huntsman sat astride a steed of mist; he was a warrior magician, a master harper who could touch the strings of the world itself and take command of the rhythm of the spheres. That power of Chaos which *could* threaten disintegration and destruction could be turned to other work, if only its music could be learned and understood.

He did not realize immediately that the music of the storm was not the only music which he could sense now, for the storm's music was so vast and complicated that it swallowed up all other possibilities – but the deeper he went into the forest the more aware he became of a much subtler set of strains and melodies which were *not* part of the storm at all but something distinct – and more fundamental. It was, he guessed, the music of the land of Plennydd, which was itself but a tiny part of the music of the Mother of All Things.

He had been able to sense that music before, but only when he was seated at the great harp, exploring with the inquisitive voice of its strings. Now he sensed it directly, and knew that in coming into the forest he had brought himself as close as he might to the protective arms of the Mother, and to the fountainhead of all druidic magic.

Even here, Chaos could not be kept at bay, but at the interface of land and storm, where the realms of different gods touched and overlapped, there was the potential for a fusion of the power of Chaos with the power of the Motherland – which Trystan Harper might accomplish, if only he had the wit.

Once he was sure of what it was that he had to do, Trystan was able to concentrate upon it, and follow the labyrinthine patterns which were part and parcel of its composition, just as he had done with the music of the storm, whose master he already was. He understood well enough what he was doing to be unsurprised when the blue light of day began to pour through the forest canopy, and the dark trees around him began to turn vivid green as they burst into leaf.

This time, it was no mere image of Bavian which appeared; Trystan discovered instead the place into which that unlucky father of bards had been delivered by his own attempts to fuse the magic of Chaos with the magic of the Mother of All.

Here, as in the ruins of Caer Plennydd, Bavian kept close company with a monstrous tree – and like the tree of confusion which had grown in Herla's realm it had boughs which could move like snakes.

But this was a much cleverer tree, whose branches could reach out to seize a man and hold him captive, and send special shoots into his flesh to drink his blood. Bavian was its captive, and had been its captive while hundreds of years had passed in the world of time; it fed upon him without ever consuming him, as though he were a milch cow.

The bearded man hung in mid-air, entwined and tightly held by thousands of slender branches. His face was so strained that Trystan could not doubt the painfulness of his position – but when Trystan approached, the magician smiled.

The tree, which evidently did not like its victims to be cheerful, squeezed Bavian in its many arms and made him gasp in agony – but still he smiled, defiantly and indomitably.

'My son!' he said. 'Thou hast found me at last. Of all my sons, thou art the finest – the one in whom the music of the heart is both loud and sweet. One day, I knew, there would come to Morien a man who was capable of mastering the music of the storm, and though I know too well what it has cost thee to be that man, I am greatly glad to see thee now.'

'I do not know what I have done,' said Trystan, looking round to see whether the Lady Melicent was still with him. She was – and it was obvious that she too could see

Bavian's plight, for her expression was fearful and pitying in equal proportions.

'For the sake of Mother-love,' she whispered, 'cut him down.'

There was nothing which Trystan would have liked better to do, but he had no sword.

'How?' he said desperately.

Bavian gasped again as the cruel branches squeezed him, but still he would not be silent, would not be cowed. 'Blood of my blood,' he said, 'thou knowest how. The power which I sought is thine, and thine to wield as thou wilt.'

Trystan, hearing the music throbbing in his breast, knew that he had indeed the power to command and control this spawn of Chaos. He urged his horse forward, and reached out his naked hand. The tips of the branches recoiled from him, and turned into gaping snakes' heads which hissed fiercely as they spat venom at him.

The venom burned his hands, but only momentarily. Careless of its fangs, he grabbed one of the snake-headed boughs. Instantly, he was in touch with the entire tree – not merely its supernatural substance but the black and twisted soul which lurked in the heart of its wooden being. The music of that soul was harsh and savage and wounding, but the music of his own soul was stern and majestic and calming.

The two souls flowed together, and merged.

The tree was immediately changed, into a great and handsome oak – and Bavian was standing beside it, joyfully bathing in the rays of sunlight which shone through its gaudy crown.

'My son!' he said, again, in a voice thrilling with satisfaction. 'Blood of my blood, thou makest me proud to be the father of thy kind.'

The magician stepped forward then, reaching out to his deliverer, and Trystan reached down to take the proffered hand and clasp it as one ought to clasp the hand of a long-lost kinsman.

'The Truth,' said the first of the bards, 'against the World.'

'The Truth against the World,' echoed Trystan Harper.

'Are we saved?' asked the Lady Melicent plaintively. 'Is this the dawn which was promised? Are we delivered from evil?'

'Aye,' said Trystan, as his face darkened again with the memory of the Storm Hunt and the chase. 'Is it over? Is Herla safe?'

He knew as soon as he saw the expression in Bavian's eyes that it was not so simple.

'My lady,' said the magician, with a peculiar softness in his voice, 'we are most certainly safe. Though we are still outside time, the world which you lost is only a step away. But King Herla and his companions forsook the land unthinkingly, and were tempted into that vault of heaven which is the Storm Warriors' own. For them, there can be no way back, unless…'

'Unless what?' asked Trystan harshly.

'Unless you and I go up into that same realm, to try our best to save him. But if we do that, we forsake the aid which we have so far had from the music of the land – we will have only the music of the storm to work with, and to work within. I believe that we can defeat the Storm Warriors – though even that must be uncertain – but I am not sure that we can defeat the others which might borrow substance from the clouds. If we ride to Herla's aid, my son, we may lose all that we have gained, and Herla too.'

'Do you instruct me not to go?' asked Trystan bitterly, noticing that the magician had abandoned the intimate form of address and now called him 'you' instead of 'thou'.

Bavian shook his head. 'I have no right to instruct,' he said. 'You have released me, and I will follow you wherever you desire to go. I only seek to warn you that we cannot go to Herla without exposing ourselves to dreadful danger. I think that the god who sent this storm will be glad to have another opportunity to send you to your doom.'

'What must I do?' asked Trystan tersely. 'I will go alone, but you must advise me what to do, most noble founder of the bardic order.'

'You know already,' answered Bavian, with a sigh, 'for you have done it once already, in a slightly different fashion. Nor will I let you go alone – you and I, together, must take the music of the storm and remake it. We must turn the music against its maker, and turn its magic to our own end.'

'That is no answer,' said Trystan. 'I say, again, how? Do you have a harp here?'

'There are no harps here,' said the magician dourly. 'Only hearts and voices. We must sing, sir bard – but our voices will be nothing but a spark to ignite our hearts, and the waking of our hearts will be nothing but a spark in its turn. No one man could do it, had he all the power and learning of a thousand lifetimes, but two hearts in harmony are more powerful by far than one. You may leave the lady here, for no harm will come to her now that you have brought the glade to summer life – but you and I must go back to the cold night. Dawn has not yet come to the world above the world, and we must bring it.'

So saying, Bavian strode over to the Lady Melicent's horse, and reached up to lift her down. Having seen what had happened to Emyr Siun she might well have been reluctant, but she trusted the big man. She reached out her own arms to touch his shoulders – and when he set her down on the forest floor she remained as solid as ever she had been.

'Thank you, my lady,' said Bavian softly. 'You do me an honour. Please stay by these trees – the Mother of All Things is about you here, and will keep you from harm while we make shift to dismiss the storm. You have been very brave.'

She looked up at him, and shook her head, very tiredly. 'I was not brave enough to wed the elf,' she said, 'as my father commanded me to do.'

'You were brave enough not to,' answered Bavian, speaking as if he were a father himself. 'And that was the greater bravery by far, for it was the bravery required by virtue, and by common sense, and by Agam's Code.'

Then he mounted the horse from which he had taken her, seeming even huger in the saddle of the lean courser, and said: 'We must go up, my friend – up into the clouds and higher still. I think that you know how to find your way, and which song you must sing – but the most important thing of all is to remember that we are two together, and that our enemies, though they may number hundreds, are each and every one apart and lonely. Every one may have a heart of ice and stone, but ice may melt and stone may crack. Art thou ready, blood of my blood and mind of my mind?'

'I am ready,' said Trystan – and spurred his mount to leap upwards in astonishing fashion, through the leafy canopy and out into the troubled air where the snow still swirled and the wind still moaned its everlasting song of grief.

Trystan and Bavian, following the contours of the storm's music and the storm's magic, began to croon their lullaby. They did not sing loudly, but they sang as one – and though it seemed impossible that a thing as vast and mighty as that tempest which raged over Morien could ever be calmed at all, their music began to insinuate itself into the music of the storm, and to change it just a little.

That very tiny change which entered into the music of the storm as they rose was not imperceptible for long, because it was rapidly redoubled and redoubled again, magnified and amplified by the storm's own power. Trystan, listening while he sang, was struck by a sensation of tremendous awe that such a thing as Chaos could be so easily possessed, and so easily subverted.

AS THE STORM Huntsmen thundered towards him Herla threw down his bow. He did not try to draw his sword again, but urged his mount to dive into the clouds and take him out of the trap which had been fashioned for him. But the horse could not dive, for the carpet of cloud which had supported it for so long supported it still, no matter how agitated it was by the renewed wind.

Herla looked up into the sky, as if to ask belatedly for help. He wondered why the stars, which were so fiery and so fierce, had not the faces of *all* the gods written in them. Why was it only the vile master of the Storm Hunt who could be seen there? Where was the Mother worshipped by the druids, who was cruel only to be kind and always brought spring to follow winter, instead of allowing the sun to continue its southward march until all the world was plunged into eternal night?

No face appeared – not even the face of the god who had offered him one last chance of reward.

Knowing that death was inevitable, Herla looked down again at the converging spear-points, which glinted with reflected starlight. He felt neither fear nor dread, but only calmness – as if this were what he had secretly sought all along.

The rumours were right, he thought. I was never fitted to be a king.

Incongruously, there floated into his mind the words of a song – a song which he had not heard for twenty years, and which had never been sung to him by his own mother, but only by the nurse who had tended him. It was, he knew, a song of the common folk – a peasant song. It was gentle, and simple, and spoke only of fellowship, not of glory or grandeur or duty or heroism. He remembered now that it had come into his mind before, not long ago, when Trystan had played the elves' harp in Thoron's hall. Why it had come back to him then he did not know, but it had, and it had helped to calm his anger and his bitterness, and thus had helped to prepare his mind for the fight against the elf captain.

But it cannot serve me now, he thought, as he watched the spear-heads. I am only a babe, after all, before this army of the risen dead, who have grown old and ugly outside time.

The violence of the storm was still increasing, but there was a change in it; it was not so cold. The clouds were seething, and vapour came up in such sudden profusion that he felt a pang of disappointment that he would not, after all, see that multitude of spear-blades slice into him from every side and cut him in two.

Then, while he was still bracing himself to *feel* the impact, the air was filled with screams. The bright spear-points dissolved into grey confusion, returning to the cloud from which they had been formed – and when he looked into the sunken eyes of the huntsmen he saw fear flickering and flaring there, while their mounts and their bodies lost the imitation of flesh which they had put on.

Within the space of a moment, the host which had threatened to impale the king a hundred times over was transfigured into a crowd of swirling, screaming shadows which had no weapon solid enough to hurt him. The wind took up their screams and amplified them, as though the storm itself were screaming.

Herla began to fall. The clouds through which his mount had been unable to dive no longer provided any support, and the world above the world was a world no longer, but only a ghostly appearance in the sky.

The Storm Warriors of Slaanesh must have been well used to confusion, and no strangers to the sound of screaming, but there was in their own screams a special quality of terror unlike anything which the king had ever heard before. Herla knew that it could not be any ordinary fear because he knew that these were the undying, who had forsaken life for something else – but it was beyond the power of his imagination to guess what all this meant.

He still expected to die, because he supposed that his fall must end with a crashing impact upon the surface of the earth, which would either turn him instantly to shadow or splinter all his bones. But then his descent began to slow, and the stallion's thrashing hooves found new purchase –

and he was suddenly borne up again, once more in the icy clutch of the raging snowstorm.

The stallion stumbled, and nearly rolled over, but Herla fought to pull him upright, and he came.

Herla could not understand what was happening, but it was obvious that the storm was reasserting itself. The silly tune which had come into his head faltered, and was lost – and though he tried to remember it he found, annoyingly, that he could not.

It was as if the voice of his own thoughts, and the will within that voice, were being drowned out by the screaming of the storm – the *agonized* screaming of the storm.

He could no longer tell whether he was falling or rising, and for a minute or two the snowflakes were so thick about him that he could see nothing else. He rejoiced that there was some semblance of solidity beneath the stallion's feet, but he knew that it was not the earth; he was still among the storm clouds, riding in the sky.

Then the air began to clear again – but he did not find himself beneath the starry sky; instead, he was confined in a narrow margin between two limitless faces of cloud, one above and one below. The snow was all drawn back into one bank or the other, but the emptiness which it left behind was terrifying.

It seemed to Herla that there was an infinite and solid mass no further above his head than the ceiling of the great hall of Caer Plennydd, which might at any moment fall upon him, catching him like a grain of wheat between two enormous millstones, grinding him instantly to dust.

When he saw the other riders ahead of him he drew his sword, making ready for a fight – but then he saw that these riders were not Storm Huntsmen, and were themselves beset by strange shadowy forms which were beginning to loom out of the clouds above and below.

One of the riders he did not know at all, but the other was Trystan Harper.

As Herla rode towards his friend at a headlong gallop he saw that the shadows which struggled to take on substance were far more monstrously mis-shapen than the warriors of the Storm Hunt. Some had a form which was not too different from the human, but they had great scissored claws instead of hands and vast green eyes compounded like the eyes of blowflies; their mounts were not horses but great scaly two-legged things with pointed snouts and licking tongues. Others were like gargantuan horned insects in the body – often with scorpion-stings extending behind them – but they had heads like lizards, and they too had eyes of green.

Green was now the only colour which showed in this realm of grey shades, but it was not the green with which the Mother of All dressed the earth in spring; it was a pale, luminous and malevolent green which was the embodiment of everything *unnatural*.

Trystan Harper, who had no weapon, was trying with all his might to fend these attackers off with his hands – and Herla saw to his amazement that the bard was succeeding, at least to some degree. There was raw power in the harper's touch, from which the daemons recoiled – but they continued to multiply in number and to press home their attack.

The other man was less intensely beset, but he was also less able to repel the creatures which tried to scratch and sting him.

The air was full of unearthly music, as though the entire host of daemons had joined together in some frightful battle song, which was as much a weapon as their multitudinous claws and stings.

Herla rode precipitately into the fray, cutting about himself with his sword – and as he did so he was overcome by an urge to sing himself, and to show these monsters from beyond the world what kind of battle-song *men* could sing, when their blood was up and their hearts had been stirred by the rhythm of the harp.

Herla cut and slashed and sang, utterly heedless of his own safety; utterly committed to the battle. He heard his

voice united in strength and melody with the voices of his
fellows, and was possessed by a gladness more intense
than anything he had ever felt before.

I am the warrior of the storm! he thought, wild with
exultation. I am the Storm Huntsman, and daemons are
my prey!

One of the mounted creatures was brought so close to
him that he could feel the foul heat of its breath as it
slashed at him with serrated claws. Herla ducked under the
wild swipe, and blocked the claw with his sword.

The impact was close enough to the hilt of his weapon
to save his head from being split, and as the huge claw ran
away, pulled wide by its own momentum, Herla brought
his sword round and stabbed as hard as he could – and
watched the point run between the daemon's ribs to
impale its unbeating heart.

The daemon fell, screaming as the Storm Warriors had
screamed, and Herla sang.

A second horrid rider loomed out of the mist, this one
with a more spear-like claw extended – but Herla was
ready now, and he thrust the sharp claw away with his
right forearm, ignoring the pain of the blow, before thrusting his sword into his opponent's scaly throat.

As this one fell away and another came at him, Herla
remembered his own words: I claim my right as a man,
to face an honourable opponent, be he man or daemon
or petty godling! He remembered, too, the laughter
which had greeted his protestations. Now, the tables
had been miraculously turned, and though no one
could call these opponents honourable they were there
to be fought as a man should fight – bravely giving his
all.

Herla laughed as the other stabbed with its spear-claw,
missing the target altogether by virtue of its own stupid
carelessness, and wove the laughter into the rhythm of his
battle-song. Herla gave the daemon no second chance, but
thrust his pointed sword through the creature's vile green
eye and into its brain.

Alas, the turn of the dead thing's head and the diving of its scaly mount contrived to tear the sword clean out of Herla's hand – but it was with triumph and not with alarm that he cried out as he saw it disappear. Three he had cast down, as he had promised to do, and the blood was singing in his veins – singing a song of valour and right-eous wrath, of honour and Mother-love.

He did not know why he sang so loudly and so proudly, but he knew that Trystan and the other man were singing too, and that was enough. He joined his voice to that of his friend, and to the voice of his friend's friend – and the dae-mons cowered away from them, hurt and afraid.

Then, as Trystan Harper grappled with the lizard-head of one of the huge insects, the sting which the creature had behind came over like a whiplash, and buried its point in the neck of the bard's horse.

The horse screamed, and threw its rider – and in the moment that he was hurled so precipitately from his sad-dle, Trystan's voice faltered and broke, and the world grew darker, as if the sky were falling.

The unknown man howled in anguish and dismay, and for a moment the song was lost.

Herla did not know why, but he knew that if his own voice could not bear the burden of the song, if only for a moment, *all* was lost. Shouting with all his might he thrust the black stallion forward, and reached down his right arm to snatch Trystan Harper up and away from the cloud which waited so avidly to receive and consume him.

As he did so, a second sting lashed out from the clouds above, aiming for the bard's unprotected back – but Herla struck out with his empty left hand to intercept the sting, and felt its envenomed point go clean through the palm.

As Herla heaved Trystan up across the neck of his horse, a great claw descended in the wake of the sting, and slashed him from shoulder to navel as though it were the blade of a battle-axe – but somehow, it did not seem to matter, because some incredible mad confusion was already carrying them both away into a whirl of golden light.

WHEN THEY CAME to rest again Herla looked down at himself, and saw that he was bleeding very badly – yet, oddly enough, he felt no pain at all, not even in his left hand, which had been punctured through.

I am not dead! he told himself. The claw just grazed me, and did not slice my ribs in two. I am alive, and though I bear a scar as long as my arm, I am king in Plennydd still.

As the mists cleared in magical fashion, he saw that the golden swirl which had gathered him in had been the stain of the dawn upon the grey vapour. He was on a high hill in his own land, and could see Caer Plennydd in the east – not in ruins, but with its walls as high and proud as ever, and banners flying from its towers. It was autumn again, with Samain still to come, and he was in the world which was his own.

He dismounted from his horse, and helped Trystan down. He was delighted to see that the bard was unhurt.

He saw the unknown man riding up the hill towards him, with the Lady Melicent behind him; they were riding like the wind, desperate to reach him.

Herla raised his empty fist into the air, and sang out in triumph and in joy, to share with his best and truest friend the knowledge that they had won, and had come home in spite of everything.

But then, absurdly, he felt himself melting away in the rays of the sun, as though he were turning to shadow just as poor Emyr Siun had done. He felt his body turning to mist – and for one moment, as though it were a last assertion of his true identity, he was flooded by the pain of the wounds which he had taken, the injuries which had torn him apart and filled his being with poison.

He heard a voice cry: 'No!', and was surprised to find that it had not been his own, but Trystan Harper's.

'No matter,' he whispered, his mind flooding with understanding even as he felt himself slipping away. 'You came to save my life, but I had to give it up to save your own. We both did right, and it was certainly not for nothing, for we have sent the Storm Hunt to oblivion, and destroyed a host of daemons which would otherwise have plagued the race of men.'

Herla felt that he was all shadow now, with no substance left. Somehow, he could still see Trystan and his friend, and the Lady Melicent with them, but he could not see himself. And though he had no more voice with which to speak the words, he tried with all his might to say something else to the stricken harper.

What he wanted to say was: I wish that one of us had saved the other's life a long time ago. It would have made us one before now, and made this moment all the sweeter.

It must have been an illusion of sorts which had made him invisible to himself, for he felt himself taken up in Trystan Harper's arms. It must have been illusion, too, which told him that he could not say the words which he wanted to say, for he certainly heard Trystan's reply, which was: 'We *are* one, and always have been, and it was because we were one, and more than one, that we prevailed – against the elves, against the Storm Hunt, and against Chaos itself.'

EPILOGUE

ORFEO LAY BACK upon the couch, shivering. It was as though his account of King Herla's stand against the powers of Chaos had somehow given new life to the poison which was lurking in his own body. His gashed leg was healing, after a fashion, but the wound would leave an ugly scar – and in the meantime, he was still beset by occasional fevers and fits of dizziness.

Alkadi Nasreen gave him water to drink.

'Enough,' said the caliph. 'That is the end of it, I know. I am learning something of the story-teller's art, you see – I know when a story has reached its proper end. There is more to be said, I know, but the story itself is ended.'

Orfeo drank gratefully and then lay back again, looking up at his benefactor from beneath slightly hooded eyelids. He felt exhausted, as he always did when a story into which he had pitched himself heart and soul had reached its climax; there was also a strange aching sadness in him which protested the injustice of a world which made valour and heroism so very costly.

'Aye,' he said softly. 'It is ended.'

'Perhaps I can help complete the matters of mere detail,' said Alkadi Nasreen, 'and put my new-found competence in tale-telling to a proper test. I hope that I am right in deducing that Trystan did not marry his one true love, Queen Morgana?'

'Quite right,' answered Orfeo. 'Queen Morgana married Lin of Gwron.'

'As she had to do,' agreed the caliph. 'Else Plennydd, stripped of so many of its knights, would have become a satellite of her own land, Alawn – which the men of Gwron would have seen as a threat. Did the elves keep their word?'

'They did,' answered Orfeo, recovering now from his brief exhaustion. 'They did not need to wait for a ship, for they completed their own before Trystan and a company of men-at-arms from Caer Plennydd rode to their house of stone in search of an answer to that question.'

'And what of Godwin Conwy, who had been seduced to their cult of evil worship? Did he sail with them, or did he inherit their house?'

'He sailed with them – at least, that is what everyone believed. In any case, he and his wife never came home from the elves' house, and have never been seen again. His other daughter married a cousin of the Aglavins, and they kept the ringhold; the house which the elves had built is shunned, however, and is believed to be accursed.'

'And what of Trystan and the Lady Melicent? Did they marry?'

'Yes,' Orfeo confirmed. 'They were more tightly bound together by the adventure which they had shared than they could have been by any infatuation excited by a whim. They left Plennydd after discharging certain duties. Trystan chopped down the tree which had grown from Thoron's seed with his own hands, and added its wood to Herla's funeral pyre. He threw the elven bow on the same fire – but the stolen cup was never found, and is rumoured to continue its dark work in the Isles of Albion.

'When the bard had done those things, and made certain that the elves had gone, he thought it best to go away and never to return, lest his presence cause the queen embarrassment or heartache. He went first to some secret conclave of the bardic order, which released him from his position of duty in Plennydd. Afterwards, he went to Albion, and then to Bretonnia, to search those places for honest elves and warn them against their wayward kin.'

'And Bavian – did he go with him? Or did he take his place in Plennydd?'

'Neither. He had his own path to find. Whether he sought again to find the kind of immortality he desired, my informant did not know. I think he would have done. Once a man has become entangled with the worlds beyond our own, he is never content with the life which men were intended to live.'

'The man who told you this tale – he had a harp of his own. Did he lay claim to be this Trystan Harper?'

'He did,' replied Orfeo.

'And did you believe him?'

Orfeo smiled wryly. 'Oh yes,' he said. 'When I met him in l'Anguille he was accompanied by a woman who bore the name Melicent. Yes, I am sure he was the Trystan of the story.'

The caliph nodded. 'And do you believe those honest elves he hopes to find will take his warning seriously?'

'Some of them, at least, have taken note of it. When I heard this tale from the harper's lips we were in the company of elves and, curiously enough, one of those present was addressed by his fellows as Senduiuiel.'

'Senduiuiel?' the caliph asked in surprise. 'That same kinsman that Kerewan spoke of to the harper?'

'Perhaps. He did not admit as much, though plainly he knew of Kerewan. Certainly he and the other elves present listened to the harper's story with every evidence of belief. When the harper and his wife departed, they were bound for Marienburg, to carry their warning to those elves who dwell there. Senduiuiel elected to travel with them.'

'So,' said the caliph. 'And do you think that the harper –
and this Senduiuiel – may yet encounter the wizard
Kerewan again?'

'I believe that they may,' replied Orfeo softly.

'Perhaps in Marienburg?'

'Perhaps. And if they do, then the tale of that meeting is
one I would be thankful to discover someday.'

There was a silence before Alkadi Nasreen said: 'It is a
dark tale, is it not, this tale of Morien? Like the one you
told me of the doom of Zaragoz, it is mostly darkness and
destruction. Trystan has survived with a warning that may
yet be acted upon – but he has lost his true love, Morgana,
and become an exile from his native land just as that
unfortunate warrior Hallam did before him. And what,
after all, did the harper achieve when he went to save
Herla, except to secure the man a warrior's death instead of
a hog's? I know that they care more about such matters in
the cold northern lands, and reckon a good death a mighty
achievement, but death is only death after all.'

'I have told you before,' said Orfeo, 'that in my reckoning an ending is happy when the greatest good of the
greatest number is secured, even if those who secure it
receive inadequate reward. Trystan has survived, as you
said, though he is no longer the bard of his realm – and
the gentle affection he shares with Melicent may, in the
end, prove more rewarding than any passionate con-
summation of his love for the queen could have been.
But what Trystan and Bavian achieved when they went
back into the storm to help their friend was certainly not
negligible, just as that which was achieved when Herla
and Trystan stood by Agam's Code against all the
entreaties of the elves and their god of luxury was a considerable victory.

'Trystan and Herla saved the kingdom – and, perhaps
all Morien – from subtle dissolution by the elves into a
tiny empire of confusion. Later, with Bavian, they hur
the Storm Hunt very badly. Now, the north wind hardly
blows at all over the hills of Morien, and when it does i

blows far less terribly than it had before. The Hunt of Slaanesh survives, and will in time be rebuilt, but before the conclave of the bardic order set Trystan free he taught them something of what he had learned, which was absorbed into their lore – and Bavian must have remained, in his own peculiar fashion, to aid its preservation. Now the music of the bards may be proof against the worst excesses of the Storm Hunt, and Morien will be a happier land for it. Because of that, Herla did not die in vain – as he knew himself, at the end. And he was probably right to argue that the blows he struck against the daemons which were sent to harry Trystan were blows which all mankind might count to their credit.'

'Perhaps,' said the caliph grudgingly. 'But I must disagree that the good which has come of his death is enough to make the end of the story happy. On the other hand, he was not a happy man, was he? He was one of those who go through life as though beneath a cloud, ever hurrying towards death.'

Orfeo shrugged his shoulders. 'I dare say that you are right,' he conceded. 'But even though he was a perverse creature, who cared too little about his own death, Herla was a true hero among kings. Any man can be reckless, but only the best of the reckless spend themselves in securing the safety of others. You will remember, perhaps, the fifth item in Trystan's version of Agam's Code: that the strong must defend the weak who cannot defend themselves, *against any and all oppressors*. If the kings who rule us cannot or will not do that, then the farmer and his son spoke truly – we are better off without them.'

Alkadi Nasreen smiled. 'The point is not lost on me, my clever friend,' he said. 'Am I not the best of kings, extending my protection to you while you lie there as weak as a babe? Have I not promised to send you on your way, so that you may continue to spread morality throughout the world with your cunning tales? But you have your own adventure to undertake first, have you not?'

'We all have our own adventures to undertake,' said Orfeo tiredly.

'Not all of them take us into the heart of the dark continent, with the *hashishin* at our heels. You must beware, my musical friend, that you do not become a Herla instead of a Trystan. It is good to know one's ancestry, especially if it has been wickedly kept secret, but it is reckless to go too far in quest of such a discovery. After all, you could not be a hero by your own kind of reckoning if you died in the deep southlands, without any good accruing to anyone at all.'

'You are pleased to mock me,' observed Orfeo faintly – though he could not entirely suppress a smile of his own.

'You have mocked me these last few weeks,' said Alkadi Nasreen soberly. 'I know that you have done it for my own good, but you have teased me very sorely with your tales – even the ones which do not touch upon my own life. You have tormented me more than you know with your elaborate account of these forces of Chaos which threaten the world in so many different ways, and to which my own brother sold his soul.'

'Enlightenment is rarely comfortable, my lord.' said Orfeo, in a whisper. 'We all have dreams of an ideal world, and the more we discover of the one which we inhabit the more woefully the real seems to fall short of the ideal. Yet all my tales are tales of victories which men can win over the powers of Chaos.'

'Victories! Oh yes, they are victories – but how tiny, and hard won!'

'If you want me to tell tales in which the entire world is set to rights forever by the bold efforts of a single man, I can do it – but you know as well as I do how false and stupid such tales are. We live in the world, friend caliph, and we know that it has not been set to rights and is not likely to be. What we need is instruction in the business of how to thrive in a world whose uncleanness and hostility must be endured. No victory is tiny, my lord, and however hard won it may be it is better by far than a defeat.'

'It is sometimes hard to know the difference between victory and defeat,' countered Alkadi Nasreen. 'If Trystan and King Herla had listened to the temptations which were put before them by the elves and the god of luxury, would they not have considered themselves victors over harsh circumstance? Would they not have congratulated themselves on their fine decision, and laughed at those who preferred the hardships of the Code they had abandoned? You say that my brother was defeated because the daemons which he sought to control were turned against him by another – but is he not simply dead, just as your victorious Herla is simply dead?'

'All men die,' said Orfeo. 'But some remain masters of their own souls and some do not. Some, whether they adhere to Agam's Code or another, contrive to enhance the lives of those among whom they live, while others merely add to the world's burden of miseries. The first is victory, the second defeat.'

'By that reckoning,' the caliph observed, 'the majority of victors win nothing for themselves, while those who satisfy their desires are almost all to be reckoned among the ranks of the defeated.'

'It may sound paradoxical,' answered Orfeo. 'But when the satisfaction of one man's desires can only be achieved by condemning others to deprivation and suffering, it is better that the one man's desires go unsatisfied. If we cannot accept that, then we cannot live together as a true community, we cannot prosper in our collective projects, and we have in the end no defence against the ravages of Chaos.'

TEN DAYS LATER, Orfeo was taken by dark and secret ways to a place outside the walls of Arjijil. No one went with him but Alkadi Nasreen, Caliph of Mahabbah and the Twin Seas, who swore that he had told no other man that Orfeo was still alive.

Awaiting them beyond the wall was a handsome milk-white courser with a good Estalian saddle and a pack which contained – as well as provisions for the journey – a rapier, a lute, a scroll, an amulet and thirty Imperial crowns. Orfeo therefore left the citadel with all that he had possessed when he arrived, and more. He had always been a lucky man, in that respect – though he also took with him two new scars, upon his shoulder and his thigh, which would no doubt produce aches and twinges as long as he might live, to remind him of this strange place and its peculiar master.

'Look after Maro, my lord,' said Orfeo, as he mounted up. 'See that no harm comes to him.'

'The boy shall be my ward,' promised Alkadi Nasreen. 'I will treat him like a son and a friend. He is lucky to have come under your protection for a while – and whatever becomes of you, when you go into the hot and evil south-lands, you will know that you have lightened the burden of his life.'

'Thank you for that,' said the player.

'You will not forget your own promise, I hope?' said the caliph. 'You will return here, when your quest is over, to tell me every detail of your adventure.'

'I will,' answered Orfeo. 'I owe you that, and more, and I am a man of my word. We will meet again, Alkadi Nasreen, unless my death prevents it – or yours.'

Alkadi Nasreen frowned at that, but made no complaint.

'I wish you the best of good fortune,' said the caliph, as Orfeo pulled the rein to make the horse turn away.

His only reply was a seemingly-languid wave of a slender arm.

Alkadi Nasreen, Caliph of Mahabbah and the Twin Seas, stood and watched as the horseman cantered away. He stroked his beard thoughtfully, and did not turn away until the pale blur of the animal's rear had been entirely swallowed up by the dark shadows of the dunes. Then he went back into the dark tunnel from which he had come, and made his way back towards his lonely citadel.

'I think that was the best man I ever knew,' he said, aloud but in a very soft tone. Then, after a moment's hesitation, he added: 'Either that, or the greatest liar on earth.'

ABOUT THE AUTHOR

When asked why he dresses entirely in black, Brian Craig claims to be in mourning for H. P. Lovecraft, but the real reason is too dreadful to reveal. The rumour that he joined the British Antarctic Survey in 1993 'to get away from it all' is false; he failed the medical and had to join the French Foreign Legion instead. He is not allowed to discuss the reasons for his dishonourable discharge therefrom in 1999, but he is glad that he will now have more time to write and play cricket.

Brian Craig is the author of the three Tales of Orfeo – *Zaragoz*, *Plague Daemon* and *Storm Warriors* – and *The Wine of Dreams*, as well as the Warhammer 40,000 novel *Pawns of Chaos*. He has contributed short stories to a range of anthologies, including the *Dedalus Book of Femmes Fatales*, edited by Brian Stableford. He is 28 and only looks older because his troubles have aged him.

More Warhammer from the Black Library

THE TALES OF ORFEO
by Brian Craig

Tales of high adventure and mystery, recounted by Orfeo the minstrel.

ZARAGOZ

RIVEN BY POLITICAL intrigue, the countless petty kingdoms of Estalia are a dangerous land to travel through. When he rescues a mysterious priest from brigands, the minstrel Orfeo is drawn into a deadly power struggle for the citadel of Zaragoz. He is forced to use all the power of his wits and skill at arms to survive enemies fair and foul, human and monstrous.

PLAGUE DAEMON

IN THE WILDEST reaches of the Border Princes, the kingdom of Khypris is thrown into turmoil when barbarian tribes descend upon its rich, fertile lands. Soldier of fortune Harmis Detz finds himself fighting more than mere human enemies when a cruel twist of fate sucks him into a far more desperate endeavour – to find the real source of evil that threatens Khypris.